She kept struggling, nearly in panic. "Leet, please—"

Finally, he loosened his hold. She rolled to her hands and knees and pushed up, meaning to crawl out of the tub.

He grabbed her against his chest, soothing with his voice and hands. "It's okay, sweetheart. Just stay in the water." He stroked down her back, then through her hair as she settled against him. "Look, you still have icicles in your hair. Just let the water warm you up. Please, Sadie."

She finally gave up and let him have his way. She pressed her face into his chest and kept it there even as he moved to turn on the hot water. The warmth finally made its way through her boots to her toes and they, too, began to hurt like they were on fire. "Ow." She rubbed against him and let the tears come. "Ow, ow, ow."

Leet held her with one hand and worked his fingers into his pocket with the other. He tore open the alcohol packet with his teeth and opened the syringe. He ripped her outer shirt loose from half its buttons, slid it down her shoulder, and pulled at the sleeve of her t-shirt to bare her upper arm. Then he stuck the needle in—fast was supposed to be better—and pushed the plunger on the syringe to empty it into her arm.

"Ow!"

That one was particularly loud and annoyed, too.

"What was that?"

"For pain. Denny gave it to me."

"But what was it?"

Belatedly, Leet thought to read the label. "Morphine."

"Morphine? How much?"

He looked again. "Twenty milligrams."

"*Twenty*? You gave it all?"

"Yes. You were crying, remember?" And it had been killing him. Having her argue with him was much better. She'd stopped crying, stopped moaning even, and that was worth the world to him.

"It's going to put me to sleep, Leet. I was up all night."

Already, she sounded drowsy. He cuddled her against him and pressed his lips to her wet head. Then he pulled her a bit to his side and drew one foot up so he could wrestle off her boot with one hand. She was quiet and even a little co-operative as he did the other. "That's good, baby. We'll get you tucked into bed, nice and warm, and you can sleep."

"But—"

Her head drooped against him now. He tucked her damp hair behind her ears—they were pink now, just as Denny had said. Her fingers, too. "You're warm now, Sadie, aren't you? Let's get you out of there and into bed."

"But—I have to get my son."

Her son. Well, hell.

"Come on." He lifted her out of the tub, but had to prop her against him to keep her on her feet. He rubbed her hair with a towel, wondering. He'd called her "baby." He'd kissed her. Even now he wanted to press his lips against her damp hair—and did. He was in trouble.

"Leet—"

"I'll take care of it." He dropped the towel and held her face between his hands. And then, God help him, he kissed her again, once, his lips hard against hers. "I will. I promise."

She lifted her gaze to his for just a moment while he rubbed the kiss into her lower lip with his thumb. Then her eyes closed, and she swayed into him again.

He finished the job he'd started on the buttons of her shirt and peeled it off her. When he started to pull the tee from her jeans, she slapped at his hands.

"You can't undress me."

"Okay," he said, all reason. "Do it yourself."

She lifted one hand to her waist, but it just hovered for a moment before it fell to her side.

"You're starting to shiver again. You have to get out of these clothes or else back in the water to stay warm."

She groaned a protest, making him think that was a no.

He left her pressed against him at the hip then arched back so he could strip the t-shirt off over her head. Her bra was a pretty pink, kind of sweetly sexy. Did married women, *mothers*, still wear bras like that?

He was going with no on that one, too.

He reached behind her and unfastened it. He had a little experience there that came in handy now. He brought it around and lifted it away, even as she started to complain again.

"It's okay," he said. "I'm not looking."

LUCKY *Man*

Rebecca Skovgaard

Cassandra — I'll
have to find a place
for you in my next
one! Enjoy —
Beck

Whimsical Publications, LLC

Florida

To purchase the authorized electronic edition of *Lucky Man*, visit
www.whimsicalpublications.com

Cover art by Traci Markou
Editing by Brieanna Robertson

Published in the United States by
Whimsical Publications, LLC
Florida

ISBN-13: 978-1-940707-32-7

ACKNOWLEDGEMENTS

To Dennis, Byrl, and Jeff. This one is for my brothers, particularly the smart, handsome one who gave football advice. (Hah! That has them *all* wondering.) Along with Old Ray, you three really formed the basis for whatever understanding of men I can claim. I love you all. And, oh, yeah—go, Packers!

CHAPTER ONE

Leet Hayes stood and looked out his window. Whoever had said it was Thursday before you felt like moving after a Sunday afternoon professional football game must not have been thirty-four. Or a quarterback sacked three times. In one half.

It was Thursday morning, and even now every part of him hurt.

Still, it wasn't much of a complaint. He'd spent most of the last three days grinning. Sometimes, he'd shake his head, disbelief still strong, and then grin some more.

There was no way that the last play of the game, the game that should have ended their season, turned on an unforced fumble. No way that fumble should have been picked up and run with, lateraled, and run some more for a game-winning touchdown, a come from behind, mother-of-all-upsets victory.

No way should the New Hampshire Metal, the league's fledgling team only four years old, have a berth in the wild card round. No way should they be three games away from—no. He couldn't say it. Didn't want to even think it. No way.

He'd meant to drag his sore self out of bed and hit the hot tub until he felt half-human. Then he'd start the workout that would get him limber and ready for final practices on Friday and Saturday. The team had work to do. He had work. There was that problem with the sacks.

But he'd stopped at the window and then hadn't moved. Unusually warm weather the last two days had robbed the Vermont countryside of its celebrated winter beauty. Rain in the afternoon had left a drab brown, muddy mess. A Nor'easter had come in, though, and cold temperatures overnight had brought this miracle—a sparkling, crystal wonderland. Trees and bushes, even blades of grass, were glazed with ice. The little creekbed alongside his property, dry much of the year, now held a tumbling, frozen waterfall with whimsical little ice bridges and stalactites. And the sun, holding its own so far against the dark clouds coming in from the east, set it all ablaze.

A rare fluke of nature had produced incredible, unique beauty. It held him. He stood some more, dressed only in a pair of ragged gray sweats. The slate floor was cold against his feet, but the sun beat warmly against his chest through windows that were floor to ceiling along the full length of his bedroom. The glass was cold against his hand when he leaned forward to look more closely at his favorite sugar maple. The way those branches arched up—

He had to get to the studio. The workout would have to wait.

Sadie Benjamin thought about the degu. It was a little known and underappreciated fact that pregnant degus, uniquely in the mammalian kingdom, contracted—and therefore gave birth—mostly during the day. Apparently, where they lived in the Andes, little baby degus would turn quickly into popsicles if they were born at night.

Unfortunately, in this one regard, Sadie was a midwife to human females, who, like all mammals but the degu, contracted most at night. Therefore, she spent many a night up waiting for babies to be born. Therefore, she was on this lovely, winding road that was now exceedingly treacherous, thanks to an overnight freezing rain. Every other sane woman was no doubt snugged up right and tight in the warmth and safety of her own home, instead of taking her life in her hands with risky winter driving, while totally sleep deprived.

Still, it wasn't much of a complaint. Sadie loved her work. And the entrance of little Madeline Ware into the world had been a particularly lovely birth. Her family had called it her coming out party. Her older brothers and sisters had held a slumber party in the living room—looked over by two of their aunts—snuggling off to sleep in their comforters more or less in order of age, youngest—two—to oldest—eleven—all five of them. The parents, Beth and Sam, snuggled quite similarly in their own bedroom, warmed by a woodstove. And the hard work of labor—a task Beth took on in her usual matter-of-fact way. One more chore in a farmwoman's life. Nothing she couldn't handle.

Madeline came with the sunrise. She took to her mother's breast like a champ, too well occupied to notice as the siblings came, wrapped in their blankets, to meet her. A part of the family for this moment, Sadie watched with them as the sun lit up their yard and outbuildings with amazing sparkle. Freezing rain—lovely to look at, a bitch to drive in.

Sadie wasn't far down the Wares' mountain before she regretted her decision to leave when she had. She'd helped the aunties with the big farm breakfast and sat down to share it with the whole family. She'd thought about lying down for a nap, but the clouds rolling in held snow. She hoped to be home before it came.

The snow and the regret came together, dramatically so. There were no pretty, gentle flakes as warning but blizzard conditions within a minute. The sky darkened and the wind howled. She battled whiteouts and gusts that threatened her control of the vehicle. But it was too late to turn around—the ice on the narrow gravel road made going downhill very dangerous, and uphill entirely impossible. Even in her trusty four-wheeler, her descent down the mountain had as much slip and slide as the average water park.

At the base of the mountain, she crossed the White River. She halted there—taking a few calming breaths in the momentary silence and shelter of the covered bridge. The county road on the other side was paved and relatively flat as it followed the river south into the Junction or north toward Oak Mill Basin and home. But it curved with the river, sometimes running very close—in these conditions, dangerously close—to water's edge.

On the far side of the bridge there was a pull-off area used by fishermen and the occasional skinny dippers. She could park there and wait out the storm. She was provisioned for it, as always. She had an emergency flashlight and blankets, water and protein bars, and her e-reader. She could last for days.

And probably would have to, if she stopped. Off road, she could get plowed in and not be able to move again until the cleanup efforts got well beyond the basics. Home called—the boys, the moms, and her own bed.

Gingerly, she left the cover of the bridge and turned north. In other conditions, she would enjoy the drive. The river was nearly frozen over. Sheets of white ice, sometimes in smooth layers, sometimes heaved into haphazard slabs looking like they tumbled from some giant game of pick-up-sticks, lined either side. The center was cold, green water. The current was fast now with the runoff of yesterday's rain.

She was less than a half hour into the storm and already the road had a good two inches of snow cover—and more where the wind formed drifts. The snow made for better traction than the ice, so she gradually picked up a little speed. But she knew there could be patches of bare ice, so she proceeded with due caution.

Not true for the car she saw suddenly coming toward her—too fast along the outside of a curve. She wasn't even sure that she'd seen it—the glare of headlights in snow was there for just a couple seconds. Enough for her to think it was traveling too fast, enough to cause her to lift her own foot from the gas pedal—and then it was gone.

She got to the curve and was alone on the road. With a sinking feeling, she passed it. She knew she hadn't imagined the headlights. So she pulled off the road—far off, for safety—and squirmed around to look at the road behind her. There it was. A patch of bare ice at the worst spot—outside curve, and a slide of several feet down to the river. She could see tire tracks through the snow at the road's edge.

She patted her waist to make sure her cell phone was there and grabbed the gloves on the seat beside her. She climbed out, struggling against an uphill slant to the road, the wind, and the ice, and went around to the back hatch for the blankets and flashlight. But before she left the SUV, she went back to the front and leaned on the horn. Three short, three long, three short.

SOS. Or was that OSO? She didn't know, so she did it all a couple more times just to be sure.

Leet looked up from his work and shut down the torch.

The snow had come in fast, changing the landscape outside his studio in moments. But the image of that maple was in his head now and, very slowly, emerging in the steel he worked. He'd been immersed in it—he felt the stiffness in his body again as he straightened and stretched. He didn't even know how long he'd been working. Or what had brought him out of it.

And then he did. There'd been a sound—a car horn. It was gone now, and he didn't even know how much time had passed. He replayed it in his head—three blasts, long ones, then short ones. He was moving even as he understood what it was. He had his work boots on and left it that way. He snagged his cell phone from the table at the door, then grabbed coat, hat, and gloves on his way through the mud-room. He was dialing as he slid into his coat.

Not 9-1-1, but his best buddy and the local law, Will Hunter. Will picked up on the fourth ring—Leet's boots were sliding through the ice and snow on his long driveway down to the road by then—and said, "I'm busy," by way of answering.

Leet ignored that. "Someone's signaling an SOS—down by the river, I think." Awkwardly, one-handed and keeping the phone at his ear, he pulled his cap on.

"We got a 9-1-1 call. I'm headed there, ambulance, too. But we're not moving very fast—the roads are shit. There's supposed to be a car in the water. Can you get there?"

"I'm halfway down. Do you know where they are?"

"The caller said she was a couple miles north of the bridge."

"I'll call you back."

Leet landed on his ass a half dozen times before he reached the road. He searched in both directions but didn't see anything. "A couple miles north of the bridge" could be in either direction. He ran to the left, toward the hazardous curve that seemed the most likely suspect. In a hundred yards—that was a distance he knew well—he saw he'd guessed right. There was a car, hazard lights on, pulled to the side of the road. It was empty. But an emergency light flashed off the other side of the curve. He opened his phone and headed across—cussing as he slipped again on the sheet of ice, and then some more to Will as he described what he saw. A small sedan, more in the water than out. One person, a woman, lying flat out on the ice, talking to—reaching for—someone through the back window of the car.

He closed the phone on Will's warnings—nobody goes in the water, no heroes, don't put anyone else at risk.

Sadie lifted her fist and rotated it, signaling the boy to roll down the window. He was maybe seven or eight, and still belted in. That was good.

She was spread eagle on the ice—it was flat here, and thick, but the warm weather of the last days had weakened it and undercut it over the water. The car had broken through the edge of it into the water, its front end submerged. It held precariously to a cantered slab of ice by part of its rear axle. The woman in the driver's seat must be waist deep in water. She was unconscious—her head was slumped against the steering wheel, and she wasn't moving. Blood seeped from a gash above her left eye. In its way, that was a good sign. There was blood, too, on the spider-web fracture of the driver's side window.

The boy looked back through the window, fear glazing his eyes. There was a toddler crying in a car seat next to him. Sadie nodded, encouraging, and moved her hand again. Finally, he did as she instructed. As the window lowered, Sadie gave thanks the beat up old car didn't have power windows.

She took a calming breath and nodded again. "My name's Sadie. I'm going to help you. You're all going to be okay."

The boy's panicky breath indicated a certain lack of trust in her assurances.

The ice creaked loudly underneath her, and Sadie had her own doubts. *Smart boy.* Still, she'd learned before to keep a cool head in an emergency.

She kept eye contact and spoke slowly, calmly. "I want you to slow your breathing down." She lifted a hand. "Slow your breathing. Like this." As she'd done in a hundred labors, she showed her own gentle breathing pattern. In a few moments, he was with her, quieting. "Tell me your name."

His breath hitched once before he spoke. "Jeb."

She nodded. "Good job, Jeb. Is that your sister next to you?"

He nodded back. "Gracie."

"And your mom?"

"She's not moving. Is she dead?" Tears threatened now in his voice and in his eyes.

"No, she's not, Jeb." Sadie was pretty sure that was true. "I'm going to help her. But first we have to get you and your sister out."

She lost him then—he closed his eyes and started crying. She reached her hand out. "Jeb. Jeb."

A deep voice came from behind her. One with much more authority than she'd ever found. "Jeb. Look at us."

Sadie lifted up a little bit and squirmed around to look behind her. Golden brown eyes, like a lion, looked back. They belonged to a big hunk of man.

"I'm Leet."

"Sadie." He lay flat out on the ice, too. If he stretched his arm out, he could reach her foot. Too close when they were on a layer of ice that kept groaning in ominous ways. "Stay back. In fact, don't move."

He nodded. "Got it. Rescue squad is coming." Then he looked beyond her and used that voice again. "Jeb. Man up, dude. We need your help."

Sadie lifted her brows at him. *Man up*?

"He knows what I mean." That was more to her, using, like, his indoor voice. And indeed, Jeb was quiet now. Even Gracie had paid attention. Those lion eyes were on her now. "You've got the lead. Take it."

Sadie mentally shrugged. Maybe young boys in danger responded differently than women in labor. She wouldn't quibble.

She turned back to the car. "Jeb," she said. "I want you to move slowly, everything you do. Don't move until I tell you to. Do you understand?"

Jeb nodded, but behind her, she thought she heard a murmured complaint—"Faster."

Sadie nodded back. "Unfasten your seat belt." She nodded again as he complied. "Move gently. Turn to Gracie and get her out of the car seat."

For no rational reason, Sadie held her breath while Jeb got this task done. "Good job. Now bring her close to the window. You're going to have to hand her out to me."

Gracie cried again and struggled as Jeb brought her to

the window. Smart girl, too. But her resistance wasn't help-ing. Sadie wriggled forward, her chest leaving the ice, dan-gling over water as she reached toward the car. An iron grip took hold of her ankle, tight around her boot, and kept her from going any further.

She tried to shake him off. "Let go."

"No." That was his quiet voice, implacable nonetheless. Then he used the other. "Jeb. Push her out. Do it. We've got her."

That part was just barely true, as Jeb gave Gracie a shove, and Sadie nearly missed her. Gracie tumbled toward the water, and all Sadie could do was snag her quick around one boot. Gracie went into the water and Sadie's arm with her, nearly to her shoulder. She was anchored only by that grasp on her ankle; one rough jerk there brought them back onto the ice.

Poor Gracie sputtered, too shocked to do more. Water poured from her snowsuit. Before it could freeze, Sadie laid her on the ice and pushed her toward Leet. "Blanket!" she yelled—pointing to the two she'd dropped as she'd run to the river.

"I know!" he yelled back, grabbing Gracie off the ice and skittering back to the edge.

"Wrap her in it! Tuck her inside your coat!"

"I got it! Get Jeb!"

She turned to do it, aware of what they both saw but didn't say out loud. The car was sinking lower, tilting more off the ice. He yelled one more time. "And stay out of the goddam water!"

Bossy man, but still, no quibbling.

Sadie lay flat on the ice again and inched back toward the car. Her wet hand stuck to the ice, leaving a layer of skin and blood when she tore it away. She muffled her own curse when she saw Jeb.

He was hunkered down in his seat, barely visible through the window. His hands covered his face.

"Jeb. She's okay. Come on. Let's get you out of there."

He shook his head, still not looking.

"Come on. Your turn. Then we'll get your mom."

She wasn't even surprised when Leet's voice took over. "Jeb, get your ass out of there now!"

Jeb lifted his head, looking like the world bore down on

his shoulders. But he turned onto his knees and moved to the window.

"Good boy. Gently. Don't jump."

Again, Sadie moved as close to the edge of the ice as she could. Again, she felt that solid grip on her ankle. She'd have objected, but she was entirely certain that while Leet held her, he'd also have Gracie tucked against his chest.

Accepting that, she reached toward Jeb. She got him with one hand and started to pull him toward her before she felt a tug on her ankle.

"Stop."

More input from the boss.

"Sadie, he's too heavy for you to pull out one-handed if he goes in. Let's trade places."

"No. I've got him. I'm not letting go."

"Shit."

She could hear his sigh.

"All right. Go out a little further. I've got you. Get both hands stable on the door. Jeb can climb out over you."

It worked fine, except that Jeb didn't want to let go. He clung onto her back like a monkey.

There was a little humor in Leet's voice then. "Hold on. I'll reel you both in. Keep your head up, Sadie, and your hands off the ice."

He was right. One hand still bled, and there was an ache above and beyond cold numbness on her jaw where she'd connected with the ice the last time.

He got them in and wrapped the second blanket around Jeb, head and all. He sat the boy down, tucked Gracie into his lap, and covered in both blankets. "You did good, Jeb. You're the man. Sit here and keep Gracie close. We'll get your mom."

On his knees there on the ice, he faced Sadie. His coat, suede and lined with very inviting fleece, still hung open. He grabbed her hands and pulled them around his back, hollering out as he slid them under his sweatshirt, ice cold against his bare skin. Then he wrapped his arms around her, bringing her into his warmth. She shivered and tried to stifle a moan at the profound sense of comfort it gave.

He took the hat from his head and shoved it onto hers, covering her frozen ears with his hands.

But that left her back open to the air. "Don't." Her words

shivered out. "Put your arms around me again."

She could hear the smile.

"You bet." He pulled her close. "We need a plan. A quick one."

Shakily, she nodded. "She's gonna have to come out from the back seat. I'll go into the car behind her, undo her seatbelt, then lay the seat back. We should be able to pull her out from there. She might have some kind of spinal injury, so we have to keep her as straight as possible. It would be better to wait for a real rescue team and a board, but we don't have the choice." They both looked again at the car, lower still in the water. "There's no time."

He nodded; she felt the movement against her head. "Agreed. Except I'll go in after her."

She looked up at him. "No. You're too big to maneuver in there."

She knew she was supposed to feel cowed by the look he gave her back. "I've got moves."

She grinned just a little. *No doubt.* But they didn't have time to squabble. Anyway, she had the winning argument.

"If I go after her, and end up in the water, you'd get me out. You could promise that, couldn't you? I could trust you to do it." She knew he could see where she was going and didn't like it.

"Yeah." It was grudging. He *really* didn't like it.

"I can't make the same promise to you." He held her gaze, held her with his hands, frozen fingers at her neck and jaw, until she tore herself away from his warmth. She gave him a fist pound on his shoulder. "You know I'm right. Let's go."

Inwardly, Leet cursed again. In fact, a whole litany of curses marched through his head. It felt nothing but wrong to let her go. She'd torn skin and was bleeding from one hand—the one that had gone in the water—and the other was white, looking about half a minute away from frostbite. Her whole body was shaking with cold—they'd be lucky if she could manage everything she needed to do inside the car.

But she was tough, and smart—she'd already shown that,

and he could see it in those dark blue eyes. And she was right. If he lost the woman in the water, or if he went in himself, there was no way Sadie could fish either one of them out.

He was tempted to force her to wait. Will and his rescue team would get there eventually. And Will was right—always the first rule of rescue by amateurs was never increase the number of people in jeopardy.

But Leet wasn't one to stand by when someone was helpless and in danger, and clearly, Sadie wasn't either. And hard as he strained to listen, there wasn't even the faintest hint of sirens. In any case, Sadie was ten steps ahead of him. She had her coat off and was sitting on it as she tried to pull her boots off with her frozen hands. Boots now with blood on them.

"Stop," he said, and moved to her. "I'll get them. Tuck your hands in your armpits."

He'd slid over on his belly but lifted up on his elbows to work the laces. Their gazes met as he loosened them and tugged the boots off, but neither spoke. When he was done, he wrapped his fingers around her toes for a minute. "Keep your fingers moving. Your toes, too." He swallowed hard but had nothing more he could say. She nodded and rolled over onto her belly. She crawled to the car with him just behind her.

Water filled the back seat now, nearly to the window. Sadie didn't pause but kept moving, past the edge of the ice. He grabbed her ankles again and stabilized her as she reached for the window opening. She got there, slid her hands through the window onto the back of the seat, and kept pulling herself through.

Leet got to the edge of the ice, holding her ankles now over the water. When he let go, she'd fall into the back seat of the car, into the water there. He couldn't make his hands release her.

"Let go."

He heard the words, knew what he had to do, but couldn't force himself to do it.

"Leet—"

Finally, she kicked her feet a little, and he did what he had to. And suffered through it as the shock of cold water brought her breath out in a harrowing huff. She tucked her feet under her and, squirming in the small space, reached between the front seats for the latch of the safety belt. She nearly had her head under water to do it.

"Talk to me, Sadie. You can't stay in there long. You only have a couple minutes before you're not going to be able to move. If you can't get the buckle, just get the hell out of there."

"I've got it."

"No, you don't." She was still struggling to reach it, he could tell. Her breath came in labored gasps edged in panic. He thought his might sound the same. "I want you to get out."

"I *almost* have it."

"Sadie—"

"Shut up."

He was on the verge of going in after her when finally, *finally* she lifted up, the seat belt loose. He raised his head for a moment and knew he heard a siren. About damn time.

"Good, good. Now lean her back in the seat."

"I know."

She reached around near the front door for the seat lever and began to tilt it back.

"Stop, Sadie."

"No. What?"

"Stay on this side. Don't let the seat get between you and the door." She'd moved further away from him to bring the seat back. She was out of his reach now, her exit blocked by the seat and the unconscious woman.

"That won't work." Inside the cramped car, she struggled to maneuver the woman's dead weight toward that small window opening. Blue lights flashed now, lighting the scene eerily, and he knew he had help.

Water reached the level of the window and started to pour in from the river.

"Sadie, goddammit! Get out now!"

"Help me! Get a hold of her!"

And suddenly, he could. The car was sinking fast now, but the water helped lift the woman. He lunged forward at the same time he felt the weight of another large body wrap around his legs. If he had a guess, that would be Will. All through high school, Will had been his wingman, on the field and off. He could always count on him.

Leet got a handful of the woman's coat and heaved with all his might. As he pulled her, fast and rough—spinal injury be damned—onto the ice, he found he had more help. A figure in rescue-squad yellow hunkered next to him and took over, pulling her further away from the edge of ice.

Leet looked behind and confirmed it was Will who had him by the legs. "Don't let go, Will!"

"What? What the hell you doing?"

But Will didn't hesitate to follow him, keeping hold even as Leet thrust back toward the water. The car was all but under. Sadie's hand stretched through the window, fingers just out of the water. She was trusting him.

He got her by the wrist, but she was being pulled down and forward as the current took the car. He wouldn't let go, and so, sliding on the ice, he went with her. Another foot closer to the water.

"Will. Don't. Let. The. Fuck. Go."

"I got you, man."

He had her wrist, and all he could do was hold on. He could feel her struggle against the car and the current. "Sadie!" Every curse he'd ever heard or spoken left his lips as he yelled at her, for her. Suddenly, he felt her go limp and let out a wail of grief and frustration. And then she was free, in the water. One more second and he had her out and in his arms.

He wrapped her against him while she struggled for breath.

"I had to let go." She was frozen, shivering, her lips barely moving.

"I know."

"I had to just give over."

"I know. I get it. You scared the shit out of me, but I fucking get it." He touched her everywhere, his fingers sticking as her clothing froze. Her hair was turning to icicles. He held her tight against his body as he moved them away from the water's edge. "Will—"

He looked around. The two guys from the rescue squad had the woman on a board, heaving her up toward their vehicle. Will had Gracie held in one arm while the other was around Jeb's shoulders, pushing and half-carrying him up the bank to the road.

On his own with her, Leet let go of Sadie enough to shrug

out of his coat and wrap it around her. Then he loosened her laces and shoved her boots over her frozen socks. He lifted her in his arms and hauled her up the bank.

Up by the truck, one of the rescue workers had taken charge. Leet got a look through the blowing snow and recognized him. Denny Rendeau was a mechanic, a beer drinker, and a Metal fan. They shared a pitcher and a pool table once in a while down in the Junction, at the Tap and Mallet.

Denny's gaze took in Sadie and him as he and his partner slid a stretcher with the woman into the back of the truck. He left his partner there and went to help Will with his twin burdens. He carried Jeb up over his shoulder and pushed him into the back of the truck, then motioned Will to climb in behind with the toddler. He closed the doors practically on Will's butt just as Leet arrived with Sadie.

Leet shot a hard look at Denny. "She needs help."

Denny nodded and looked at Sadie. "Is she injured or just wet and frozen?"

Leet gestured toward the doors. "Open up, Denny."

His friend didn't budge. "Answer my question, Leet." Apparently, Denny could be tough, too.

"Frozen."

Denny nodded again. "She needs to get warm. You can do that better than I can, even if we weren't full up. As it is, I'm gonna need Will to drive us in so Frank and I can take care of the three we've got inside." He nodded his head up the road. "Your place is as close as any help we're gonna get here. The rig coming up from the Junction is in a snow bank, so we're on our own. Put her on her feet. She's gotta move or she *will* freeze. Get going with her. I'll get some things from the truck and be right behind you."

"Shit." Leet watched him disappear into the truck, then looked up into the snow-filled sky, wanting to howl. "Sadie—" He couldn't bear to let go of her, to put her down.

Sadie shivered out a breath. "I heard him. I can do it."

Leet sighed hard and let her feet slide down. He had to half hold her as her knees buckled.

"I can do it."

She sounded like a petulant two-year-old putting her own shoes on the wrong feet, and somehow, it sounded good to him. She took a staggering step before he pulled her hard against his side.

"Sure you can." He spoke that and sundry curses under his breath as he began to lurch up the road with her. After a dozen stumbling paces, she started to move with greater co-ordination. He took that to be a good sign and warmed to-ward Denny just a little.

In another minute, Denny was with them. He stopped them to throw a blanket over Sadie's head and torso, and another around Leet, then got them moving again. He talked as he pushed them along, helping along Sadie's other side. "You got a hot tub, right?"

At Leet's grunt, he continued. "Get her in it, fast as you can. Dump her in, clothes and all. That'll take the water tem-perature down a lot so you'll have to refill it. Keep it good and warm but not hot—she'll be sensitive. She's got frost-bite, at least on this right hand. Check her other hand and her feet, too. And her ears. Where the tissue is white and hard, she's frostbitten. Don't rub it. Just let the water warm her. If circulation returns, the area will turn warm and pink. If it doesn't, she's gonna have to get in to the medical cen-ter. That's not an emergency, though. Just keep the area clean and covered until you can safely get her in." He paused and looked around Sadie to him, raising an eyebrow. "You have that, Leet?"

Irrationally, Leet wanted to punch him. "I have it."

Denny heard the tone and grinned for just a second. "She's gonna have pain. A lot. Give her this." He moved in front of Leet and stopped him. He slid a syringe and an alco-hol swab into Leet's hoodie pocket and patted it. "Get her in the water, then give her this. Deep into muscle. I've gotta get back to the truck." He left a hand on Leet's shoulder for a minute. "Good luck, man."

Sadie knew what was coming, and still she hated it. Leet had her in his house—she'd glimpsed an acre of glass, wood, and stone as he pushed her up his never-ending drive—and he was going to dump her into his hot tub. Just as that—that *guy*—Denny had told him to do.

But she didn't want to be in water again, maybe ever again. She was one big pile of misery, and she wanted to just fall down where she was—*not* in water—and cry.

That was what she had wanted every step of that horrid climb up his stupid mountain. At one point, she'd just stopped—or her feet had stopped. Leet had dragged her several steps before he even noticed.

"Come on, blue eyes. *Move*," he'd said.

Sadie flailed at the blanket that covered her. "I can't see."

Leet wasn't the least bit sympathetic. "I don't care. I've got you. So just move it."

There was that attitude again.

"I can't *breathe*." Sadie knew it to be a pitiful wail.

But it had worked. Leet stopped pushing at her. With a certain exasperated gentleness and an almost bit back sigh, he lifted the blanket from over her head. He tucked it around her like a hood, leaving just a small space for her face. He peered at her for a second, then for no reason she could understand, he pressed his lips against hers in a kiss. She was just beginning to warm to the idea—his lips, after all, were *warm*—when he pulled away. He wrapped his arm around her and pushed again. "Now. *Move.*"

He'd dragged her through the house without seeming to care at all that they left a trail of river water, ice, and mud on his lovely slate floors.

He held her to his side while he dropped their blankets and unwrapped her from his coat. Shaking uncontrollably with cold, she looked at the water with dread.

"Leet, don't—"

"Sorry, baby. Take a breath." He sat on the ledge—the tub was huge and surrounded by windows and slate tile—and pulled her into his lap. Then he swung around and tumbled her in.

She went under. It was ecstasy and agony at once. The warmth of it was like heaven, and had her body shuddering out its relief from the cold. But her fingers screamed in pain, and she thought maybe she did, too, as she surfaced. He was there, nearly inside the tub with her, holding her down.

"It's okay. Stay under, keep your ears under."

But Sadie couldn't bear it—the feeling of the water taking her again—and fought him.

"Sadie. Sadie, I've got you."

She kept struggling, nearly in panic. "Leet, please—"

Finally, he loosened his hold. She rolled to her hands and knees and pushed up, meaning to crawl out of the tub.

He grabbed her against his chest, soothing with his voice and hands. "It's okay, sweetheart. Just stay in the water." He stroked down her back, then through her hair as she settled against him. "Look, you still have icicles in your hair. Just let the water warm you up. Please, Sadie."

She finally gave up and let him have his way. She pressed her face into his chest and kept it there even as he moved to turn on the hot water. The warmth finally made its way through her boots to her toes and they, too, began to hurt like they were on fire. "Ow." She rubbed against him and let the tears come. "Ow, ow, ow."

<hr />

Leet held her with one hand and worked his fingers into his pocket with the other. He tore open the alcohol packet with his teeth and opened the syringe. He ripped her outer shirt loose from half its buttons, slid it down her shoulder, and pulled at the sleeve of her t-shirt to bare her upper arm. Then he stuck the needle in—fast was supposed to be better—and pushed the plunger on the syringe to empty it into her arm.

"Ow!"

That one was particularly loud and annoyed, too.

"What was that?"

"For pain. Denny gave it to me."

"But what was it?"

Belatedly, Leet thought to read the label. "Morphine."

"Morphine? How much?"

He looked again. "Twenty milligrams."

"*Twenty*? You gave it all?"

"Yes. You were crying, remember?" And it had been killing him. Having her argue with him was much better. She'd stopped crying, stopped moaning even, and that was worth the world to him.

"It's going to put me to sleep, Leet. I was up all night."

Already, she sounded drowsy. He cuddled her against him and pressed his lips to her wet head. Then he pulled her a bit to his side and drew one foot up so he could wrestle off her boot with one hand. She was quiet and even a little co-operative as he did the other. "That's good, baby. We'll get you tucked into bed, nice and warm, and you can sleep."

"But—"

Her head drooped against him now. He tucked her damp hair behind her ears—they were pink now, just as Denny had said. Her fingers, too. "You're warm now, Sadie, aren't you? Let's get you out of there and into bed."

"But—I have to get my son."

Her son. Well, hell.

"Come on." He lifted her out of the tub, but had to prop her against him to keep her on her feet. He rubbed her hair with a towel, wondering. He'd called her "baby." He'd kissed her. Even now he wanted to press his lips against her damp hair—and did. He was in trouble.

"Leet—"

"I'll take care of it." He dropped the towel and held her face between his hands. And then, God help him, he kissed her again, once, his lips hard against hers. "I will. I promise."

She lifted her gaze to his for just a moment while he rubbed the kiss into her lower lip with his thumb. Then her eyes closed, and she swayed into him again.

He finished the job he'd started on the buttons of her shirt and peeled it off her. When he started to pull the tee from her jeans, she slapped at his hands.

"You can't undress me."

"Okay," he said, all reason. "Do it yourself."

She lifted one hand to her waist, but it just hovered for a moment before it fell to her side.

"You're starting to shiver again. You have to get out of these clothes or else back in the water to stay warm."

She groaned a protest, making him think that was a no.

He left her pressed against him at the hip then arched back so he could strip the t-shirt off over her head. Her bra was a pretty pink, kind of sweetly sexy. Did married women, *mothers*, still wear bras like that?

He was going with no on that one, too.

He reached behind her and unfastened it. He had a little experience there that came in handy now. He brought it around and lifted it away, even as she started to complain again.

"It's okay," he said. "I'm not looking."

Her breasts were beautiful, firm and high and just more than a man's handful. The nipples, erect now as she was chilled again, were rosy pink, thrust out like ripe raspberries. How he wanted to suckle.

If she had a husband, where the hell was he when Sadie was out there in the water, needing rescue? It was Leet who pulled her out of the water, gave her the bum's rush up his mountain, and was peeling her wet clothes off now. That had to count for something.

He yanked his own wet sweatshirt off before he pulled her back against him, shuddering when her breasts pressed against his bare chest. Even as he was, sloppy wet and half-frozen himself, his dick began to stir. Manfully, he tried to ignore it.

He unzipped her jeans and tugged them down her hips. They clung, and she sagged, and altogether it wasn't easy. Finally, he sat down with her in his lap and held her in one arm so he could use the other to wrangle off her thick wool socks—toes pink—and then maneuver her legs free. And then he didn't look some more.

He held a lot of woman in his arms. She was tall—five-ten or eleven, he guessed—with long, sleekly muscled limbs. She had good, firm shoulders and those breasts, well, he'd already *not* looked at those. He wasn't looking at her ass either, though he knew it was extremely shapely, too—that had pretty much been the view of her he'd had down at the river. Not that he'd noticed then either. They'd both been busy. Now he could see—or not—the generous curve of her hips. He stroked this thumb over her there, just where her belly turned concave. And *didn't* look where her mons had just a little drift of hair, a shade darker than the ashy blond of her head.

He stirred some more and, God's truth, tried hard not to look. She had an athlete's body, he admired that. And the rest—well. He was, indeed, in trouble.

She didn't wear a ring. He'd made note of that out there on the ice, very soon after he'd developed an appreciation for her shapely butt. Before he'd held her in his arms. Before he'd called her baby or kissed her.

With a heavy sigh, he brought them both to their feet. Her eyes opened watchfully, and she stood more or less on her own, silent, while he wrapped her in one of his giant towels. Then he took her back up in his arms and carried her to bed.

He had a lot of choices. The hot tub he'd brought her to, the one that was always filled and warm, was in his gym, which also doubled as his studio. That area was huge—taking over half the square footage on this level and more, given that part of the studio was open to the floor above to accommodate his larger works. Oddly, the gym and studio worked well together. Both required open, flexible space. He used the exercise equipment during breaks in his work, and others did as well.

Very often he had students working with him, or there, at least. He had a lot of equipment for metal work—more than most sculptors could afford early in their careers. For that, he had his first career to be grateful to, and he was. And he was happy to share. Sometimes, he'd have area college or university students taking a concentration semester in studio metalwork. Or adults pursuing an old dream or even just indulging themselves in a hobby. For any who wanted it, he had a living space off the far end of the studio—a handful of dorm-like bedrooms and a great room with a kitchen area. That part of the house was empty now, just after the holidays when people were still home with family.

Upstairs, above the level of his own living space and alongside his own bedroom, he had a full guest suite and another guest bedroom as well.

He had lots of empty beds, lots of places he could take her.

But he didn't consider, didn't pause for even a second as he carried her to his own bed.

She took to it readily, curling on to her side, tucking her hand up under her cheek. He sat next to her and brushed her damp hair back—ear still pink.

"Where's your son?" He spoke quietly, almost a whisper as her eyes drooped.

"At the high school." She spoke sleepily, also quiet.

"Sadie, I'm sure they closed the schools for the storm."

"He goes early for practice. I talked with him on his cell this morning, while it was still dark. He was on his way then. Before the storm."

Had he been with his father, who lived somewhere else? Leet liked the sound of that.

"I'll get him. What's his name?"

"Jace Freeman."

"Okay. You sleep. I'll go."

"Wait. What are you driving?"

He had plenty of choices there, too. But he knew she had a four-wheeler still down by the river. "I thought I'd take your rig, get it off the side of the road. That okay?"

"Yeah. That's good. I left the keys in it."

Of course she did. Smart, competent woman.

He slipped his fingers in between her cheek and her palm and squeezed her hand for a minute. "It was nice to meet you, Sadie Freeman."

She opened those damn blue eyes and smiled just a bit. "My last name is Benjamin."

He kissed her cheek. "Sleep, Sadie Benjamin."

A different last name than her son. He liked the sound of that, too. He straightened as she drifted off, then he quietly pulled out some fresh clothes. He worked off his wet boots and jeans in the bathroom and got dry and dressed. She was soundly asleep when he left the room.

Jace Freeman. He played that name in his mind until it clicked. Then he called Ray Morgan. Ray had been his football coach through high school, nearly a father to him. After college, Leet had married Ray's daughter, making Ray his father-in-law. That relationship had been a good one—better than Leet had with his wife—and they kept it even now. Did a man stop being your father-in-law, just because your wife died?

*C*HAPTER TWO

Sadie rolled over onto her other side, snuggling deeper under the blankets, and took pleasure in simply being warm and dry. When she peeked out, she saw it was dark outside. She must have slept for hours.

There was nothing but window along one wall, and she could see snow falling—still heavy, but gently, quietly now. The wind was gone. It was a lovely sensation, to almost feel out there, to almost be a part of the storm, but still to be safe inside, and oh-so warm. In his bed.

She thought about that for a while.

It had been an extraordinary day. A lovely birth. That wild storm. She'd heard thunder, she knew, when she'd pulled off the road at that curve. And then the rescue—baby Gracie, nearly lost in the water, Jeb so bravely climbing through that window over ice and water. Leet holding on to her before he let her go into the car, into the water. Letting her know he'd have her.

And then the water. Cold like she'd never known, like ice down into her core. The helpless frustration as her fingers wouldn't do what she needed, how she had finally used them like a club to batter at the seatbelt latch. Then the woman was gone, and the car and the water took Sadie. All but for that grip Leet had on her wrist. A grip she knew, she *knew*, would never loosen, until he had her in his arms.

Leet. She really had to think about that.

They'd bonded, she knew, like people did in a crisis. She'd experienced it before—it was similar to the camaraderie she'd felt among the staff at the labor and delivery unit when, together, they'd handled an obstetrical emergency. It was a good, solid feeling, an effect of adrenaline and high emotion. It helped form good working relationships.

Leet had felt it, too, obviously. They'd been thrown into the rescue together, strangers forced into sudden intimacy. He'd saved her—his strength pitted against the river. He'd held her as she shook with cold and pain. He'd undressed her. Of course they would feel connected.

It was adrenaline and high emotion. She understood it.

He'd kissed her, more than once. He'd tucked her naked into his own bed.

And honestly? None of it had felt wrong.

She could be in trouble.

⁓◞⧸⧹

Sadie tottered into the bathroom—she was waking up, but she still felt the effects of the morphine. She was pleased to see her overnight bag there. She always kept it in the car so she'd have the toiletries and a change of clothing she might need in the case of a prolonged labor.

The bathroom was on a par with the rest of the house she'd seen—lots of glass, stone, and wood. There was another hot tub—not the deep, hold-a-party sort that he'd tossed her into before, but still big enough for two, even if one of the two was as big as an ox. Better, for her purposes, was the shower. Slate again, a bench seat, and showerheads from all directions.

And, as it turned out, endless hot water. The tub had no appeal, still bringing to mind those awful moments of being pulled under in the river. But the shower was glorious, and she wallowed in it to her heart's content.

Wrapped in a warmed towel—the man didn't stint on creature comforts—she padded back into the bedroom. Lights on, she took a good look around. She found it lovely. The bed—king-sized, of course—was a deep mattress floating like an island on a platform of burnished wood. The same wood framed the huge windows and formed a wall of shelves interspersed with a door on either side, likely closets, at the head of the bed. Opposite, the wall was of stone, interrupted only by a fireplace and a large flat-screen that could be viewed from either the bed or a recliner—black leather, extra-large—near the windows. The dressers and the table next to the recliner were more sleek wood.

Masculine, but lovely, entirely comfortable and welcoming.

And curiously, the long padded chest at the foot of the bed held another of her bags. When she opened it, it was clear that Leet had been to her home and that one of the moms had helped him out. It contained a couple days' worth of her clothes—sweats and jeans, sweaters and t-shirts, undies and fluffy socks—just the things to wait out a winter storm. Though she noted it wasn't her *practical* underwear that had been selected.

On a hunch, she went to one of the doors in the wall. When she opened it, lights came on to reveal a deep walk-in closet. It extended from where the wall met the windows to, she guessed, the center of the bed. It was filled with Leet's clothes—on hangers or in built-in drawers and cubbies.

Around the bed, on the side that led to the bathroom, she found an equivalent space. It was not, she was undeniably relieved to see, filled with a woman's clothes. It did give her pause, however, though no real surprise, to find a few items of her own clothing. Again, winter weather gear—snow pants and parka, snow boots. It looked suspiciously like she was expected to ride out the storm here in Leet's house. Even, if one were to make assumptions from the obvious, in his bedroom.

She slipped into some clothes—a long-sleeved tee, sweats, and a pair of socks—and left the room.

The door opened to a balcony. On her left, the balcony made a right turn, passing a couple doors that were presumably to more bedrooms. Then stairs descended to an open living space. It had a seating area around a fireplace, another around a television/gaming console, and a long dining table set along the windows.

Beyond that and one floor down, she could see, was the area where Leet had first taken her—that huge room she'd seen filled with exercise equipment and metal sculpture under construction. A gym and a studio, apparently. The far end of it was open to the living area above and, from where she stood at the rail, she could see the tops of some of the sculptures.

Trees, she realized. She'd almost thought it a dream, mixed in with that memory of the glittering, ice-coated trees she'd seen with the sunrise and then those harrowing minutes she'd spent thawing out in the studio.

He built trees. At least, she had to assume he was the sculptor. And they were gorgeous. As she recalled, only a handful were complete. One she could see was a majestic birch that reached nearly to the ceiling of the upper lever. Its trunk and branches were constructed of silver metal, almost white, rough and peeling like birch bark, pocked with dabs of brown. And leaves—there were thousands of them. All proper birch-shaped, but of varying materials. Most were simple, flat cutouts of shimmering metal in tones from silver to copper. But scattered among them were true leaves—intricately cast with the jagged edges and network of veins as seen in nature. And more—faceted crystals cut into leaf shapes that scattered light in all directions.

She remembered looking up at it when he'd held her, naked, in his arms. It had seemed surreal then, shifting her in time and place to the aftermath of the early morning ice storm.

Now, she remembered other trees—many still unfinished. Small ones, in the shape of dwarf Japanese maples or weeping cherries. She recalled a mid-sized one, a pussy willow with narrow, curling leaves and catkins made of dark glass. And another huge one—a maple, with branches just being built out from the sturdy trunk.

Organizing it all in her mind now, she knew it was incredible, beautiful work.

And the sculptor sat below, sunk deep into a leather couch, controller in his hands, vigorously and vociferously competing with another avid gamer. That was her son Jace, who appeared to have no qualms about trash-talking back to his much larger, adult opponent.

Leet was every bit as loud as Jace, but sat more sedately, held down as he was by the weight of her other son, four-year-old Tino, who was passed out on his lap and drooling on his chest. He had his feet propped on an ottoman table that still held the remains of a total guy-party—torn bags of chips, mostly empty, a bucket of chicken from the local grocery, and a bunch of dead soldiers—empty bottles of soda and, in two or maybe three instances, beer.

Bemused, she watched them for a couple minutes before she headed down the stairs. Leet spotted her first and let the controller fall, his attention fixed on her.

He looked extremely appealing. He was dressed in soft denim worn white at the stress points, an olive sweater that looked like it might have been army-issue, if the army had an equal eye to fashion as function, and bright knitted socks. He held Tino and had been engaged with Jace as though it was natural. As though he was enjoying himself.

And when he looked at her, that felt natural, too. His eyes scanned her, focusing with concern and, she could see, appreciation. When he was done looking, he held her gaze, open and calm.

Then Jace elbowed him in the arm. "Come on, man. Get in the game. I just powned you."

Leet elbowed back and got his attention, nodding his head toward Sadie.

Jace jumped up and clambered over Leet's legs. "Ma!"

He came to her with an enthusiastic hug. At fourteen, he was just a couple inches shorter than she. In another year or two, she'd be looking up at him. She was smart enough to enjoy his childlike enthusiasm, not seen so much these days, and hugged him back, hard. For sure, it wasn't every day he'd drop a video game to hug his mother.

Over Jace's shoulder, she met Leet's eyes. He looked a bit cautious, but stood, Tino drooped against his chest, and approached her.

"You have my boys."

"Uh, yeah," he said, looking like he'd scratch his head if he had a free hand. "I picked up Jace like I said I would. We had nearly a foot of snow by then and the roads were sh— slippery. When I got him home, we discussed it with your, uh, moms." That appeared to cost him a bit. "Another couple hours and we were all going to be snowed in wherever we were. We thought you'd probably rather have the boys with you. Otherwise, it could be a few days before you got back together again. I think we were right, too. We've got nearly three feet out there now. Nobody's gonna be moving for a while."

She glanced at Jace, who nodded and seemed to be trying to contain his eagerness. That must be a heck of a game system Leet had.

"So we're snowed in here, with you."

Leet met her gaze solidly, giving nothing away. "Yeah. It seemed best."

She nodded, aware of Jace, beside her now, quietly watching their exchange. "That's fine."

Tino turned his head on Leet's shoulder—maybe Leet wouldn't notice the drool spot on his sweater—and opened sleepy eyes. When he saw her, he reached out and was in her arms, snuggled into the crook of her neck. With one "Mama," he was asleep again.

Leet had stepped closer to her for the transfer. He stayed close now, leaned in, and put his lips to hers for just a moment. "You look good, Sadie. Are you feeling all right? Any pain?"

"I'm fine."

In blatant retreat, she took a step back, but he held her elbow. "Are you hungry? We've got...uh."

She followed his eyes while he glanced at the table and then to Jace. "We probably should have cleaned up, eh, dude?"

Jace grinned. "Yeah. We could've told her we had salad."

Leet grinned back. "You think she'd have bought that?"

"Maybe," Jace claimed, then giggled as Leet poked him. "Well, get started on it."

Jace did, filling his arms with empty bottles and bags of chips. Leet shrugged with a superior smile as Sadie raised an eyebrow at him.

"Why don't you see what you can rustle up for your mom while I help her put Tino to bed?" He turned to Sadie, still holding her arm. "Okay?"

When she nodded, he headed them back to the stairs. He opened the first door at the top and reached in to turn on the light before waiting for her to enter. She started in, then stopped and looked back at him when she saw the boys' bags there, their own pillows, and Tino's raggedy stuffed bear on one of the beds.

Leet gave her that steady look again but didn't speak. She couldn't really argue with his decision to keep them all there, and he was apparently done explaining it. She carried Tino into the bathroom and kept him on his feet long enough for him to brush his teeth and use the toilet.

"Come on, buddy."

He climbed into bed, snuggling with his bear, and Sadie tucked him in.

When she leaned in to kiss him, he kept her there with a

hand on her cheek. "Mr. Leet said you're a hero."

She smiled and ruffled his hair. "We saw some people in trouble, and Mr. Leet and I helped them out. We were just doing the right thing, just like everybody should do every day."

"You said that before. Do the right thing every day. That's what a hero does."

"That's right." She kissed him again. "You going to be able to sleep here?"

He looked around the room and pointed to the other bed. "Jace will sleep there, right?"

She nodded. "Yup."

"You'll leave the light in the bathroom on?"

"Yup."

"And if you have to go, Mr. Leet will stay with us, like the grandmoms do?"

"I'm not going anywhere tonight, sweetie."

"What if a baby wants to come out?"

"Hmm," she said, and nuzzled him. "No baby with any sense would want to come out on a night like this." She surely hoped that was true. "I'll be here." She reached to turn off the bedside light. "Now, sleep."

"'Kay. Good night, Mr. Leet."

Leet answered from the door, where he leaned, shoulders filling the doorway. "Night, Tino. Sweet dreams."

With another kiss, she stood and approached Leet. He stayed in place, watching her for a few moments before he stepped back and let her pass.

In the kitchen, they found Jace competently handling some canned soup and a grilled cheese sandwich. He served it up and got a kiss for it from Sadie as she sat on a stool at the island.

Leet got a beer and watched them as Jace sat next to her, asking about the rescue. They leaned toward each other, heads almost touching. Her blond hair, dry now and swinging to her shoulders, contrasted sharply with Jace's tight, dark curls in neat cornrows, beaded at the ends.

Jace played football—a stand out quarterback, according

to Ray, with great hands and a lot of promise. Jace recognized Leet the moment he'd parked Sadie's car outside the gym. When Coach had given him leave to go with Leet, Jace had barely been able to contain himself. For sure, he'd gotten the story of Sadie's actions in the rescue, heard a hint at least of the jeopardy she'd been in, and been assured of her safety, but after that, it was all football.

Leet knew he had a significant case of hero-worship going on. It seemed okay to him, because he had a lot of admiration for Jace, too. He was a bright, enthusiastic, loveable kid, after having a start in life that would have been ruinous for most. Ray told Leet as the boy had collected his gear. His father had died of an overdose in prison, his mother violently at the hand of another boyfriend. He'd been passed around from one poor and overburdened relative to another. Until he'd been rescued at age nine by a young midwife who'd seen the light still in him, maybe just barely flickering.

A midwife he watched now, who, in the opposite extreme of her son, not only failed to recognize him, but *didn't even like football*. Jace could play football, his adoptive mother had told him. But it was a game. It wasn't *life*. He could be an athlete, but he was a *student*-athlete. It was school that required his serious attention. He could only *play* football.

Jace had related all this with every expectation that Leet would understand and sympathize. "Yeah, mothers," they'd said in unison. You couldn't expect them to get it. And Leet had agreed, with Jace's urging, that it might be better if Sadie was kept in the dark about his profession.

But Leet wouldn't mind if she'd share just a little bit of the admiration for him that her son had. He knew that she wasn't particularly pleased with the whole snowbound sleepover arrangement. She'd accepted it with fair grace, but she was clearly wary of him. It wasn't the usual response he got from women these days.

Especially not from hot, single women—which latter fact Jace had not hesitated to share. No husband, no boyfriend. There was that issue of the two moms, but that wasn't so much genetic, was it?

She hadn't seemed immune to his kisses, exactly, but she hadn't really returned them either. She was—wary.

She was going to have to get over it.

Sadie ate with real appetite. He knew she'd burned a lot

of energy as her body had fought the cold. She said no to a
beer when he offered one, but warmed his heart when she
absentmindedly took his from his hand to wash down the last
of the sandwich.

Jace was serious as he listened to Sadie's account of the
rescue. She was honest with him and gave a lot of the details, but still left out the worst of it. Jace didn't hear that she
was still in the car as it sank. And he heard a lot about Leet's
role.

Eyes twinkling, she took his beer to swig again. "After we
got the kids out, Leet tried to warm me up. He put my cold
hands under his shirt, against his skin. You should've heard
him. He squealed like a girl."

Jace snickered and punched Leet's arm.

Leet took his beer back and pointed it at her. "You take
that back."

Sadie and Jace exchanged a look and burst out laughing.

They kept laughing even as he got them in headlocks
against his chest and managed to noogie both of them,
though the one was more of a caress.

Sadie left her hand on his chest for a long moment when
he let them up, and the glee in her eyes settled into something softer as their gazes met and held. She slipped away
from him and took her dishes to the sink. As she passed Jace, she whispered, "Like a girl," just loudly enough for Leet
to hear, too. The boy stifled another chuckle when he caught
Leet's eye and made a show of helping with the clean-up.

Hiding his own grin, Leet did the same, bringing in more
trash from the living room. When Sadie put the last of the
dishes in the washer, Leet took over, filling the detergent cup
and setting it to run.

Jace watched him finish up and spoke sympathetically.
"Guess you do live alone, huh?"

Leet caught his mischievous eye and winked. "Oh yeah."

Sadie put her hands on her hips, the towel she'd been
using dangling. "Wait. Are you two implying that if he lived
with a woman, he wouldn't know how to run a dishwasher?"

Leet and Jace looked at her, all fake innocence. "Well,
yeah."

Jace was quick, so the towel ended up hitting Leet's
chest. He gave the kid credit, but quietly, a thumbs up behind his back.

Leet moved out of the line of fire when Sadie pointed a finger at Jace. "You're going to bed."

Jace pretended to be chastened. "Yes, ma'am."

The two stepped together for a long, affectionate hug. Jace looked up, just a bit, into his mother's face. "We get to sleep in, right? Snow day, tomorrow?"

"I'm thinking." She kissed him. "Sleep tight. Love you."

"Me, too."

Jace gave Leet a fist-pound, chest-thump combo before he took himself off upstairs.

Then Leet was alone with Sadie.

He watched her carefully, making her nervous as she gave a last, unnecessary swipe to the counter.

"You've had quite a day of it. Are you really okay?"

She stopped puttering and looked back at him. Steeling herself a bit, she walked around the counter to face him. "I really am." She stood close, working to keep eye contact. "You saved my life. I knew you would. I knew you wouldn't let go. That saved me."

He took her hand and lifted it, peeling back the long sleeve she'd deliberately worn to cover the bruise that wrapped around her wrist. He fit his hand over it, matching. Her heart fluttered, feeling the intimacy of his mark on her.

"I know I hurt you. But, no, I wasn't letting go."

She nodded. "Thank you."

"You're welcome." He brought her hand against his chest, over his heart. "But don't ever do that again."

She smiled a bit and shook her head. "No, I won't."

Still holding her wrist, he toyed with her fingers with his other hand. "Do you need to sleep?" She shook her head and followed as he turned. "Good. Come sit with me."

He settled her on a deep sofa, lifted her feet onto another long ottoman table, and laid a chenille throw over her legs. Then he turned to the fireplace and lit the fire. When he came back, he sat on the ottoman, facing her, and lifted one of her feet into his lap. "So, I figured out the boys aren't your biological kids."

She saw the humor in his eyes and smiled back, though

it took a bit of effort since, as he spoke, he was slipping her sock off the foot he held. "No. Jace lost both of his parents and really had no other family who could take him in. He had an aunt who was just a few years older than he was. I met her when she was pregnant. Jace came with her to her pre-natal appointments, even to the hospital when she was in labor. He just had nowhere else to go. He was nine.

"When my patient left the hospital, she was going to stay with the baby's father. Jace wasn't welcome. He was just left there, in her postpartum room, when she packed up the ba-by and walked out." She paused, watching as he put her sock back on and switched to her other foot. She realized he was checking her toes for frostbite. She nudged his hand away. "I'm okay, I told you."

"Denny told me to check. And I will." He ignored her re-sistance and took off the other sock, giving her toes a squeeze before replacing it. "What about Tino?"

"Much the same. I actually delivered him. Seffie was just fifteen when she came to my practice already pregnant. She wouldn't speak of the baby's father. Often that means incest or rape. She never said. She's twenty now and actually doing okay. She lives with an aunt, attends community college. The aunt works hard, and has five children of her own. Seffie sleeps on the living room sofa. They just didn't have room for Tino."

"And so you took him."

Sadie shrugged. "Most girls who have babies when they're that young are poor all of their lives. They have little hope for the future—they may not even finish high school. They'll never have a job that lets them support themselves and their children."

"And they pass that same legacy on to the next genera-tion."

She nodded. "Yeah. Seffie—I should say, Josefina, is so bright. Born into a different family, she could have been any-thing, done anything. She has a small chance to break the cycle. But she couldn't do it and keep Tino, too."

It had been obvious to her, the right thing to do, was all. She was a little uncomfortable with what she saw in his eyes. She wasn't a hero. Giving him a direct look back, she shrugged again.

He smiled but let it go. "You're a midwife."

"Yeah." She was familiar with the question behind that statement. "I take care of women during pregnancy and then deliver their babies. I was working at a clinic in Brooklyn. I took in Jace and then Tino, and we were a family. The inner city thing wasn't working so well for us then. So I moved up here."

He was a good listener, sitting quietly, resting his elbows on his thighs, his eyes on hers.

"I guess you met my moms."

She could see him have to step up to that.

"Uh, yeah."

"They moved back here to Vermont when they could get married. You know, they're—" She left it hanging.

He tightened his jaw a bit. "I can say it."

She snickered. "Go ahead then."

He let it out on a breath. "They're lesbians." He objected when she laughed. "Hey, my mother could be a lesbian. You don't know."

She leaned forward conspiratorially. "She could be. Do you think she is?"

He *almost* wiped the automatic denial from his face and had her laughing again. He retaliated by swatting her leg, but then left his hand there, gently massaging her calf muscle. That was distracting enough that she had to force her attention back.

"Anyway, it was better here, for the kids, and for me, too. One of the moms—Jocelyn, not my bio mom—had grown up on a farm here, and she's taken it over now. They have plenty of land, so we built a small A-frame for the boys and me. I mostly do homebirths here, and practice alone, so I'm on call essentially all the time. It works that the moms are right there. They take over for the boys if I have to go out. I couldn't do it without them."

He nodded, but she was aware that his thoughts were elsewhere. His hand had moved higher up now, stroking above her knee. He'd snugged closer, settled directly across from her, with one of her feet at either side.

He was so attractive—that large, muscled body and male, handsome face. Unruly chocolate brown hair curling at his neck paired with those surprising warm, golden eyes. And a powerful, take-charge attitude softened by unexpected gentleness and humor.

To say nothing of intent determined sexuality.

She suppressed a shudder, willing herself to focus. "You—" She paused and had to try again. "You don't really know me."

His hands slid along both legs now. "You mean, you're aware that I want you, and you think I'm just after your..." His gaze traveled slowly up from where he watched his hands, finally reaching her eyes. "Extremely delectable body."

Sadie couldn't suppress that next tremor. "We met in very unusual circumstances. There was a lot of—"

He slipped forward so he knelt between her knees, spreading them. He slid a hand along her neck, stroking her cheek with his thumb.

"Of adrenaline and emotion. It's not surprising that we'd, that we'd—"

He reached behind her and pulled her forward, bringing her face to face with him. His lips hovered over hers, his breath a soft stroke. "Want each other?"

Sadie shivered as his lips followed the line of her jaw. "Leet," she whispered, feeling lost.

"Sadie." He kissed her neck, lingering, then rested his forehead against hers. "I do know you." His thumb brushed the pulse at her neck. Behind her back, his arm enclosed her. "You went into a freezing river to save a stranger. You took a couple kids into your heart, your life, just because they had no one else to love them. You're compassionate and strong and competent. And courageous." He slid his palm to her lower back and pulled her even closer, pressing her against the erection that strained his jeans. "Plus, you're beautiful and fucking sexy as hell. God, *yes*, I want you."

He took her lips aggressively, sucking and nipping, invading with his tongue. He held her head, captured and vulnerable to his plundering. He slid his other hand under her bottom and steadied her as he rubbed his hardness against her, stimulating her ruthlessly.

Sadie moaned, nearly panicked by the onslaught of his passion and her uncontrollable response. Sharp excitement shot through her, unlike anything she'd ever experienced. This was new to her, and overwhelming.

She struggled a bit. One hand—how many did he have?— now cupped her breast, stroking until he aroused her nipple

then tugging and pinching, sending further shocks of exquisite pleasure coursing through her body. "Leet," she panted,
when his mouth left hers to bite sharply at her earlobe.
"Leet!"

She arched against him, actually rubbing back against
the pressure of his hard cock, pushing her breast more fully
into his hand. Her body seemed to have a mind of its own,
responding, *initiating* even, in ways she couldn't have imagined.

"What?" He lifted her breast and was moving his head. In
a moment, she knew, his mouth would have her nipple. Des-
perately making a stab at sanity, she slipped her fingers over
his lips. "*What?*" he asked once more, his mouth reaching
her breast despite the barrier of her fingers. He rested
against her and shot out a couple deep breaths before he
raised his head to look at her. "Baby." He looked at her but
didn't stop sliding his arms around her, squeezing her
against him here, then there. "Sadie, are you okay?"

She gripped his sweater at his shoulder, a clinging motion committed neither to pushing away nor pulling toward
that precisely represented the chaos of her emotional state.
Shaking, she forced herself to meet his eyes. "I'm afraid."

His gaze searched hers for a long moment. Then he
leaned back, separating them just a little. "You've done this
before, right?"

Had she? "Yes, but—"

That settled him back some more. "But?"

"Not like this, not so—" He waited, but what could she
say? Not so devastating? Not so stunning?

She'd had boyfriends, twice, in college. They'd been
nearly as inexperienced as she, and their few furtive times
together had been touching and sweet and not entirely satis-
fying. Then in graduate school, she'd been so busy, and in
her work that followed, well, being a midwife hardly brought
her into contact with many eligible men.

Plus, she had her sons to think of. She really wasn't the
type for casual sex. And if it wasn't to be casual, then it had
to be thoughtful, careful. Not like this, so gripping, so overwhelming.

She'd ducked her head and she felt him now, fingers
along her jaw, lifting to get her to look at him. "Sadie? Not
so...what?"

"So fast, so overpowering, Leet." She still felt excitement thrum through her and felt it in his hands where he touched her. They were both still wanting. She touched his face and saw his eyes burn. Belatedly, she was aware she was hardly discouraging him. "I don't have much experience." That might not have discouraged him either, judging by the flare in his eyes.

He slid his hand back to her breast and rubbed slowly, almost thoughtfully. "But you've done this—made love before, right?"

Mesmerized by his touch, she nodded.

He found her nipple and squeezed, making her arch up against him. "Have you, uh, had orgasms?"

Sadie cringed—how were they having this conversation?—and then shuddered as he tweaked her nipple again. "Well," she said, "not with a man."

"Whoa." Leet backed way off, not touching her at all, pushing the ottoman behind him back a full foot.

She couldn't believe she found it in her to laugh, but he was in such a comical panic. She grabbed his hand, brought it against her belly. "I don't mean that. I'm heterosexual, Leet."

He'd be mortified to know he was blushing, but it didn't keep him from rubbing her abs. "All the way?"

She nodded.

He nodded back. "All right then."

Moving quickly, all strength and grace, he lifted her and rotated. When he sat, leaning against the back of the couch, he had her on his lap. Her knees were at his sides, straddling him. At her center, she rested right against him, still hard, and he nudged her until they were settled just so.

He stroked his hands over her—gentle strength, warm, arousing. "We can go slower. We can just—kiss," he said, as though he was speaking of something harmless.

Sadie knew, with him, it wasn't. But she let him pull her to his mouth, let him softly take her.

"We'll leave our clothes on."

But it hardly mattered. The way he touched her, she felt it on her skin, as though it burned through her clothes.

"Trust me. You did out there on the ice, remember?"

"I remember."

His kiss *was* soft, and slow. His lips rubbed against hers, just a touch, and then slightly abrading. He kept at it for a long time, gentle with his lips, soothing with his hands. Sadie relaxed into it, only just aware of his occasional slight movements that kept him hard against her, just a touch of friction that kept her body stirred.

Much later, his mouth opened, and he drew her in, pulling first on her lower lip, then her upper. His tongue slid between her teeth and explored her mouth. His hands moved over her with greater intent.

"Touch me, Sadie," he commanded as he went deeper. "Somewhere, anywhere."

She'd braced herself against his shoulders. At his urging, she slipped one hand along his neck, reaching for the curls at the back. She tangled her fingers there, taking a firmer grip in his hair when he shifted to pull her closer, not just a little friction then, but a good, hard pressure. She put her other hand against his chest, feeling the strong, quick beat of his heart.

His hands slid down her back and grasped her hips. His fingers kneaded into her bottom as, with a deep groan, he arched up into her. He was so hard, and large, and rubbed against her so effectively she cried out.

"Kiss me. Keep kissing."

Sadie gripped his hair with both hands now and pressed into his mouth. Beyond her power to control, she rubbed back against him, moving her hips to slide along his full length. She wore only a thong and thin sweats, and the chafing from his jeans was exquisite torture.

He moaned again. He moved one hand along her ass, fingers digging right into her center, bearing down as they rocked roughly together. With the other hand, he took her breast, squeezing and pulling at the nipple. He drew up a fold of her t-shirt and slid his fingers inside her bra, the shirt rough as he knuckled her. He spread his fingers so the nipple popped through and then closed them around her, tweaking her with his thumb.

"Ah." Sadie was lost once more. "Leet." She bucked against him, reveling in his response, staggered by her own pleasure.

"Sadie." He arched his back off the couch, thrusting up. Through her sweats, his hand twisted into her thong, tugging, pulling it tight against her, adding to the stimulation.

Each breath now was a pant, a groan. Their mouths lost contact, and she burrowed into the crook of his neck and shoulder, breathing in his scent, scraping her teeth against his skin while he did the same to her. The pull of his fingers at her nipple became rhythmic, matching the movement of their hips. Which was faster, rougher.

Then they spasmed together, loud and hard. Three more times they ground together before stilling, Sadie feeling too sensitive then to touch. They held each other, breathing harshly, until Leet sank back into the couch with a huff. He brought his hands to her head, holding her against his heaving chest.

As their breathing slowed, he lifted her head to bring her face to face with him. He watched her carefully, intently.

Lost, Sadie thought yet again. He was so—much, so appealing, so strong, so compelling. And yet, also gentle and tender and now—vulnerable. She couldn't help but smile, and that brought relief to his face.

She slid both hands to his neck, stroked his jaw with her thumbs. "You kiss, uh, pretty good."

He huffed out a laugh, then glanced with chagrin at his fly and the wet stain there. "I haven't done that since junior high."

"Let me guess. Elsbeth Thomas, sexy class nerd. In the library."

He grinned, entirely charming. "Nope. Prissy MacAvoy, smokin' hot cheerleader. In the bleachers."

They both laughed as she rolled off of him. He held her hand while she settled next to him. "I need a shower," he said as he nibbled at her fingers, still watching her.

She sternly suppressed the little quiver that his lips caused, the reaction she knew he was looking for. "Okay. I'll clear my stuff out of your room."

He stood up and pulled her with him, holding her loosely. "Not necessary. I'll go downstairs. I shower down there as often as not after I work out. After I work, I mean."

He kissed her and started to turn away, but she tugged at his arm. "Leet, I'm not sleeping with you tonight."

He gave her a long look and a heavy sigh. "Fair enough. I'll take the guest suite then." He stroked his hand through her hair. "I'm going to really, really enjoy the thought of you in my bed, even if I'm not there with you."

Sadie checked on the boys, relieved to find them both sound asleep. She took the book that had fallen onto the bed from Jace's hands and set it aside with a smile. He was in the midst of a science fiction classics kick right now. Before Sadie, no one had ever read to him. It had taken weeks for him to even lie still for a bedtime story. And then, like a light going on, he'd gotten it and had never been without a book since. It was one of many things about him that made her proud. She was even proud of his remarkable skill and grace on the football field, though she took pleasure in that discreetly. She'd seen too many young men in the city who thought of sports as their only way out when it was the answer for only a very few of them. And even then, it often ended badly. Still, she knew he loved it and would never think to keep him from playing. As long as school came first. And she was lucky that way. He was a great student. She kissed his forehead and then Tino's, and, shutting off the light, left the room.

She went down the stairs to the living area, then down one more flight to the lower level. The huge space was an odd, and oddly appealing, combination of sculpture studio and workout room—extensively equipped in both cases. To the back there was a curve of glass block—from beyond that came the sound of a shower running. On either side of the glass block was a bench with pretty wooden lockers and cubbies. In front, along the floor-to-ceiling windows, was the hot tub she'd, well, *survived* earlier in the day. Beyond the windows, she could see nothing but the night and the storm—and snow drifts reaching halfway up the glass. Many of the windows, she realized, were really sliding doors. In warm weather, this space would open up to the outdoors.

She knew little of it, but she recognized a forge in a separate bay that opened into the back of the house. A crane hung overhead there, suspended from ceiling beams on a track that ran the length of the room. There was an area for welding, enclosed on three sides, filled with tanks, hoses, torches, and protective gear. Large workbenches circled the area, each with an array of tools—hammers of an amazing variety, cutters, power tools for polishing, she guessed—it seemed endless.

And the workout equipment was similarly numerous and varied. Several machines for aerobics—a treadmill, elliptical, bike, and rowing machine. And weights—free weights, weight machines—also seeming endless. There was a large mat, speed and heavy boxing bags, exercise balls, and a wall strung with jump ropes, elastic bands, and other things with functions she could only guess at. Viewing screens hung from the ceiling, in case the scenery out the windows was not enough entertainment. The area rivaled a high-end fitness center.

She moved about in the studio, appreciating again the remarkably fine work and beauty of those metal trees. She ran her fingers along the leaves of a weeping cherry that was about her height, nearly finished. The leaves hung free, chiming in response to her touch. Outdoors, it would be a visually and audibly dynamic, complex sculpture—a quiet wind chime in a gentle breeze, clamorous in a windstorm.

Clearly, it was a working studio, the equipment extensive, maybe even indulgent, but used to incredible effect. The same could be said of the workout area—it may be a bit over the top, but it didn't lie idle. Not judging by Leet's physical form.

He was large, yes, but heavily muscled in addition. His strength was obvious in the ease with which he'd pulled her from the river, lifted her over him when they'd been upstairs. He'd hauled her up his drive—nearly carrying her the whole way without appearing winded in the least.

His body was beautiful, itself finely sculpted, and further, strong and graceful. Not just pretty, but ultimately *useable*, powerful, at his command. She'd played volleyball in college and had spent a lot of time in gyms. She'd seen guys working hard to build muscle, but seldom had she seen it combined with such athletic grace.

And, *oh yeah*, beautiful. She saw it now as he walked out of the shower area, scrubbing at his wet head with one towel, another slung low around his hips. He was all firm, sleek muscle—his arms, lifted to his head, his abs as they ran from his ribs to disappear behind the towel.

He was moving to a locker but stopped when he caught her looking. He was nearly naked, but didn't seem uncomfortable to have her there. She couldn't say the same, though. She felt a blush on her cheeks and started to turn away.

"Sadie."

She turned back just a little and met his eyes.

"I don't mind you looking at me." He ran the towel in his hand over his shoulders, then dropped it on the bench.

She took a breath, trying not to stammer. "You work out a lot. Your body is very—muscled."

The corners of his mouth lifted. "Metalwork is not for pussies." He said that, and then dropped the towel from around his waist. He faced her, watched her watching him.

She stood, unmoving. She tried to swallow, though her mouth was dry. His eyes darkened, and his penis, lying along his upper thigh, thickened and stirred. Lengthened.

After a long moment, he turned toward a locker. Moving very slowly, he opened it and rummaged, giving her plenty of time to appreciate his very nice ass. He turned back to her, watching her as he slid his legs one at a time into a pair of sweats. He had to stretch the waistband out to bring it over his penis, then adjusted himself with his hand in a lingering kind of way.

When he was done doing that, their gazes locked. She wasn't sure who flinched first, but in a moment, they were both laughing. He slid his feet into a pair of leather slippers and walked over to her.

Tenderly, he pulled her into his arms, his bare chest not quite touching, just a little pressure below where his hardness came in contact with her belly. He kissed her forehead and stroked her hair. He still smiled, but their laughter subsided.

"I can't help it. It wants you."

"And you have no control over it."

He raised a hand. "God's truth."

She rolled her eyes and turned away, aware of his hand sliding over her, keeping contact until she was out of reach. She moved into the studio area with him behind her, catching up so he could keep a hand at her back. Apparently, he liked to touch. She motioned to some of the trees.

"These are amazing, Leet. Really, nothing short of amazing." She looked back at him. "It's your work, right?"

He nodded, apparently more interested in watching her

than looking at his art.

"You must sell them." He didn't speak, his gaze still on her. "Don't you?"

He took a moment to respond, his attention lingering on her. "Uh, not yet, really. It's kind of a second career. I'm supposed to have a show this summer, though. We'll see what happens then."

"They'll sell, Leet, I'm sure of it. You'll have trouble keeping up with demand." She stroked that cherry tree again. "The work is so detailed, so painstaking. Each one must take weeks of work, months."

He shrugged. "A lot of it is drudgery—I make a *lot* of leaves. I get some help. I often have students here. They help me out in exchange for use of the studio. It works out for all of us."

She went to the pussy willow. "I love this."

"Yeah. I had a glass student join me on it. It turned out okay."

"*Okay*," she scoffed. "It's beautiful, Leet." She sighed and looked at him. "I'd be your first customer, but I'm afraid I could never afford even one."

He kissed her and slid his hand down to her bottom, pulling her close against him again. He rutted into her a couple times, a flicker of laughter in his eyes. "I'm sure we could find a way for you to work it off." He chuckled as she swatted him and pushed away, but then he grabbed her hand. "There are more outside. Come look."

He went to the end of the studio near the forge, keeping her at his side. He flicked a switch that lit up the outdoors— an area just outside sheltered by a large, upper level deck and, beyond that, an expansive yard. She suspected there was a pond buried under the snow in a depression thirty or forty yards out and then a gentle incline leading up to a more rugged, forested hillside.

Largely sunk in snow, and covered still in thick layers of ice, some of his sculptures were visible in the yard. They circled the pond and were scattered around the hill.

But nearer, in the protected terrace beneath the deck, was a veritable forest of his work. Here, they were bare, sheltered from the ice and snow. And the lights, shining from above and below, lit them up like she'd imagined them on a sunny day. It was a glistening, glittering wonderland, just like she'd seen nature produce only that morning.

Sadie laughed in delight and kissed his cheek without thought. "Leet, it's this morning's ice storm. Just as gorgeous, only permanent." She looked at him in wonder. "And you made it."

He held her with one arm, elbow at her back, hand cupping her nape. "I'm glad you like them, Sadie." His eyes were serious then, showing none of the laughter that had been in them before.

He walked her to her room—his room—with that same arm around her, that same serious mood. He stopped at the door and kissed her, gently, but taking his time at it, putting some feeling into it.

It was a heart-melting kind of kiss, and Sadie was not immune to it. She knew it would take very little for him to change her mind about where he was spending the night. She felt a little relief and a little regret also when he stepped away from her. And then some fear as he spoke.

"That was some hot sex, Sadie, that *kissing*, we had before. Very appealing, very compelling, in and of itself. I'll never say no to more of that. But the fact is, I'm falling for you."

She shook her head, denying his words or the heat that shot through her, she wasn't sure which. "No, Leet. It's too soon to think that. It's too much...part of this day."

"You think that if you want to, Sadie. Another day isn't going to change it. I don't think a week or a month or a year will, either." He took one more step back. "You sleep well in my bed. I'll be thinking of you there."

When she tucked herself in, she thought that might have been a curse. She was surrounded by his scent, haunted by the knowledge that he was thinking of her here, in his bed. She thought she'd never sleep. She thought that for nearly a full three minutes, when she drifted into slumber.

ℭHAPTER THREE

Sadie woke at dawn, the sky just beginning to lighten, a little sunrise color visible over the ridge outside of Leet's windows. She felt warm and rested and very alive. There was something in the way that Leet had touched her that woke her body, something in the experiences of the remarkable day they'd passed that aroused her—what—her spirit? She wondered for a moment if, in seeking a simpler, safer life for her little family, she'd disengaged too much from her own life. Certainly, she'd been aware of the mildly concerned looks that the moms exchanged periodically. They wanted her to be happy, she knew, and they weren't certain that she was.

She was, though. She loved the boys and her work. The combination gave her life a great deal of fullness.

Yesterday had given her life a great deal of excitement. She couldn't and wouldn't choose to go into a frozen river every day. But she could, it appeared, choose Leet. At the least, she could open herself to the possibility of a relationship with him. There would be excitement in that and, as had been made obvious, significant pleasure.

The desire they'd had for each other, that needing, wanting thrum their bodies had found for each other, had been almost scary-strong. Very, very appealing and compelling. She hadn't felt quite safe.

So, was safety what mattered most to her? She wouldn't have thought so, but here she was, quelled by the power of her attraction to Leet. It would take a certain amount of courage to face up to it. Courage wasn't a thing she thought she lacked.

Still, she also had the responsibility of two young lives dependent on her. Having her sons did not give her an excuse to retreat from the challenges and possibilities of her own life. But they were a reason to act with caution.

There it was then. She should proceed. But with caution. A shower seemed like a safe first step.

The next step also seemed very easy when she went downstairs and found Leet and Tino together in the kitchen. They were busy. Leet worked at breakfast—it appeared waffles were on the menu. And Tino sat on the counter, directing and entertaining him. Leet wore low-slung jeans and an unzipped hoodie, confirming that he could look good in anything. Tino was still in his pajamas, with athletic socks covering his feet and running up over his thighs. Apparently, they'd forgotten his slippers.

They were a pair—discussing the finer points of, it seemed, bacon. One of which was that all real men loved it. Tino thought women did, too, but granted Leet's point that it was optional for them.

Leet's eyes met Sadie's, but he kept up his end of the conversation—which had moved on now to the obvious superiority of Vermont maple syrup, particularly in regards to waffles.

She joined them.

She went to Tino, enjoying his always pure, enthusiastic greeting. He threw his arms around her and accepted her kiss, then laughed and arched away with her prolonged nuzzle.

"Umm." She nuzzled some more and blew a raspberry in his neck, bringing another gleeful laugh. "What's that smell? Is it—bacon? I love it when my men smell like bacon."

Still trying to escape, he squealed. "Leet made me eat it! For the man club!"

She chuckled and kissed him more sedately. "Did you sleep well?"

"Yeah. But Jace was mean to me when I got up."

"He was?"

"He told me to shut up and go away."

"Ah, that was rude, wasn't it?"

"Yeah."

"I'll talk to him. But remember when we figured out that teenage boys like to sleep in? And that they're grumpy if you wake them up?"

"Yeah. Leet wasn't grumpy, though."

"Oh." She cringed and met Leet's eyes, glad for the humor there. "Sorry."

He nodded. "No problem. It was *nearly* morning. It turns out we like the same cartoons."

"And bacon."

"Yeah, dude. High five."

He was close enough then that he could slip an arm around her and turn her a little away from Tino and into him.

"I smell like bacon, too, you know."

She returned the smile in his eyes. "Do you? Well, then." She lifted up and leaned into him, closing in on his mouth, then blew a raspberry into his neck.

He laughed, but kept his hold—with his hands and with his eyes. He spoke quietly. "It's a new day, Sadie. I'm still falling."

"Leet." Her heart skipped a beat, but she held still as he lowered his mouth. His lips were soft but hungry—and bacon-flavored. How could she resist?

And so she didn't, but slipped her arms around his neck and kissed back.

He let out the softest of moans and held her at the waist—discreetly, but firmly enough to let her know he was getting hard. He lifted up only when Tino swung his foot against his arm. It took him a moment to let go of Sadie's gaze and look at Tino. "What?"

"If she kisses you, it means she loves you."

"Yeah?" His gaze came back to Sadie, hot now, and with a wicked gleam of triumph. "Good to know."

Sadie closed her eyes but couldn't stop the blush that warmed her cheeks.

"And if she kisses me a lot?"

"She loves you a lot. That's what she said for me."

"Better and better." It was just a murmur, just a moment before his lips took hers again. This time, he held her gently. The kiss was soft, cherishing. Moving. Enough so that it caused Sadie to shiver.

He leaned back, but held her face until she lifted her eyes to his. Courage, she thought. It took more than she would have guessed.

Finally, he seemed satisfied and gave her a pat. "That a girl." Then he lifted a brow at Tino, responding to the ever more persistent nudge from the boy's foot. "What, little man?"

Tino raised a brow back. "*Waffles*?"

Leet huffed out a laugh. "Yeah, all right." He turned Sadie around, keeping his hands at her waist. "Stay right there for a couple minutes."

She wiggled a little against him. "Right here?"

He grasped her hips to still her movement. "Not helping, you witch." He sidled away, moving a little stiffly and keeping his back to Tino. On his way, he dragged his hand across her bottom, a provocative grope included.

"Mama."

It took a moment. "Yeah, baby?"

"He called you a witch."

Her breathing wasn't steady, but she managed a small laugh. "Did he? I guess older guys get grumpy, too."

Jace joined them before they were finished with breakfast, and so, when it was done, the waffles were demolished and the bacon long gone.

They ate together, then cleaned up the kitchen, Tino enjoying giving directions while he rode on Leet's back. Sadie and Leet toasted each other when Will Hunter called and gave them an update on yesterday's mishap. The kids were fine and with their dad. The mom was at the medical center, out of ICU, and expected to recover just fine.

They were easy together—Jace gradually waking up and becoming human, Tino constantly chattering, and Sadie appearing comfortable and, Leet thought, happy. But nervous, too, he could see. She watched him interact with the boys, but her smile would waver when he'd catch her at it.

Still, she was facing up to what was there between them. He could hardly hold her hesitation against her. As the morning progressed, he was aware that twenty-four hours before, they hadn't even known each other. It wasn't rational that the desire he had for her, and more, the *feelings* he had, could have grown to seem so right so quickly.

It was beyond anything he'd ever experienced.

He'd loved his wife, Suhayla. She'd been a part of his life since high school, when Ray had become his coach. Suhayla was Ray's daughter—stepdaughter, really, and the young girl had been a kind of team mascot. She was always there, her big, dark eyes watching as the only father she'd known shaped boys into football players and young men.

Then, when Leet had come back to visit after his junior year at UVM, Suhayla wasn't a girl anymore. She'd spent a year at the Fashion Institute studying design. She still had the big, dark eyes, but everything else about her was different. From the elegant up-do of her lustrous black hair to the painted red toenails peeking from her strappy, sexy heels, and all parts in between, she was different.

She seemed to see him differently, too. He was a year away from a career in professional football and his future looked good. Daughter of his coach, the person closest to him in the world, she seemed to fit perfectly.

He hadn't touched her until they married, and that was after he had a contract to play ball. They had a romantic, intense relationship for his first couple years as a pro.

But they'd lost that, and then she'd died.

Since then, sex was easy. He hadn't been looking for a relationship, and there were plenty of women who were generous with their bodies around pro-football players. He didn't take advantage of it to the extent that many did, and he liked to think that he was careful with the women. Hearts were not involved—he made certain of that, and he felt everyone got what was wanted.

Nothing in his past explained what he was feeling for Sadie. He wanted her physically—all kinds of want, and endlessly. Just a touch, or even a look, and he'd get hard. And he knew, *knew* to his very core, that when they came together, it would be like nothing he'd ever experienced. He was sure it would be the same for her. And that in itself was over the top for him.

But it was hardly even the beginning. He wanted her as his. He wanted her in his life, for his life. He wanted her as his wife. Her sons as his sons.

Damned if he could explain that. Certainly, he was a long way from convincing her of it. Nonetheless, it was true. He didn't have a moment's doubt—really, from the second he'd pulled her from the river, she'd been his.

She didn't believe it yet.

But this morning, when he'd held her, Tino impatiently kicking his feet behind her, he knew she'd begun to face up to the possibility. She was those things he'd said of her—strong and brave. She wouldn't let her fear hold her back for long. He was going to trust her to get there.

He watched her tug at Jace's braids, then smile back at him. He turned away to adjust himself yet again. The wait could kill him.

Sadie put a movie on for Tino and then made some calls. She checked in with the moms—they were busy with their hired hand, digging out from the snow, milking the goats, and setting up a batch of cheese. She also called in to the medical center. She had a couple ultrasounds to follow up on—all was well there, and she talked to the ob-gyn residents on the labor unit. She often covered a shift on the unit—evaluating women in labor, helping with the births, assisting when needed with c-sections. It helped her keep up to date, kept her skills up, and made for friendly terms when she had to transfer a laboring woman to the hospital, as was occasionally inevitable.

The residents were all hot about a Sunday afternoon football game—she'd been hearing all fall about how great the local team was doing. They were throwing kisses to her over the phone when she agreed to take an extra shift and cover Sunday afternoon and evening. Apparently, watching the games required a certain amount of partying.

Finally, she called the three pregnant women she had who were due in the next couple weeks. They were all happily sitting out the storm, no signs of labor threatening. She rescheduled their prenatal visits for the next week. She felt confident that the roads would be passable before she was needed anywhere.

Then she went to join Tino, taking a blanket to snuggle in with him. She'd left him in the huge recliner in Leet's room. After breakfast, Leet had told her he needed to do some work downstairs. He invited Jace to use the gym, but asked Sadie, a bit cautiously, if she would mind keeping Tino upstairs, out of harm's way. Of course she agreed, aware that they were all three unexpected guests, and she didn't want to interfere with Leet's work. The kiss he'd left her with had taken any sting out of the request.

For Tino, it was the promise of sledding when they were done.

Apparently, the man-work happening downstairs required the accompaniment of extremely loud music. Rock when, she guessed, it was Leet's turn to choose, and rap when it was Jace's. Jace seemed to get to go first. Anyway, the volume was enough to send Tino and her to the far corner of the house where, with the door closed, they could hear each other and the movie.

She and Tino had both dozed off, but Sadie opened her eyes at the sound of the bedroom door opening. The house was quiet now with the music gone, and Leet stood in the doorway watching them. He was freshly showered—hair still dripping wet and chest bare again above his loose sweats. The man didn't care a lot about clothes, and she didn't mind. He padded over and knelt alongside her.

He rested his forehead against hers, touching her lips gently with his. "My sleeping beauty."

She nestled into him. "Umm. A smart midwife never passes up a chance for a nap."

"I'll remember that." He slipped his hand under the blanket and covered her breast—the one that Tino wasn't lying on. "Sometime when we have an afternoon alone." He rubbed his thumb over her nipple, bringing it to a hard peak. She arched a little, letting out an unsteady breath. His eyes burned, showing her he knew what he was making her feel. "I've got a very trustworthy method for putting a woman to sleep."

"Yeah?" She squirmed again as he pinched a little. "Talking her to death?"

He leaned his head harder against hers and slipped his hand down, inside the blanket, until he reached the juncture of her thighs. He didn't stop there, but pushed his fingers in between her legs, roughly stroking against her jeans, pressing in. "Nope. No words required. None more than four letters, anyway." He reconsidered. "Maybe five. Sometimes just three."

He put his lips to her ear and gave her a sample.

Sadie suppressed a shiver and leaned away from his mouth. She slid her hand down to his wrist, but he kept rubbing at her, despite her grasp, letting her know her strength was no match for his. Letting her know that when he stopped, it was his choice.

When he did, he rotated his hand to take hers and brought it out to his lips. His heated gaze held her while he kissed and sucked her fingers. "Tonight, Sadie." Then he stood, that strength and grace again. Appearing not to care at all that his sweats tented out, tightly gloving his very large erection, he walked to his closet. "Come on. Wake that boy up. We've got sledding to do."

Dragging the sleds to the top of the hill outside Leet's yard was a huge chore but also part of the fun. Drifts of snow were over Tino's head, and they all were swallowed up in it as they "accidentally" tumbled each other to the ground. Leet had a couple saucers the boys used and a more sedate toboggan they could all four fit onto, though the young ones preferred the speed of the saucers. That generally left Sadie alone with Leet. After a few runs, a good path was made, and there was nothing more sedate about it.

Leet sat on the toboggan with Sadie between his legs, laughing as the boys crash-landed at the bottom of the hill. Jace had built a jump to add excitement to the course. Clearly, the more spectacular the crash, the more fun they had.

Sadie knew she was in trouble when she heard Leet's voice in her ear—"I think we can land that, don't you?" just as he pushed them off. They built up more speed than they ever had, and Sadie started to scream as they raced past the boys trudging back up with their saucers. She got nothing back from them but jeers to go faster.

Inevitably, Leet headed them toward the jump. She could feel the rumbling laughter in his chest even as she cursed him—out loud, which appeared to have the effect of making him laugh all the more.

They took the jump off center and lost the toboggan from

underneath them as they were in the air. Leet had her wrapped in his arms and took the brunt of their landing. Then he rolled with her a couple times, making sure, she was certain, that they ended with him on top, his full bodyweight pressing her deeply into the snow.

They were laughing even as they brushed snow from each other's faces. Even as the brushing turned to kissing. Leet pulled a glove off to caress her face as he took the kiss deeper. When he lifted to gaze at her, the laughter was gone.

"Sadie." His eyes were dark, intent.

Sadie sobered, too, meeting his gaze. "Yeah."

Then he gave her hair a tug. "You squealed like a girl."

She swatted at his arm, well-padded in his snow gear. "I don't know what you're talking about."

Suddenly, his cold hand was under her jacket, against bare skin, and there was, in fact, squealing to be heard. Laughing again, she pushed at him until he rolled, and she was on top. "Well, at least I *am* a girl."

His hand, still under her jacket, pushed up toward her breast. "So you are." He flipped them once more, keeping his hand in place. "And isn't that a fine thing?"

He kissed her again, sloppily, noisily, and then just rested against her, looking around. "It's beautiful out, isn't it? I'd forgotten how much fun it is to play in the snow."

He discreetly removed his hand as more squealing and hollering heralded the arrival of Jace and Tino. They landed all akimbo in the snow a few feet away. In another moment, they were piled on Leet's back, and there was a bit of wrestling until the two boys challenged each other to another run.

In the silence they left behind, Leet and Sadie lay on their backs, enjoying the blue sky.

When Leet's cell phone buzzed in his pocket, he rolled to his side to watch her as he answered.

"Hey, Wes."

He leaned over her, propped on an elbow, but had fingers free to trail through her hair.

"I'm sledding…. Yeah. I've got a couple kids here." His fingers stroked her cheek now, and his knee found its way between her legs. "Yes. There is a mother involved."

His eyes were dark again, and he slid his lips over hers. "Yeah." Once more, he lifted up. "Yeah. I'll be able to get out tomorrow. The highway's clear now, and the plow made a first pass by here this morning. I'll plan to leave by nine." Leet nodded and made a couple more noises of agreement. "Okay. See ya in the morning, man."

He slid the phone back into his pocket, his gaze on Sadie. She knew a bit of regret at the seriousness on his face.

He slipped his other hand along her face and held her. "I have to leave tomorrow. I'll be gone a few days." He touched her lips with his. "I'm sorry. It's a work commitment I can't change."

"Of course, Leet."

"I really don't want to leave you."

"Leet, this isn't…we're not…" *Well.* She wasn't sure how to finish either one of those thoughts.

He brought his weight over her again, that knee still pressed between hers. "It's not. We're not. But still." His lips found hers again, more than a touch now.

Sadie slid her arms around him, taking the fullness of his kiss. When he lifted up to look at her, she spoke with a sigh, owning the truth. "I don't want you to leave me either."

He liked that, she could see. His gaze burned into hers, and there was a grim satisfaction in his expression. And a new tension in his body, a new intention. He rocked her a bit side to side to get his arms under her. With one arm he cradled her hips, lifting her up against his sudden erection, blatant even through their snow pants.

He groaned deeply, her name and a curse seeming as one. His mouth ground against hers, his tongue delving deep. He rose up onto his knees and sat back, bringing her up onto him, her weight all settled over his groin. He looked over her head, up the hill, and gave a heavy sigh.

"Your cursed sons will be here in a minute." He gave a wry smile, but it clearly cost him, and he settled her a little lower down his legs. He looked up at the sky, searching. "Pulling you from the river, half-frozen. Holding you naked but unconscious in my arms. Making breakfast in the kitchen with your four-year-old. Rolling with you in a snow bank." He cast her a blaming look before he got—painfully, it seemed—to his feet and then pulled her up. "And that's not even half."

"What?" she almost laughed, but he seemed so serious.

"All the inappropriate hard-ons I've gotten since I've met you."

She was quiet for a minute, but her lips twitched. "Pulling me from the river?"

"Shut up."

She did laugh then, watching as the boys came tearing toward them. "That's really not my fault, dude."

He squeezed her hand and tugged her back a bit as the boys landed, sending snow flying. "It sure as hell is."

She kept laughing even as he tossed her a look—*especially* as he tossed her a look. He picked up Tino and threw him over one shoulder then pulled Jace to his feet with a single hand. "Yo. Do you guys skate? We could clear the pond."

Leet had skates of every size tucked into some of the cubbies in the studio/gym. The pair that fit Tino, he said, had been used a couple years back by one of his brother's kids. Apparently, that family visited from California every year over Christmas. Jace, whose extra-long feet were still waiting for his height to catch up, fit into a pair Leet's friend Will used.

Sadie and Tino made a game of clearing the pond. Mostly, that meant Tino got a free ride on the snow shovel. Leet and Jace made a real job of it. With skates already on, they pushed shovels full of snow across the whole length of the pond, building up walls of the stuff that took all of their combined efforts to move. They were grunting and sweating, stripped down to just sweatshirts now, working hard. It reminded Sadie of one of the exercises Jace's team used as a workout during practice. Her suggestions for an easier way to do it had been rejected with little grace and rolling eyeballs. Apparently, as a woman, she was not expected to get it.

Tino's heart was open and easy, so his happy acceptance of Leet was natural and no surprise to Sadie. But watching Leet and Jace work together—*very* together, both clearly committed to what they were doing, even if Sadie *didn't* get it—made her a bit anxious. Jace didn't generally open up to others easily. He was the only African American in his class; his early life experiences had been very, very different from those of his peers in a rural Vermont high school. She knew it was only on the football field that he really felt a part of the kids around him. That was the reason she'd agreed to let him play varsity at his young age. His coach seemed to understand it as well, and she trusted him to watch out for Jace.

So Jace's seemingly instant comfort with Leet, his clear admiration for him, came as a surprise. Jace had little contact with adult men outside of school, except for the occasional shared chore with the moms' hired hand. And that one hardly counted. Canaan was a veteran of the war in Afghanistan. The moms assured her he was gentle and trustworthy, but he seldom spoke or even made eye contact with her. Jace seemed perfectly comfortable working with him from time to time, but she couldn't think they had a relationship.

With Leet, he seemed to just click. Jace admired him and totally related to him. It was clear in the way they worked side by side, communicating with more grunts than words, and in the way they played and teased, with that male posturing they had of strutting and crowing.

She could almost feel left out, except that it gave her such pleasure to see. And they included her—and Tino—generously in much of their playfulness.

Sadie and Jace's relationship had taken time to build. He'd not been trustful initially—had never learned that humans might *be* trustworthy. It had taken a long time for him to let her into his heart. She was there now, and she knew she was important to him.

So she'd worried that he might mistrust the relationship that seemed to be developing between Leet and her. But that was apparently not the case. Leet was not the least bit hesitant to display his affection for her, his attraction. Jace seemed not to care at all. He seemed entirely, *suspiciously*, unconcerned.

Sadie wasn't quite sure what to make of it. And so, when the snow was cleared and Leet had gotten Tino into a pair of skates and was helping him skitter across the ice for the first time, she body checked Jace into the snow bank the guys had built around the rink.

"Hey!" He rolled to get up and retaliate, she was sure, but she plopped down beside him and held him down with her. They sat back in the snow, propped against each other, and watched Leet and Tino.

Finally, she spoke. "I like him, Jace."

He looked at her with a smile and nudged her shoulder. "I know. He likes you, too."

"You okay with that?"

He smiled, meeting her eyes, seeming achingly more grown up than she'd recognized. "Yeah," he said. Then he nudged her again. "He asked, too. Well, kind of."

She sat up at that. "When? Tell me."

"Yesterday. When he picked me up from school." He looked back to watch as Leet talked Tino back to his feet after his first fall. "After he got done asking me if you were married or had a boyfriend." He smirked a bit then. "He didn't ask if you were a lez. Guess it was before he met the grandmoms."

They both snickered at that.

"Then he said he was gonna make a play for you. He didn't really ask if it was okay, he was just letting me know."

Man to man, she thought, with no pretense. She knew Jace understood that and appreciated it. She nodded. "What did you say?"

"I told him good luck. You ain't been with a man since I've known you."

"Hey," she said, and felt an embarrassing blush. "That's not true."

"*Yeah*," he said, and there was a bit of the street in it, a thing she rarely heard these days. "It is."

"Humph." She searched her memory for an exception, without real success. "Well, it looks like that might be changing."

"'Bout damn time," he said, and was up and gone before he got the reprimand he'd know was coming.

―――⌐◝⌐――

Dark still came early, so they skated under the lights while the moon rose and stars came out. They played a little ice rink fox and geese then Jace and Tino practiced slides into the snow bank. During that time, Leet and Sadie made a fair show of skating together face to face. Leet had grown up playing pond hockey, he said, and did a good job of keeping Sadie on her feet. If she let him do most of the work, she could manage a backwards skate while they glided around the pond. Leet seemed content just to hold her, moving in sync with her, and she was, too.

It was quiet and peaceful and lovely.

Her ankles were wobbly long before the guys were ready to call it quits. Sunk into the snow bank, burrowed into her parka, Sadie alternately watched an impromptu hockey practice and stargazed. And maybe dozed, because at some point, she opened her eyes to find the three of them peering down at her.

"Told ya." That was Jace, never one to mince words.

Leet chuckled. "I'll never doubt you again, man." He reached down for Sadie. "Come on, sleeping beauty. Time to go in." He had her up and in his arms almost before she was awake. "I can't believe you fell asleep in the snow."

"Hah," Jace snorted. "Don't ever take her to a movie."

Leet shook his head, still holding her. "Tell me you don't fall asleep during movies."

Sadie was awake enough now to engage. "Shut up, Jace." Though she said it with a grin. "Maybe once. And it wasn't a *good* movie."

"Only once that she admits to. And she can't tell you if it was good *because she was asleep*."

Leet was chuckling again as he turned them all toward the house. Sadie considered trying to defend herself some more—if it was a good movie, she wouldn't have fallen asleep. Probably. But Tino was pulling at her hand, starting the little dance that meant he had to get to a bathroom PDQ.

"Come here, sweetie." She set him down on a stone wall on the terrace and tugged his skates off, then unzipped his parka. "Can you handle the rest?"

"Yup," he said as he tore off into the house, not quite managing to outrun her pat on his bottom.

Sadie figured there was at least a fifty percent chance he'd make it. She looked up to see that Leet had been watching them. They shared a quiet smile. He sat down to unlace his skates, and she did the same.

"Mom." Jace was already out of his skates and had his boots back on.

"Yeah?"

"The pizza shop in the village is open—we checked. Leet says I could ride with him on a snowmobile. We could bring home pizza for dinner."

"On a snowmobile?" She looked up at Jace, all full of enthusiasm, then at Leet who met her gaze squarely. She was
nervous about snow machines, and Jace knew it. Two win-
ters past, a classmate of his had died in an accident on one.

Leet came over and stood next to Jace. "I'm careful. I
took the safety course and got certified. We'll wear helmets.
I know the trails. And nobody else is going to be out."

He spoke quietly, without heat. But he stood with Jace.
And the look in his eyes told her he knew that a concern for
Jace's safety wasn't the only issue. Or even the main issue.

Sadie stood, too. Jace had used the word "home," refer-
ring to Leet's place. Suddenly, she was very aware that she'd
let things go too far.

She looked from one face to the other, Jace's hopeful,
Leet's determined, steady. She took a breath and let it out
slowly. "Jace, would you please wait inside?"

He opened his mouth—an objection, of course, but Leet
put a hand on his shoulder and spoke first. "She's right, Jace.
Your mom and I need to talk. But I don't have anything to
say to her that you can't hear, too."

He stepped closer to Sadie. She held her ground with a
little effort, but had to tilt her head back to meet his eyes. He
reached out and took her hand in his but did nothing more
than loosely hold it.

"I'd like to think I'm above using your kids to get to you,
Sadie." He looked around at Jace for a minute and then
turned back to her. "I don't know. I have to admit there's a
lot that I'd do to make you mine. But the thing is, I get that
you're a package deal." He stepped closer then, so she felt
his next breath on her cheeks. "I like the package, Sade. *All*
of it."

Sadie swallowed hard and then did step back. "I can't
risk that much, Leet. I can't have the kids get attached—"

"They'd damn well better get attached. I'm getting attached to them."

Sadie pulled her hand away. "No. I like you, Leet, a lot.
But I don't really know you." She looked at Jace. "*We* don't
really know you."

Leet took his own step back, turning halfway to face Jace,
too. He ran a frustrated hand down the back of his neck then
spoke to Sadie. "You do know me. You just don't trust yourself to believe it yet. I get that, too. It's your job to consider

whether it's possible I'm a skank. You want to protect your-self, but even more, you need to protect your sons. I can hardly object to that. Though I'll say, it's killing me." He turned, hunched forward, hands dug down into his pockets. "Jace. You know I'm not a skank, don't you?"

Jace looked at her and nodded, but Sadie shook her head and stepped closer to Jace. "Leet—"

Leet broke in. "No. I mean it. I'm saying it's not just what he'd like to be true. He actually *knows* it's true." He looked at Jace, prompting. "Tell her, Jace. Tell her how you know it's true."

Sadie watched, breath held, while some message passed between the two males. Then Jace turned to her and put a hand on her shoulder. "He's right, Mom. Coach let me go with him. When he picked me up at school, I mean. That means he's okay."

Her breath came out in something—a laugh, a cry? She pulled Jace into a hug, then leaned back to look into his face, then Leet's. "And that's all it takes? In this 'man club' of yours, you just need Coach to vouch for him, and you know he's okay?"

The two of them looked at each other, then back to her and spoke as one. "Yeah."

Sadie sighed and rested her head down on Jace's shoul-der, aware again how close he was to being a man. After a moment, she let him go. "All right. Go. I want pepperoni."

"Okay!" He turned, ready to high-five Leet, but subsided at another of those unspoken signals. "Thanks, Mom."

"Yeah, yeah." She looked at Leet, who had a very satis-fied-yet-humble-in-victory face on. "Be careful with my boy."

His eyes positively glowed as he nodded. "Yes, ma'am."

"Jace, hold on tight."

He wasn't so skilled yet at the humble part. He smirked. "To what? Leet? Or the pizza?"

She tried a quelling look. "Both. You have two hands, don't you?"

His grin held. "Well, *yeah*. How else would I catch a foot-ball?"

She rolled her eyes and turned away, but she could see their victory dance in the reflection of the windows.

They had pizza and watched a movie together. With the pizza devoured, they ended up all sprawled out on the couch. Sadie made a special point of staying awake, but Tino was a goner before the movie was half over. He fell asleep first tucked in between Sadie and Jace—Jace got the drooling end. Then he woke enough to crawl over Sadie and plop his head onto Leet's abs. Laid out across her, he managed to keep his feet in Jace's lap.

Sadie smiled. He had them all. All was right in Tino's world.

It felt pretty good in hers, too, she had to admit. She had Tino lying across her, staking his claim to all three of them. Jace was on her left, impressing her with his maturity but still perfectly comfortable to let her put her arm around him and tuck him into her side. And naturally draping an arm across his brother's feet to secure them in his lap.

And on her right was Leet. She leaned into him the same way Jace leaned into her. Her head rested against his chest where she could hear the slow, strong thump of his heart. His arm was around her, tucking her close, but long enough to reach Jace, too. He'd tugged his braids a couple times when they were razzing each other. And other times, she saw, he simply rested his fingers on Jace's shoulder. His other hand had fingers gently twisted into Tino's curls.

Leet had been relaxed since he and Jace had gotten back from the village—undemanding. Sadie suspected it was a tactical lull. She had felt, what? *Besieged*, ever since she'd woken up from her drugged sleep in his bed yesterday. Leet was storming a castle. And she was the castle.

It wasn't something she had any experience with. Oh, she'd known determination and strong will. Her mothers had them, and she did, too. Her mothers had struggled to find and secure the kind of life they wanted, to have love in their work and their personal lives. To face the world together, openly and honestly.

And for Sadie, much the same. She'd worked hard to develop skill and wisdom in a profession she loved. She could fight, too, and had. To wrest Jace from a foster system that would never give him the one thing he needed—a family. To place herself so that Tino's mother, too young to raise a child, would see her as his best chance. To convince her to put his good above all else.

But for her and the moms, it had been a feminine kind of approach. They'd all done the thing that had seemed right and good, first one step and then the next, until they'd gotten what and where they wanted. If there had been missteps or detours, well, that was part of the process, and part of what led them to where they were.

A journey. Not a battle.

Leet was all male. He'd found something he wanted, and he was going to have it. She could see it thrum inside him. The watchful evaluation of the enemy and development of strategy. The marshalling of resources and securement of allies. The tactical reassessment after testing enemy strength.

The deep satisfaction in battle. The determination to see victory.

This strategic retreat probably *was* killing him. She smiled and rubbed her cheek a little against his chest. Immediately, his hand came up, fingers stroking along her jaw. Retreat, but not surrender. He was still battle alert.

When the movie ended, Leet hauled Tino up to bed, and they tucked him in together. Jace, male-bonded ally that he was, also said goodnight, claiming fatigue. He felt guilty enough to at least avoid eye contact with her as he told that whopper.

Without asking for consent, Leet took her hand and led her downstairs again. He settled her on the couch by the fireplace with a light kiss.

The scene of last night's battle. Lull over.

"Want a glass of wine?"

"Sure."

"White? Riesling?"

At her nod, he went to the kitchen. When he came back he clinked glasses with her—his wine was a dark red—and stepped away to start the fire. Then he looked her over from where he was.

"Sadie, I want to finish this night with you in my bed. Actually, there's nothing in the world I want more. Are you going to fight me on that?"

Well, there was an aggressive tossing down of the gauntlet. But she heard the concession he was reluctantly offering. She could counter offer if she wanted to. He'd...*listen*, at least. And she had to give him credit—he was asking from twelve feet away, touching her only with that hot gaze of his. He could have been much surer of her answer if he'd spent two minutes beside her on the couch, "engaging" with her as he had last night. He wasn't using every weapon in his armament.

And wasn't that a brilliant strategy. If she agreed, it was a surrender, not a defeat. That was what he wanted.

She spent a moment debating it. But really, she couldn't compete with his skill and natural aptitude for this sort of battle, and her heart wasn't in it anyway. She would do what came naturally to her. The thing that seemed right and good. See where it took her.

"No."

His eyes lit and he took a moment to savor it.

"Good. Then I want us to talk for a bit."

Well. She hadn't expected *that*.

Leet set their wine glasses down and nudged her around until they were lying on the couch together. He was on his side, back against the couch, and had her tucked up next to him. They were propped enough that they could both watch the fire. He had one arm around her, behind her shoulders. He slipped his other hand under her shirt—determined to be content to just let it rest there, enjoying the smooth skin and taut muscles of her abdomen.

She was a quick learner. He knew she'd caught on to his strategizing. He accepted that it was foreign to her. He suspected she didn't have much experience with men. Not just sexually—in that realm, it appeared she was all but virginal, and it turned out that was a heady, freaking turn on to him.

But in her life in general. Presumably, she'd been raised by two women. And her work was with women, mostly, obviously.

He understood the significance. Oh, his parents were heterosexual, for what it was worth. But his mother had never served as a source of experience and insight into the world of women. His parents just hadn't had much interest in raising their two sons. Their real baby was the cardiology department at the medical center. He hadn't even lived with them since he was fourteen, when he'd jumped ship and crossed state lines to play football with Ray Morgan.

Since then, football had pretty much been his life. And that was pretty much a male world. Granted, there was cheerleader Prissy MacAvoy and her ilk, but the occasional, lighthearted foray into the...*lives* of women didn't mean he knew anything about them. He was fully aware that he knew very little about how women thought, how their hearts worked. His experience in his marriage had served to drive that point home.

Presumably, it was the same for Sadie, just from the opposite point of view.

He made her nervous.

Well, *hell*, she made him nervous right back.

All in all, those facts were probably good reasons to proceed methodically, slowly, and with caution.

That would no doubt be Sadie's preferred approach, what came naturally to her.

Too damn effin' bad. He knew, heart and soul, he wanted her. She was his. He'd do what he could not to push too much. But she'd better freaking catch up.

Leet closed his eyes for a minute, resting his head down and touching her hair with his lips, filling his lungs with her scent. Where his hand rested, just below her rib, along the cut of her abdominal muscle, he drew a little circular stroke with his thumb. Small compensation for the urgent mating instinct in him, growling, straining against its leash. Shrieking from every fiber—*Have done. Tear her clothes off and bury yourself balls-deep in her body. Stake your claim.*

She probably wasn't ready for that. She was no doubt expecting a little gentle, all mooning eyes and romance, *lovemaking*.

With any luck, their magnificent groping experience in this very spot last night had given her a clue.

Steady on. He took another breath and another, her scent, her body, imprinting on his, if not vice versa.

"Jace's coach really does know me well enough to vouch for me. He was my father-in-law."

That got her attention. She turned her head to look up at

him. "Was?"

He nodded, tucking her in again. It was a long story. "I married his daughter just after I graduated from college. She died three years ago."

Sadie huffed out a little breath. Her hand crept over his, rested there, accepting, waiting.

"Suhayla's mother was pregnant with her when Ray and she met. He coached professional football then, in D.C., back when the pro team there competed in the national championship for several years running. The team and coaches were kind of local celebrities. They often partied with the political bigwigs.

"Ray met Neelah at an embassy party. She was from a small Persian Gulf state. The ruling family had been supported by the U.S. We had a Navy base there, they had some oil—our country had an interest.

"But there'd been a revolution. The royal family got ousted, and many of them fled to the U.S."

Neelah had been the queen's personal secretary. She'd married an officer in the king's guard who'd later been killed in the fighting. She was lovely—dark hair and sad, brown eyes. Her pregnancy was just beginning to show. She was all fragility and grieving vulnerability. Ray fell hard and fast.

Leet didn't know. Maybe Neelah loved Ray back, or would have, if they'd had any time. She accepted his proposal, they married quickly, had two months together, and then she'd died with the birth of her child.

"You'd know more about that than I do. Ray said she had seizures and a stroke."

Sadie's hand was steady over his. "Eclampsia."

"Anyway, Ray was away, at an out of town game, when she died. He had this little baby girl—a preemie, she didn't even weigh three pounds—who was his only in a legal sense. "But he'd loved Neelah, really loved her. And so he loved Suhayla."

Ray couldn't forgive himself for being away when Neelah died. Leet knew it was a burden of grief that Ray would always carry. He gave up pro football and took a high school coaching job so he could raise his daughter. So he could be there with her, for her, every day.

Leet knew Ray had many regrets, but that decision was never one of them, never would be.

"I'd known Suhayla since she was a kid. I grew up in the area. My parents have a home a few miles south, across the river, in New Hampshire. I'd see her with Ray at games and practices, and I ran into her again just before I graduated from college. She was pretty grown up then. We got married and did okay for a couple years. I was working. We kind of expected that we'd have a couple kids. That she'd stay home and raise them. But she didn't get pregnant. We might have been okay if she had." He paused there and owned up to the truth. "Probably not, I suppose. As it was, she became more and more dissatisfied. She'd started school in fashion design, but gave that up when we married. She might have pursued it again, but, you know, life happened. We had to move around some for my work initially. And we thought there would be a baby."

The truth was, Suhayla had never been interested in designing fashion. She was more about *wearing* it. And perhaps, he'd come to believe, she hadn't been all that interested in mothering either. He'd finally realized that she wasn't the one hoping each month for a little pink line.

No, Suhayla had seen Leet's football career as a ticket to a glamorous life. She'd expected travel and parties and excitement. She thought that, as he worked his ass off to earn that starting QB position, he'd negotiate his way onto one of the high-profile teams. One of the high-paying teams. She couldn't believe that he would sign up with a brand new, publicly-owned team of little consequence and with next to no money. She hadn't grasped what mattered to him—to choose home. To settle where he could be near Ray, who was his true family, *their* family, and where he could live quietly, accepted as a neighbor, an occasional drinking buddy, a *local.*

An equal part of the failing was his. He'd led her into marriage with no real awareness of her dreams, her vision for her future.

"Anyway, things were already headed south between us when she met a man who claimed to be her cousin. We were in New York City, celebrating with some friends in a club when he approached her. This guy traveled as part of an entourage. Head honcho of the group, the definite alpha male, was a man named Dalid. The cousin introduced them. Dalid was an expat, one of the royal family that had been ousted in the revolution. Neelah had worked for his mother, the queen. He was a prince."

A real prince. Elegantly handsome, sophisticated, glamorous. Very seductive to a woman like Suhayla. Pretty much exactly what she'd wanted, and hadn't gotten, from Leet.

"He had money, loads of it, and he liked to party. In a big way, I mean. Private jet, villa on the Mediterranean. Sailing, race cars. Skiing in France or Aspen, or New Zealand for the off-season. Clubbing in Rio or Paris, wherever. Suhayla fell for him. I don't know, maybe it was mutual. He was so slick it was hard to tell what was real. She was already past done caring about me and made no effort to conceal her feelings for Dalid. She came home with me—I was building this place by that time. But he'd come for her, and then she'd be gone. After a while, she just didn't come back anymore. Once in a while, she'd call Ray. He'd get together with her—she'd spare a little time out of skiing at Stowe or shopping in New York. Eventually, that stopped, too."

Leet had been angry all over again about that, until it became clear that Ray had pretty much gotten past caring, too.

"Then, three years ago, the jet was lost, somewhere over the Atlantic, on a flight from Cancun to Milan. The prince was flying her over for some big fashion event. She was the only passenger on board."

Sadie rolled over to face him and slid her arm around him. Where his thumb caressed her, he slipped his fingers around her back to hold her close.

"It was a strange kind of grief for both Ray and me. I'd already given up, but I don't suppose I'd really let go. Ray still loved her, of course, but he couldn't understand her. He and I had gotten very close. Her behavior was a disappointment to him, to no small extent on my behalf. We both felt like failures. With no way to make things right."

Sadie ran her fingers along his face. "I'm sorry."

That simple. That profound. He nodded. "Yeah. I am, too."

They were silent for a long moment. "It was odd. Two weeks after Suhayla died, Dalid got married. To a young woman—a girl, really, she was only sixteen, from another royal family. They made a big event out of it. So soon after Suhayla's death—it seemed wrong."

He knew Ray had suffered over that. He'd hoped that his

daughter had at least found some happiness. But the wedding had made Dalid seem heartless and uncaring. It added to the grief. It added anger.

Leet moved his thumb over her, aware of her body heat, bringing himself back to the present.

"Three years, Leet. You must have had other women in your life since then."

He'd known that would come. Honesty would be the best policy, and there really wasn't much to hide anyway. "None with any expectations." By which he meant, none that would, or could, hurt. Until now. He looked her square in the eye. "As of yesterday, none at all." He squeezed her closer and sought her lips. "Present company excepted." Sought them and found them. "I'm done waiting, Sadie."

*C*HAPTER FOUR

Leet hadn't needed to wait so long. Sadie was glad to have heard his story, but she'd been on a slow simmer for a while now. That stroke of his thumb on her abdomen—so soft, almost like he was unaware of the movement—had sensitized her skin there. Like he'd left his mark, his brand, that was exquisitely responsive to his touch—only his. Like he'd imprinted himself on her skin.

He kissed her now, but all of her attention was still focused on that touch. She took her hand from his shoulder and followed down his arm until it lay over that spot where his thumb circled. She held it there, feeling the heat of his mark, accepting, taking it in, letting it set.

Leet lifted his head in awareness. Their eyes met and held. Somehow, he knew what had just passed.

"Come upstairs with me." His voice was rough, wanting, scarcely short of commanding. There was a mere hint of hesitation, of uncertainty, just enough that it required an answer.

"Yes."

He stood—leapt to his feet would be a perfectly accurate description—and pulled her up. With his hands on her waist, he turned her—herded her, she thought—to the stairs. His hands never left her until she stood beside his bed, or even then. An instruction, she thought, a demand—*don't change your mind. Please, don't change your mind*.

She nearly smiled, but his expression when she faced him was so serious, so intent it took her breath.

He bent to touch her lips. "Stay put," he said, then went to the fireplace to light the fire.

When he came back, his hands took her waist again. He pulled her closer, a step they both took, until her body came against his. He lowered his head and claimed her lips in one fast, hard kiss, a possession. Then he lifted to look down at her.

"Sadie." He raised a hand to stroke her hair, hold her face. "I'm going to remember this."

He paused then, awaiting her acknowledgment.

It took all of Sadie's courage to face him. She knew what he was telling her and thought she knew what he was asking back.

What happened between them this night was important, a beginning. It wasn't going to be just one night in bed together. He was entrusting her with his feelings, communicating his resolve about that.

And he was asking the same declaration from her.

He understood what she had at stake, accepted, she believed, her responsibility to her sons. He wouldn't ask her for more than she could safely give. But he would expect, would demand, all that she could.

Did he know that she had never given her heart? Would he guess that she guarded that as well?

Leet relished, *celebrated* his maleness. He had and used strength and power that was more than just the physical. He wasn't domineering, exactly, but he was definitely determined. He was not the gentle, undemanding sort that she'd been involved with before. It was clear he'd push her beyond her boundaries of comfort. He wouldn't settle for half measures, for something so meager as her affection. He'd want her, body, heart, and soul. There had been no effort at disguise. He'd let her know him, let her see him.

Well, she had strength and power, too. And courage, somewhere, that she wouldn't let fail her now. He'd seen her, too.

Finding her breath again, she placed her hands over his. "Leet. I won't forget either."

He nodded once. "Don't move." Looking only into her eyes, he unbuttoned her shirt and pulled it from her jeans. She expected him to tear if off her, but he simply folded back the left side, below her heart. Holding her gaze until the last second, he knelt before her and put his mouth on her abdomen. On that spot where his thumb had rubbed his stamp onto her.

He kissed and licked that spot now, nuzzling, circling with lips and tongue. Then he suckled, drawing her skin into his mouth, grazing with his teeth. Finally, he sucked hard, eliciting a small twinge of pain.

Her breath had trembled when he knelt and touched his mouth to her. Now, at that taking, it huffed out in a helpless moan. Her hands took his head, holding him there.

She knew what he was doing. The sucking bruise he put there would be a physical, visible confirmation of that symbolic marking he'd done before. *Mine*, he was saying. *Know it. Accept it.*

When he'd accomplished what he wanted, he spent a moment soothing with his tongue. Then he stood and held her gaze for a long measure. Abruptly, he lifted her up hard against him. He spoke roughly, urgent. "Wrap your legs around me and open your mouth."

She obeyed, and in the next instant, his tongue was inside her. He kept her tucked against him, pelvis to pelvis, as he crawled onto the bed. He pressed her down onto her back, his mouth still on hers, his erection rocking against her.

"Be with me, here." His words, his plea, came on a groan.

And she was—with him, there. Her arms wrapped around him, fingers digging for purchase in the sleek, taut muscles of his back. It wasn't enough, so she slid one hand down further, wedging it in the waistband of his jeans.

"Christ, yes, Sadie," he moaned. "Thank God."

He raised himself on one elbow, lifting up so he could look down at her. He took the left side of her shirt now and tore it aside to uncover that breast. Breathing heavily, he stared down at her. Sadie writhed once as a thrill of pleasure shot through her. Under his hot gaze, her nipple tightened, responding to his regard. Without thought, she arched up, her body offering itself. As her spine curved to lift her breast, her pelvis flexed, rubbing her center along the rigid length of his erection.

A shudder coursed through him as well. She twined her fingers into his curls as he lowered his head. He took her into his mouth, sucking hard through the red silk of her bra. The lace was rough, abrasive as his tongue stroked her.

Sadie cried out at the shaft of excitement that shot from her nipple to her core. She tilted her pelvis, nudging against him, the friction of their jeans increasing the stimulation.

Leet lifted his head again. He took the strap of her bra and tugged it down her arm until her breast was bared. He circled his fingers along the underside and cupped her. "You are so fucking beautiful."

Sadie raised her head to look. Her breast stood up proudly, the nipple jutting out and reddened already from his attention. She watched as, with a groan, he took her in his mouth again.

He sucked hard, his tongue stroking, his teeth grazing. He let go of her with his hand, moving it down to grip her bottom. He held her there, rutting against her, in time with the pull on her nipple.

Exquisite need tore through her. She arched and rocked against him. In just a moment, she would come.

He seemed to know it. He slid back, lifting off her before leaning forward and sinking his tongue into her mouth again. "Not yet," he said. "I want more. At the least, tonight, we're getting all our clothes off."

He went back on his knees, hovering over her. He reached under her back to lift her then slid the shirt off her shoulders and down her arms. While he held her, he suckled for a minute at her right breast, still covered by her bra, until he removed that, too.

He kept his hands on her then, lifting her ribcage, displaying her breasts, his for the taking. And he took. With one arm, he kept his hold on her. He used his other hand to stroke over her, kneading her breasts, chafing and pinching her nipples. He arched her up, bringing her to his mouth. With a hungry, needy moan, he sucked her deep, still using his hand to torment her other breast.

"Leet!" Sadie unwrapped her legs from behind his back and pressed her feet into the bed. She pushed her pelvis up then, flexing and rubbing against him.

Just as urgent as she felt, he lifted up, his eyes all heat and hard desire. He leaned back on his heels, his arm slipping down to hold her hips. His gaze held hers while he worked open the button of her jeans and slid the zipper down. He slipped his fingers in, wedged between the tight denim and her most sensitive tissue. He rubbed her, stimulating her with the backs of his fingers.

Sadie's breath came in a rasp. Leet watched her, pleasure in his eyes as he gave her another stroke.

"I changed my mind," he said. He tugged a little, lowering the opening of her jeans. "I'm going to make you come before I have you."

Then his gaze left hers to take in the part of her he'd just revealed. She watched as he held her suspended there and pried the opening of her jeans just a little lower. Enough to reveal the little thatch of hair she left unshaved at her mons, and then the swollen, oh so sensitive little nub at her core. He stiffened his fingers to lever her jeans back, not so accidentally prodding into her wet opening. With a hot glance at her eyes, he lifted her to his mouth.

He rasped his tongue against her, three strong strokes that had her coming. Then he drew her into his mouth, sucking hard, and had her screaming.

Sadie was lost in it, an orgasm that seemed to go on forever, that took her over, leaving her adrift in its wake. She was aware that he laid her back on the bed and slid her jeans down and off her legs. She heard him unfasten his own jeans, felt his movement on the bed as he struggled out of them.

Then he lay over her, softly stroking her breasts as he came up over her, gently kissing her.

All that before she even began to come back to herself.

"Sadie."

She could hear the indulgence, his pleased satisfaction. She didn't have the power to object.

"Hmm?"

He kissed her some more, played with her breasts with a little more intent. She wouldn't have thought she could have any further interest, but she began to stir under him again. Apparently, he knew her body better than she did.

"Tell me you're on some kind of birth control." His erection was pressing, pulsing against her thigh. He slid his hand along her side, gripping her hip to steady her as his movement became more deliberate.

It took Sadie a minute to focus on his words. "Yes. I am."

His mouth was gone from hers now, had found her nipple again. Involuntarily, she arched up to meet him.

"Are you still going to make me wear a condom?" His fingers were between her legs now, dipping inside her, finding her wetness, stretching, rubbing.

She shivered in response, struggling to follow. "What? Oh, um, yes."

He pulled away from her breast without breaking suction,

creating a rough little sting that made her breath catch. He crawled up over her, his knee between her legs, his thigh pressing erotically at her center. Keeping a rhythm there, he reached into a cubby at the head of the bed. He came back with a condom and tore it open with his teeth. Muttering, he rolled it onto himself while still nipping at her neck with hard kisses. "Okay, but just for tonight. I'm getting tested while I'm away this weekend and that will be the end of it."

When he'd gotten himself covered, he kept hold with his hand. He moved the head of his cock to her opening and held himself there. Ever so slowly, he pressed in just enough for her to feel his full breadth.

He was very large. She'd known it. She'd felt him hard inside his clothing, seen him at least partially erect before. But having him stretching, opening her body to accommodate him sent a little spasm of fear through her.

He was watching, and she knew he saw it.

Still holding himself there, he leaned over and touched her lips. "Shh, baby. It's okay. We're going to fit just fine." He slid his tongue over the seam of her lips until she let him in. He explored gently, not pressing, taking his time. As though he had a care for nothing but this kiss. As though he wasn't there, on the verge of filling her, waiting for her body to allow him entrance.

He slid his hand around until his thumb pressed against her center. He circled there, massaging. Sadie opened her mouth and let his tongue take her, let him thrust as she knew he would do with his cock. The stimulation from his thumb got stronger, making her moan, making her rock just a little.

With that movement, he slid a little further into her. She felt stretched tight, a pulling that added to the effect of his thumb. Then it was all too much. She cried out his name, urging him in crude words to do what he wanted to do, what she wanted him to do.

And he did. He entered her fully, distending her, filling her up. He slid one arm under her shoulders, holding her steady for his kiss, pressing her breasts against the firm muscles of his chest. The other he moved under her hips to hold her against him while he plundered, thrusting in and withdrawing, faster and faster until he was pounding into her.

His fingers grasped and squeezed her flesh. He arched her up under him and lifted to his knees for greater purchase. Together, their breaths turned to rough moans. They spoke each other's names in urgent appeal.

Sadie reached her limit, overwhelmed by the extreme power of this taking. She began to spasm, crying out, every muscle in her body seizing.

Leet was right there with her, his arms gripping her, his body grinding out the final strokes, his breath rasping out a shuddering climax.

He buried his head in the bed at her shoulder. He grasped the rim of the condom to hold it as he rocked against her, gentling his movement. "Sadie," he groaned. "Sadie, Sadie."

He pulled out of her and dropped the condom somewhere over the side of the bed. He plopped down, half on top of her, half beside her. He put his big hand up and turned her head so they were face to face, eye to eye, just inches apart. In the firelight, they regarded each other quietly while their breathing gradually slowed.

After a bit, Sadie's eyes fell closed. Leet stroked her cheek with his thumb. "No falling asleep, baby. You don't think I'm done with you, do you?"

She smiled, but kept her eyes closed. "No? All right then, bring it on." With that, she rocked a little against him, where he nestled against her hip.

He stirred a bit, thickening, but not becoming fully erect.

She heard the grin, a little chagrin, in his voice. "I'm not saying a little rest isn't in order. Maybe a short nap."

She chuckled and rolled over, tucking her bottom against him, enjoying the way his arms automatically circled to hold her. "A nap. I like the sound of that."

"Can I wake you with, uh, any means available?"

She placed her hand over his, weaving fingers, where he'd tucked it against her middle. Her head rested on his bicep and she smiled a kiss into the muscle. "Do your worst."

His worst turned out to be pretty good.

Sadie woke later, thrumming with desire. Leet held her breast with one hand, his palm chafing at the nipple. He was inside her, filling her from behind. She was already wet and slippery, giving way easily now to his slow thrusts. Apparently, his fingers, where they stimulated her, had been busy for some time.

His mouth was at her ear. "Hello, my sleeping beauty."

He took a pillow and tucked it up against her lower belly, then pushed into her with a little more purpose. "Lift your hair up, off your shoulder."

Sadie raised both hands to slide under her hair and twine it up on top of her head. He plundered with his mouth there, grazing at the juncture of her neck and shoulder, then sinking in with his teeth. At the same time, he shoved hard against her, into her. He rolled her so she was flat on the bed, arms up, her breast pressing firmly into his hand, her pelvis propped on the pillow. He rocked into her, urging her against the pressure of his fingers where they gripped her.

"Oh, yeah." It seemed he liked that.

His hand squeezed at her breast. He slid his palm lower, dragging against her until her nipple slipped into the vee between his fingers. He closed his fingers then, grasping the nipple.

He thrust again and then once more. Each time, the force of his movement pushed her sensitized nub harder against his fingers. At her breast, he kept his grasp firm, so the motion caused a sharp tug of her nipple.

"Spread your legs more, Sade. I want you to take all of me."

She did, and he pressed more deeply into her, impossibly deep.

Sadie's breath shivered out. She felt—possessed. So vulnerable and taken by him. But the fear that might have risen yielded to the overwhelming stimulation of his assault on her body. It wanted him, wanted more.

"Leet!" There was a plea in it, but she wasn't sure what she asked.

He seemed to know. "Yes, sweetheart."

He moved inside her, slowly, but deep, all the way. He held there, stretch and pressure peaking everywhere he touched her. All around her his muscles clenched, and his own breath came in a feral growl. "Sadie."

Then he gave over, too. His hips moving like pistons, he slammed into her, pushing her further up the bed, causing ever more stimulation against the grasp of his fingers.

Using those words he'd told her he would, he described what he was doing to her, what he was feeling. What he wanted her to do.

And she did it. She came as he told her to, endlessly,

while he still pounded into her. She screamed out her orgasm, as he instructed. Again. And again, when he arched back, roaring, seized by his own release.

And amazingly, once more, when he collapsed down on her, gently soothing where his fingers and teeth had so abused her, whispering her to a last tender climax.

Leet disengaged and moved a little to her side. His hands curled over hers where they'd burrowed into the bedding, prying her fingers open until their hands joined. He tucked his head at her shoulder so they shared the same air as their breathing slowed, little mewling sounds from Sadie gradually fading.

She kept her eyes closed, feeling surrounded by him, taken. It was a little frightening and entirely seductive.

He wasn't satisfied to let her evade him. He kissed her forehead and whispered her name until she opened her eyes and met his gaze. "You're mine, Sadie. Say it." His gaze was strong, not letting go while he waited. "Say it."

Sadie resisted for only another moment. It wasn't necessarily rational, but it was surely true. He'd marked her, claimed her in every way. Her body had accepted the obvious truth of it. The sensible urge to deny it, the desire to cling to a last thread of self-preservation, didn't counter the reality of it.

She took a deep breath, more mental than physical.

"I'm yours, Leet."

His eyes lit with his victory. "That's my girl."

He rolled to his back and lifted her over so her head rested on his shoulder. She could hear his heart, a slow, steady, determined beat that lulled her to sleep.

Leet stood in the shower, water blasting hot from all directions. He'd left Sadie asleep in his bed.

The shower wasn't his first thought. That had been to wake her with his tongue between her legs, sliding into her. Or skip even that nicety and just fill her with the boner he'd woken with. That had worked out pretty well last night.

Pretty *freaking* well. He'd taken her a third time, in the darkest hour of the night. He'd woken her with kisses as he penetrated her. He'd held her face and done nothing but look into her blue eyes as he stroked in and out of her. She'd closed her eyes to him as she neared her peak, but he'd paused until she opened them again. Then he kept going until he'd brought them both to a quiet, intense orgasm, gazes still locked.

He hardened again there in the shower as he thought about what had passed between them. Physically and, *yes*, he could say it, emotionally, too. He'd never experienced anything like it. He had a constant hard-on for her. He wanted her, powerfully wanted, all the time.

And her responsiveness made him want to crow. She had that little initial reluctance, that very sensible-Sadie resistance that he couldn't help but find endearing. He knew it hadn't been easy for her to let go of that prudent, natural caution. He'd pushed her, purely unable to take a more reasonable approach. He'd gone over the top so fast he just couldn't fathom taking weeks to date her, court her.

He'd had to claim her, now.

Her body recognized it, accepted it; that was a done deal. Physically, they'd mated, bonded.

But he knew getting her head on board, getting her heart to acknowledge what they had, would be a greater challenge. He was there already. The last time he had her, as he'd looked into her eyes, with each stroke into her body, in his mind he'd said those three words. She may have seen it in his eyes. He may have even said it out loud as he crested, losing all control with that last, final surge into her.

He understood that she wouldn't think it rational that he could be so certain, so gone, in such a short time. He couldn't defend it as especially rational himself. Nonetheless it was true, he was dead sure. He was in love with her, and he was going to stay in love.

She was going to love him back. He was pretty sure she already did, even if she wasn't ready to own it. He thought it wouldn't take anything more than some time for her to come to terms with it.

And, yeah, he might need to reveal a little more about his life than he had so far. He suspected she was probably pretty big on honesty, so that issue about football would have to come up eventually. He'd have to defend his decision to keep it from her initially—he hoped having relied on Jace's advice about that would ease his way there. Anyway, the season-ending game could come as soon as tomorrow. At most, and he was reluctant to even voice the thought in his head, the season could last three more weeks.

So he'd stick with the strategy that had worked so far. Spend all the time with her he could manage. Forego any subtlety about his desire for her. Bide his time about demanding a commitment from her. Tempt her into more of that mind-blowing sex at every opportunity.

And the next opportunity presented itself nicely, as the woman stepped all naked into the shower with him. He'd been willing to be gentlemanly about it—he'd more than taken advantage of her during the night. But he wasn't going to say no to what walked into his arms now. He already had the hard-on. She had to know what she was getting into.

Sadie had watched him through the shower door. He was a physical man. Given over now to the pleasure of the water spray, he arched and stretched his muscles, letting the water massage and soothe.

It was there in everything he did. Sledding and skating, rough-housing with the boys. Making love with her. He had physical competence and strength and took pleasure in the use of his body.

He used it very well to give pleasure, too. Sadie had been comfortable with her sexuality up until now, though she'd had admittedly little experience. She had known there was more to discover but hadn't ever been tempted to experiment further.

Leet had introduced her to a new kind of sexuality. It seemed he needed only to touch her to have her reacting, arching toward him. His desire for her seemed endless, and it drew from her an equally ready response. Twice during the night, she'd woken to his lovemaking, and her body was there, seeking, wet and wanting, before she was even aware.

Endless wanting. She'd come awake with the light, sensing his absence even before she was fully conscious. She knew a physical longing, like her body had missed him even during sleep.

She should feel more than content, more than satiated. She shouldn't be wishing for one more chance to find fulfillment in his arms.

All true, yet she'd followed the sound of the shower. She stood watching as he enjoyed the water. And smiled to see that he was erect, gratified that he'd woken wanting her right back.

She stepped into the spray, facing him but not touching. His eyes met hers then made a thorough perusal of her body before returning, heat already lighting them. His cock twitched, reaching toward her of its own accord.

Sadie took the bar of soap from Leet's hand. Running it under a spray of water, she lathered her hands. Then she wrapped her hands around him, both palms fitting along his length. She stepped closer, pressing him against her belly, stroking with her soapy hands.

His eyes rolled up and he arched, thrusting more strongly into her clasp. He set his hands at her neck, clutching tight. He bent his head and took her mouth. "You are a witch," he said before he slipped his tongue in. Then he explored her mouth while she worked him, fast then slow, teasing as his excitement grew.

He slid a hand down, molding her breast. "Baby, you're going to make me come."

She ran her hands down slowly, then up, circling the tip. She nipped at his lip and smiled. "And that's bad?"

"God, no." He slid his other hand around her bottom, squeezing as he drew her closer. "But I haven't taken care of you."

The words caught as he spoke, shuddering out, and Sadie was very satisfied with her power. She kept at it. "You've been taking very good care of me. *Extremely* good."

Leet groaned, grabbing her ass now with both hands, starting to rock against her. Sadie leaned back, letting him glide between her hands, and her tightened abs. He looked down, watching her breasts, noting, she knew, the way they bobbed as he worked himself against her.

"Sadie, Sadie." His voice was urgent, his fingers gripping hard now. In another thrust, he started to come, spurting up high onto her chest, thrusting, coming more. With a long growl, he dropped his head onto her shoulder and grasped her hands, stilling her movement against him.

As his breathing eased, he slid his arms around her. His hands stroked her back and her bottom, fingers beginning to knead. He lifted his head, looking down at her with a satisfied smile. "So," he said. "You have some skills."

She knew her grin was a bit cocky. "Guess I'm a natural."

He eyed her, up to the challenge. He brought one hand around and started toying with her nipple. "I've got some stuff I haven't shown you yet."

His hand on her bottom slipped in between her legs, fingers seeking. His fingers at her nipple tweaked, then held tight while his thumb strummed.

Familiar with it now, trusting him entirely, her body gave over. She arched a little, giving better access to his questing fingers. Her breath quickened. She felt the dampness as he found her, probing into her. She cried out as he pushed one finger deep inside her, then two. "Leet!"

She circled her arms around his shoulders, hanging on as her legs turned to jelly.

"I know, baby. I've got you." He plunged his fingers in again, stretching her. Then he pulled them out, soothing, stroking, and rubbing his way back to her bottom. "Here," he said, bending over, lowering her down. "Sit." He set her down on the edge of the shower bench. "Rest back."

He held her head as she leaned back until her shoulders met slate. Water gently sprayed against her back from a showerhead there.

Leet put his lips at her ear. "Now spread your legs. I've been dying to taste you again. Fully, this time."

His words sent a shudder through her. She looked up at him, uncertain if her new sexual boldness had carried her quite this far.

Leet simply waited, resting one arm against the slate above her shoulder. He waited, not touching her in any way. Waited for her to accept him, to trust a little further.

With a moan, she closed her eyes and separated her legs. He didn't move, didn't touch her, until she opened her eyes again to meet his gaze. Then he kissed her, lips meeting hard, tongue thrusting. He kept at it, letting her know exactly what he had in mind.

Then his mouth lifted and moved down her neck and lower until he reached her breasts. He suckled there, gently biting one side then the other, leaving more marks. Finally, he took her nipples, tugging hard on one and then the other.

Sadie's each breath came out in a pant. Her pelvis began to rock, chafing her bottom against the slate of the bench.

His lips moved a little lower, rubbing over that bruise he'd left below her heart. Then, suddenly, he was at her core, his tongue stroking, sucking as he had the night before. A moment of that and he was in her, plunging deep as he had into her mouth, as he had her with his fingers.

Sadie cried out, bracing herself with her hands, one against cool slate, the other against glass. With his tongue, he took her again and again. Sadie spread herself more for him, rocking up to open herself to him. Then his fingers replaced his tongue, and he moved his mouth to take her swollen nub in, licking and sucking. She began to fly apart, lifting herself up against him, offering herself. He made a fist of his hand, pressing his knuckles into her opening, stretching her impossibly. The tightness pulled at her, making her exquisitely sensitive as his tongue rasped over her.

Sadie's hips bucked wildly as she began to come. Leet slid his arm around her, anchoring her against him, making her take more. Again and again she shuddered, her whole body spasming. She cried out his name in desperation before finally, he stopped, slowly withdrawing his touch, soothing gently.

He slid his head up to rest against her belly, and she held him there, sliding her fingers through his wet hair while her breath gradually calmed and she came back to herself.

Herself. That seemed a different person than she had been two days ago. She held Leet to her, fingers twined in his curls, and knew her life had changed. He'd wanted her, taken her, and now she was his, just as he'd said.

It felt lovely, glorious even, and also paralyzingly frightening.

Leet lifted his head and looked at her, tuned into her enough that he seemed aware of her thoughts. She kept her hands on his head and bravely, she thought, met his gaze. After a while, he seemed satisfied and pulled her up against him. He stood, holding her close. He nudged her chin up and kissed her, taking a long time with it.

After a while, he handed her soap and shampoo, and used both himself. They washed, then dried, then dressed. Through it all, he kept his hands on her most of the time, his eyes on her all of the time.

Together. Whatever else they were, Sadie knew he was communicating that. They were together.

This time, it was Jace entertaining Tino in kitchen. He smiled and nodded good morning to Leet and Sadie when they came downstairs together. He was kind enough to at least pretend not to notice Sadie's blush, and Sadie pretended not to notice when Leet gave Jace a grateful fist pound while she got a kiss and a hug from Tino. She didn't even want to think about what arrangement had been made to assure that the young one had been kept occupied.

Leet made coffee and helped Sadie get started on scrambled eggs and toast. He talked with Jace and Tino about his trip, explaining that he would be gone for a few days but would see them both when he got back. He took Jace's and Sadie's cell phones and dialed his number into them both.

Then he ate quickly and filled a travel mug with coffee.

Sadie and Jace cleaned up the kitchen while Leet disappeared downstairs. When he came back up, he carried a good-sized duffle and a garment bag.

"You guys take your time," he said. He went to Tino and noisily kissed him goodbye. He gave one of those male handshake/hugs to Jace, and the two of them spoke quietly for a minute. Then Leet turned to Sadie. "I'm happy for you to stay here as long as you like. In fact, I'd be nothing but happy if you were still here when I get back."

The boys were loudly in favor of that, but Sadie gave them a quelling look. "No," she said, sternly eyeing all three of them. "We're packing up and going home. And now is when we're doing it. You two go get your things together."

They accepted this more or less gracefully. Giving Leet one more salute, they trudged upstairs.

Leet pulled her close. "When you're ready, just lock the front door behind you. Do you want a key, Sadie?"

She looked at him, raising a brow. "We have a home, Leet."

He looked steadily back at her. "Your call."

Those words didn't reassure her a lot that her point had

been made.

"I'll let you know when I'll be back as soon as I can. I'll see you then, right?"

He waited for her nod.

"Until then, I'll call." He kissed her, lingering. "I'll call a lot. Do you have, like, a schedule?"

Sadie explained that she was working at the hospital on Sunday. She ran a teen clinic on Monday afternoons and held her own office hours usually on Tuesdays and Fridays. Otherwise, she was on call, having to be available if one of her patients went into labor. "It can be a little hard to live with my job," she let him know. "I can be in the middle of something, anything, and have to go."

Leet nodded, seeming to accept her warning. "There are things in my job I can't control also." Metal work, he'd told her. There were a number of old foundries in the area around Concord. And he was part of a team that traveled sometimes for jobs in other cities. "Like this trip." He rubbed his thumb over her cheek. "How late will you work tomorrow?"

"It's usually seven a.m. to seven p.m. But the residents all want off to watch this football game, so I'm covering late. Probably till about ten."

Leet nodded again. "Yeah, it's a regional team. They're in the playoffs. It's kind of a big deal around here."

Sadie shrugged, nodding. She'd heard a lot about it.

"So I'll call you late tomorrow night, okay?"

She looked up at him, searching his eyes. There was regret in them. He didn't want to leave her.

Sadie knew regret, too, and was surprised by it. She'd thought it would be a bit of a relief to have a few days' separation from him. To feel entirely herself again, grounded, situated in her own life. To have some distance, some perspective on the intensity of these two days. She was sure that would be a good thing.

Still, it was hard to let him go.

He put both hands on her, holding her head. His lips skimmed over hers, over her eyes, her cheeks. "Miss me, Sadie."

She took his wrists, holding them to her, holding him. "I will, Leet. I do already."

He kissed her hard and long, then took his bags and left.

CHAPTER FIVE

Sadie packed up her own bags and herded the boys into her SUV. Leet's drive had been plowed overnight, and he'd left her rig in the parking area outside the house.

She and Jace were quiet on the way home, and she was aware that he was missing Leet just as she was. She met his glance as they reached the highway, and they held hands across the seats for a couple miles.

Tino never did anything quietly, so they were treated to a chant about Leet and skating and pizza most of the ride, accompanied by the kick of his boots against the back of their seats.

Jace gave his brother a frown, but it was one Tino knew he could safely ignore, so the concert continued, a little louder for a couple minutes. When it began to die down to a tolerable level, Jace turned to her. "Coach invited some of the team over to his place to watch the game tomorrow. Can I go?"

"It's a school night, Jace. The game will go pretty late, won't it? Plus, I'm working. What will you do about transportation?"

"If I can find a ride?"

Sadie looked at him, knowing he cared a lot about this. "I suppose we can ask a grandmom to take you. I can pick you up on my way home, but I'll be late. I'll have to wait for some of the residents to get back to the hospital after the game's over. See if that would be okay with Mr. Morgan. Or maybe one of the other parents can bring you."

"I'll work it out." Then he looked up at her, anticipating what was coming. "I'll confirm it with you before I get into a car with anyone."

She smiled and tweaked a braid. "Right."

"Thanks, Mom."

The drive up to the farm had been cleared, too. Canaan was still out in his pickup, plowing out the yard. Joss was no doubt in the barn milking goats. Sadie thought her bio mom, Marta, would be in the house. Most likely she'd be in the kitchen, baking something as an excuse to stay out of her office and the accounts that were awaiting her attention. Every day was a workday on a farm, but Marta usually stuck to household chores on Saturdays, except for around tax time.

Sadie left the bags to unload later, and they all three traipsed into the moms' kitchen. She'd been right—it was banana bread just coming out of the oven.

Marta met Sadie's eyes but gave hugs and kisses to the boys before she took Sadie into her arms. They held each other quietly for a good, long hug. Marta had been a high school volleyball coach—Sadie's high school coach—before the couple had moved to Vermont. The two of them stood at the same height, their bodies mirroring each other, Marta's just a few pounds heavier now with her more sedentary life. It was a comfort—that sameness, that sense of shared self.

Marta poured milk and sliced bread while the boys chattered about their snowstorm adventure. Leet was featured in every story. Remarkably, Tino told of the trees Leet made, describing them in a detail that surprised Sadie. Apparently, Tino and Leet had a plan for metal sculpting lessons in the future.

That had Sadie's and Marta's gazes meeting over Tino's head. That and the story of Jace's snowmobile ride.

Finally, the boys were ready to take their narrative to Gramma Joss out in the barn. Jace volunteered that he'd stay to help finish the milking or help Canaan out with other chores.

Marta made tea as she and Sadie settled into the silence. Then they sat together at the kitchen table.

Marta started by grasping Sadie's hand. "I think Leet was holding back when he told us what happened on the river. You were in danger, weren't you?"

Sadie nodded. "I was still in the car when it went under. But Leet had hold of me. I knew he'd never let go. It was scary—and frigid cold—but I knew I could trust him. He'd have come in after me if he'd had to."

Marta watched her, reading, as always, what showed in her eyes. "He's a dependable man." Her mouth trembled a little and her eyes teared up, though she smiled gently. "You're in love with him."

Sadie mentally shrugged. That was always the way of it. Mom Joss would be all practical about it—she would ask about safe sex practices and had probably already done an Internet search on one Leet Hayes. She was on the town board and had no doubt vetted him with Will Hunter and the mayor as well. Marta would see—and feel—the emotion. It wasn't the first time she'd known what Sadie was feeling before Sadie had herself.

What could she do but nod and hold back her own tears? "Probably." She sipped her tea. "It was very intense—what happened at the river, then these two days we spent together. He's so good with the boys and so—"

Marta lifted and eyebrow and nodded. "So hot?"

Sadie chuckled. "Well, yeah. But also very sweet and gentle and—"

"Manly?"

Their eyes met and they both burst into laughter. "Yes. Very manly." She waved her hand over her face as if cooling herself and made Marta laugh more. "Mom, it happened so fast. Do you think it could be real?"

"I don't know, baby. He certainly seems like a take charge kind of guy. And you've always known your own heart. Why would you doubt it now?"

Sadie shook her head. "It's just not like me, you know? I was in love before, but it's never been—"

"No, sweetheart, you haven't been in love before. Those were boys you were with in college. Leet is a man. He's strong—physically, and strong-willed, too, right? Do you realize Leet is the first man you've been with who's taller than you? You've never taken on a man who posed a challenge to you before." She squeezed Sadie's hand. "Honey, you've never taken a risk with a man before."

Sadie turned her hand over to hold onto her mom. "He scares me."

"Love should be a little scary. If it means anything, if you really matter to each other, well, then you have to change, don't you? You have to compromise to make room for the other in your life. You lose a little bit of control."

Sadie sat back, resenting it a bit when her mother smiled.

"And you don't like that, do you? It's always been important for you to feel in control. You got that from your uncle."

Sadie's Uncle Dick, Joss's brother, had been her sperm donor.

"It's not just me, Mom. I have to think about Jace and Tino, too."

"Oh, pshaw. Your boys are fine. You know they are. And you know they're falling in love with Leet, too. I just heard it from them, in the way they talk about him."

"It's too soon, too fast for them, as well, isn't it? I feel like I should be careful about this. Very careful."

Marta stood and patted Sadie's shoulder before she picked up dishes. "Yes, dear. You do that. See how it works for you."

Sadie took a deep, heavy breath. "Thanks, Mom." She *almost* kept the irony out of her voice. "And what do you know about manly, anyway?"

Marta kept her back turned as she ran water in the sink. "Oh, I know things."

It was nearly eleven when Sadie picked up Jace at Ray Morgan's. She'd had a busy shift at the labor unit—a woman with twins had needed a c-section, and she'd hardly got done helping with that when another woman arrived fully dilated and delivered right there in triage before they could even get her to a room. Catching up the electronic medical records for both of those births had taken the rest of the shift until the residents had come back.

They were in a fine mood when they arrived—their team had won, against all odds, apparently. These days most ob-gyn residents were women, but there were usually one or two men in each class of ten. For the current group, a couple of the guys were avid, if not rabid, football fans. One was a local New Hampshirite who'd gotten the whole group on board rooting for the home team.

Jace and his coach, when she arrived at Ray Morgan's

house, looked equally elated. Jace gave her a big hug when she got to the door. Ray watched the two of them, a happy grin on his face, too.

Sadie smiled back. "I see we have satisfied fans here."

"It was a great game, Mom. You should have seen it. They came from behind again after trailing almost the whole game. They had grit, didn't they, Coach?"

Ray nodded, clearly enjoying Jace's enthusiasm. He shook Sadie's hand when she put it out and gave her a wink, then pulled her in to close the door behind her. She had met with Ray a couple of times when they talked about Jace's option to play varsity. But she backed off after the decision was made, determined not to hover. She knew to respect the coach-player relationship.

"Hi, Mr. Morgan. I'm sorry I'm late like this. Thank you for keeping Jace so long."

"No problem, Sadie." He put a hand on Jace's shoulder. "We had a great time. And I think you ought to start calling me Ray now, don't you?"

Jace spoke up then. "He knows Leet too, you know, Mom."

Sadie looked from one to the other. She wouldn't have thought Leet would tell Ray about their relationship so soon. She could see how that would be a difficult thing. But clearly, Ray was aware of it.

She nodded, uncertain what to say. "Get your jacket, Jace. We need to get you home."

Ray spoke softly when he was gone. "Leet gave me a call yesterday. He sounded very happy. That makes me nothing but happy, too."

Sadie met the understanding in his eyes. "I'm glad. Thank you for saying so."

Then Ray crossed his arms over his chest. "He's my boy, and he deserves to be happy, so you'll treat him well."

Sadie was a bit startled. He was a big, imposing man, having lost nothing to age. She did her best to stand her ground and keep eye contact but was significantly relieved when he finally cracked a smile.

She smiled, too, trying to keep the worry out of it. "I'll try."

He leaned forward and kissed her as Jace came back. "I know you will. Good night, Jace. Thanks for keeping me company. Same time next week, eh? No objection, right, Sadie?"

Sadie was definitely outmatched. And she was already committed to cover for the residents again. "Right."

In the car, Jace was surprisingly quiet given his earlier enthusiasm. They were halfway home before he spoke. "You don't really hate football, do you, Mom?

"Jace, I don't hate it at all. Did I say something to make you think I do?"

"I thought you really didn't want me to play."

Sadie rolled her shoulders once and then took his hand. "You love it, don't you, Jace? It's very important to you, yes? How could I ask you not to play?"

"But you don't like it that I do."

"I wouldn't ask you to be who you're not. It's like my work—it's a nuisance, isn't it? I have to leave sometimes when you don't want me to. I miss some things that are important to you and Tino or the grandmoms. But you all deal with it because you love me, and I love my work. You wouldn't ask me to give it up unless there was something really big going on, right?"

He smiled. "Like the Super Bowl?"

She laughed. "You play in the Super Bowl, Jace, I'm definitely taking that day off." He seemed more serious in response to that than she expected. "I worry a little about your safety, Jacey. That's just something a mom has to live with, though I claim the right to expect that you'll act with some caution. I have to trust you to do that, just like I'll have to trust that you won't drink and drive or behave irresponsibly when you start to have sex. *Many years from now.*"

That at least got a smile.

"But you know what my biggest concern is."

"Yeah. School."

"Um-hmm. Not *just* school, but yeah, that's your job now. It's important to find something else that you want to do, *love* to do, I hope, that can be your work besides football. Football doesn't make a career for very many kids, and even then, it doesn't last for long. I just don't want you to count on it for your whole future."

"Yeah, I get it."

"But I love to see you play, Jace. You're so good, and it makes you happy. I can see it. I would never be opposed to that."

"So you're okay with someone playing football 'cause they love it?"

Sadie shrugged. "Of course I'm okay with that. I loved playing volleyball, Jace."

"But you made sure to find work that you love."

She nodded. "Yeah, well, the likelihood of playing professionally is pretty small for football, and just about zero for volleyball."

Jace smiled. "Maybe you gave up too easy. I've seen women play beach volleyball professionally."

"In those little bikinis? You'd have sand *everywhere*. I wasn't going there."

─────※─────

Leet was back in his hotel room when he got Sadie on the phone. He'd taken a soak in the hot tub then stretched out on the bed, letting the four ibuprofen he'd swallowed do battle with the inevitable aches and pains.

It had been a hell of a game. Really, they'd played their best game ever, nearly flawless, and it was good enough to keep them trailing by no more than three or four points behind what was probably the best team in the league, at least on paper. But his team had heart, and it had, well, metal. They'd never given up.

Then they'd gotten lucky with a punt return and surprised everybody, even themselves, by taking the lead early in the fourth quarter. That changed the dynamic—they had more to lose then, and had to balance the urge to be too careful and conservative in protecting their unexpected lead.

They discussed it on the sidelines and on the field, and agreed to keep trust in their basic game. They took a gamble on a couple long passes and played out the last three minutes of the game with a sure win.

Who'd have thought?

In one week, they'd play for the division title.

Who the hell would have thought?

He bristled with the urge to talk about it with Sadie as he waited for her to answer.

"Hey, Leet."

"Hi, baby." He rolled over, keeping the phone tucked close, and closed his eyes. He wanted every bit of her he could get through this very unsatisfactory, long-distance connection.

"How are you?"

"I'm fine, damn fine, with just one major exception."

"Does that exception have anything to do with me?"

"*Everything* to do with you. I miss you, Sadie."

"We just saw each other yesterday."

Yeah. And what a lot had happened since then. "And your point is?"

She laughed a little. "I miss you too, Leet."

"Do you? I can't say I'm sorry to hear that." How his life had changed since those moments at the river. He wondered if she had a clue. "How are the boys?"

"They're fine. Jace spent the evening with Ray, watching that football game. They were both ecstatic when I picked him up."

"They were happy about the game?"

"Oh, Jace was over the top. Really, Leet, he loves football. And that local team—everyone's agog."

"The Metal."

"Yeah. Everyone here is so excited."

"Nothing wrong with that." He spoke again into her silence. "Is there? You don't really hate football, do you, Sadie?"

"That's funny. Jace asked me exactly the same thing tonight."

"How did you answer him?"

"I don't hate it, Leet. How could I, when it means so much to him?"

"Yeah." He guessed that gave him hope.

It felt wrong to him, to keep this part of his life from her. He *wanted* to talk to her about it, ached to tell her what today's game had meant to him. Plus, he didn't want to have secrets from her. He was afraid that would come back to bite him.

A tangled web. *Well*, one week or three, this season

would be over.

"Tino said you were going to teach him to make trees."

He grinned. "The kid seemed interested. I think he liked the idea of using a blow torch."

"You're so sweet, Leet."

There was a very pretty tone in her voice that had his thoughts going elsewhere. And his blood, too. "Wait 'til you've had to douse a couple fires." Then he paid attention to that blood. "Tell me what you're wearing, Sade."

Her next words were in a different tone. "We're not having phone sex, Leet."

Prim Sadie. Like that didn't turn him on even more. "No? You ever done it?"

"No."

"Me either. But I bet we could figure it out. We're smart. Creative. What do you have on *underneath* what you're wearing?" She made him wait for it. "Who says I'm wearing anything under anything?"

"Oh, Sadie."

She laughed, but there was a little tremor in it.

"Tell me. If you could have my tongue anywhere you wanted it right now, where would it be?"

"Leet!"

"I can think of four places."

"I'm not doing this."

"All right, five."

"How is your work going, Leet?"

"Are you asking that because you're anxious for me to come home? Six."

"*Not* six. And, in part, yes. How is it going?"

"It's going great, Sadie, really great. But we lost a couple days with the storm this week. It's going to be tough to get away. Why not six?" He said that last low and urgently.

Silence. Then, "*Maybe* six."

He had an erection now that was seeking some wet, welcoming spot in the bedding, like a wild boar sniffing out truffles. *Good luck on that.* "Baby, I want you." He tried not to growl it. "I need you."

Silence again.

"If you could have my hands anywhere you wanted them right now, where would they be?"

"Oh, Sadie. That's my girl."

Leet had told Sadie he thought he could make it an early day and come home for Thursday evening, then spend the night. He'd managed it okay. The team had spent the first half of the week reviewing tapes and developing an initial game plan while their bodies rested and recovered. They had light workouts and practices on Wednesday and Thursday with more intense efforts planned for Friday and Saturday, after travel. He was able to leave at four on Thursday afternoon. The drive upstate and across the Connecticut River into Vermont took a little under a couple hours.

He was home by six.

So there he was, sitting at the dining room table in the farmhouse with Jace, Tino, and the two moms. He had only one complaint.

The food was topnotch—a green salad with walnuts, berries, and goat cheese, mixed vegetables very nicely herbed and buttered, and chicken and dumplings. Then there was pie. Two pies, because, Marta said, not everyone liked strawberry-rhubarb, but almost no one said no to apple. Leet didn't say no to either. Tino was one of the naysayers to rhubarb, but Jace was on board with both as well. Ice cream was involved also, so it was good not to be alone in that.

The company was fine for the most part, too. The moms were not as oblivious, apparently, as their daughter and were aware of Leet's football career. Marta had done some substitute coaching at the high school and knew Ray a bit as well as Leet's history as Oak Mill Basin's star quarterback. So they were able to discuss the game, though they were a bit discreet about Leet's role around Tino. They all agreed he couldn't be trusted not to spill the beans.

The moms had some concerns about the secrecy—Jocelyn especially. But Jace stepped up and claimed responsibility. Apparently, he'd talked with them about it before, on the day Leet had brought Jace home after pulling Sadie from the river.

If Sadie knew that Leet was a professional football player, she would probably have more strongly resisted developing a relationship with him. She'd have been concerned about his influence over Jace and his plans for the future. She might not have wanted someone encouraging him to pursue the game as a career, someone who had actually made a success of it himself. Leet was living Jace's dream.

Jace framed the problem around Sadie's issue with him and his future. But Leet figured Sadie would have additional objections, and he thought the moms suspected the same. Sadie knew him as an artist, and he'd planted the vague thought that he worked in industrial metallurgy as well.

She didn't have any reason to think of him as a *player* with regard to women. He wasn't, especially. But he was pretty sure she'd have more suspicion, less trust, if she knew of his pro career.

Already, he was set to close the deal with her. Already, she was moving slower than he wanted.

It would have killed him to have to spend months convincing her that he was a serious, steady man. That she could rely on him. That she could safely give her heart to him.

In general, the moms seemed to be on his side. Leet figured it was a typical mom thing, wanting the adult child settled in a good, happy relationship. He knew enough to be grateful.

And the boys were already there, on his side.

So, the only complaint he had this night was the absence of one Sadie Benjamin.

Apparently, some woman just had to have her baby that day.

Sadie had called home just after Leet had gotten there—there was some discussion with Marta about eight centimeters, something Leet didn't really care to know more about. And some hope that it wouldn't be much longer.

But Leet was working his way through the second piece of pie before her car came up the drive. He was on his feet before it came to a complete halt. He went alone into the kitchen—he was pretty sure both boys had a grandmother's hand on their shoulder, keeping them in their seats. He met her on the screened-in porch, out of sight of the dining room.

"Hi, Leet. I'm sor—"

He didn't care. He didn't care if she was sorry she was late, or how the birth had turned out, or whether it was freaking triplets. He just cared about having her in his arms, having his mouth on hers.

If she was surprised, it only took her a minute to get over it. Then she was soft in his arms and opening her mouth to him.

It was a long kiss. Very thorough. He started backing off, thinking he was done. But then it turned out he wasn't.

She seemed okay with that, too. She had her arms around him by then and was putting some muscle into it. He liked that. Sort of like the two pieces of pie, he was glad not to be alone in it.

It felt damn good. When he finally was done with the kiss, he still held her, his jaw resting against her head. They stood together that way for a long moment. "That's better, isn't it?"

She rooted into his chest, inhaled. She was breathing in his scent, just as he had done with hers. He was already hard, but that stirred him even more

"Indeed it is." She lifted her head to look at him. "I've missed you, Leet. More than I thought I would." She looked a little more, biting her lower lip. "Or could."

He slid his hand along her face and took that into his heart. He nodded, then touched his lips to her forehead. "Brave woman. I missed you, too, tremendously."

She smiled. "'Woman?' You're going to be politically correct now and stop calling me girl and baby?"

He put an arm around her shoulder and, after straightening himself a bit, started walking her to the dining room. "Probably not, as a rule."

Pleasing him again, she had an arm around his waist and touched his chest with her other hand as she laughed.

He squeezed her shoulder and leaned a little into her. "I trust you understand I fully appreciate that you are an adult, competent, intelligent woman." He stopped her just outside the dining room and spoke at her ear. "With a fucking hell of a rack."

She nudged him, though it was with a blushing kind of laugh, and went to greet her family. She trailed her hand nicely over his butt before she left him.

Everyone at the table got a kiss, though none approached the quality of the one he'd gotten. He held back his smirk on that. Marta asked about the birth—Leet tried to remember some of the questions, but knew he'd have to work up to that. Then she offered to fill a plate for Sadie. He almost fell to his knees in gratitude when Sadie declined.

"We weren't sure how long you'd be, so the boys brought over what they'd need to spend the night here." That was Joss, and he was ready to kiss her, too.

Sadie looked at him from across the room, and he knew his eyes had lit. He knew the moms were seeing the same thing, and he didn't fucking care.

Joss held Sadie's hand at her shoulder, and he saw the squeeze they shared. Sadie kissed her again. "Thanks, Mom." She went to Marta and repeated the procedure. "You, too."

Jace stood, and they held onto each other for a minute.

"Do you have your homework done?"

"Yeah, except to study for my biology test."

"Not that nasty Krebs cycle again."

Jace grinned. "No. We're done with that. We're onto cell physiology now."

"Okay. Osmosis. Active transport. Mitochondria. That's all doable. Study hard. I'll see you tomorrow."

They kissed, then Sadie lifted Tino up.

"You're going out again?"

She nuzzled him. "Yes. Sorry, sweetie. You're going to sleep here tonight."

"Another woman has to have a baby?"

"No. I want to spend some time with Leet."

"Okay, then. G'night. G'night, Leet." He remembered one more thing to tell Sadie. "Leet says when I'm older, I have to give rhubarb a chance."

Sadie chuckled. "It's good advice. Good night, baby." She handed him off to Leet. The naturalness of that action, and the easy way Tino came to him, touched Leet greatly. He got another, somewhat sloppy, apple-pie flavored kiss.

Still holding Tino, he gave a hug to Jace. "Cell physiology. Better you than me, dude. Study hard."

Then he acknowledged the moms and thanked them for dinner. He passed Tino to Joss and, a very happy man, followed Sadie out the door.

She'd only gotten about five steps out into the yard before she was in Leet's arms again. He turned her and lifted her up, so she wrapped her legs around him. His hands were on her ass, squeezing and pulling her close. She slid her arms around his strong shoulders and held on.

She had missed him. He was in her thoughts so much of the time, she'd had trouble focusing. Often, she'd stroked her fingers over that spot below her heart where he'd made his mark on her. Even as it faded, she felt the imprint he'd left.

"I love your mothers."

Sadie smiled. "They seem to like you okay, too." She could already feel his erection pressing into her.

"Your place or mine, babe?"

She had to wait for him to take his tongue out of her mouth before she could answer. "Mine's closer."

He looked over to the A-frame. "A huge point in its favor. But mine has a hot tub and a king-sized bed."

Hers had neither of those. They shared another kiss. "Your call."

He carried her to his rig. "Mine then. I won't have to worry about waking anybody up when I make you scream."

Sadie suppressed a shiver. The man had a point.

He got her to his truck. It was a big, black extended cab. With his sculpture work, Sadie knew Leet had a good practical reason for owning it but figured he'd have made one up if he'd needed to.

He leaned her back against it and rocked into her. They lingered in a kiss that went ever deeper. He moved his hand to cover her breast. She arched into him, and he moaned.

"We could manage a quickie right here," he said, his voice rough. "Just kind of take the edge off."

Sadie felt the cold from the truck fender at her back. "I'm sure you said something about a king-sized bed."

"Beds are for wusses." He rubbed a little at her breast and watched as she shuddered. She knew it was obvious to him that he could change her mind. When he saw her admit it to herself, he relented. One more kiss and he tucked her into the passenger seat.

"Do you have your overnight bag in your car?"

"Yeah. It's in the back."

"Got it." He fetched it and then belted himself in behind the wheel and backed out of the yard.

"I am sorry I left you alone with the whole family."

Leet took her hand and brought it to his lips for a kiss. "No problem. It was fine."

"You did okay with the moms?"

"I love Marta. She's a very warm, motherly sort. It was nice." And something different from the kind of mothering he'd experienced in his own home. "I think Joss likes me okay, but still has this basic desire to kick my ass. There's a chance she could do it, too."

He had them pegged pretty well. She smiled and enjoyed watching him drive. His hands were strong, competent.

"Have they been together all of your life?"

"Yes, since before they had me."

"What about, uh, your—?"

"My father? They used Joss's brother as a sperm donor." She could see his eyebrows lift. "So he's like your—"

"He's my uncle. His name is Dick and don't laugh. We're close. We both know about the biological relationship, of course, but that's not what's primary."

"Is that typical for lesbian couples who want a kid?"

"People work it out different ways. Some couples use a sperm bank and an anonymous donor. Others use a donation from a male friend or relative. Sometimes it's even an ex-husband." She watched his reaction. "Does it seem odd to you?"

He looked at her and grinned. "Well, *yeah*. But I can tell you, you have a very sweet, loving family. Much more so than anything I ever had. I'd be the last one to criticize."

"Do you see your family much?"

"We get together over the holidays when my brother brings his kids out. My parents are shaping up a little bit better as grandparents than parents. I think they're aware that they might have missed something. "But their work was very important to them. And it *was* important work—they built up a top-flight cardiology department. My brother and I couldn't compete." He shrugged. "It's what it was. We both found other things. We're all okay together now, but I can't say we're real close."

"Oh, Leet. I know of your parents through the medical center. They're very well respected. And a little feared."

He smiled and nodded his head. "Probably my mom more than my dad."

"Maybe. I saw her speak once at an OB department meeting. She didn't have any trouble handling that crowd."

Leet took the gravel road up to his house fast enough to make Sadie brace a hand against the door. Maybe that was his usual approach, but Sadie thought it might be a sign of his hurry to have her in his house. In his bed.

An old beater was parked in the drive, but he passed it and pulled into his three-car garage. There was a practical though high-end midsize sedan in one bay and something small and no doubt very sporty underneath a tarp in the third. He took her bag and came around to open the door for her. He ushered her into the house but for the most part kept his hands off her.

Inside, he glanced over to the open area above the studio. Light flashed there—welding sparks. "Looks like I've got a student here. There's a kid from UNH who was going to come back after Christmas to finish up a project before his semester starts." He took her arm and gave her a direct look. "We can ignore him."

Sadie read his eyes. "You mean he's no reason to hold back on any screaming?"

The smolder there confirmed her thoughts. "That's exactly what I mean." He still didn't touch her with any more than his hand on her arm. "I appreciate that you told your mom you didn't need dinner there. But *are* you hungry? Tell me if you need to eat."

Tell me now, he was saying. *Or it will be too late.*

"I'm okay."

"Good. I want you to know I got that testing I told you about."

She swallowed. "Okay."

Then, in very clear non-verbal communication, he nodded her up the stairs. And kept his gaze hard on her until she turned and went.

She knew exactly where his gaze was as he came up behind her.

Inside his room, she turned and looked at him. He'd already closed the door, dropped her bag on the floor, and tossed his jacket and shirt after it. He was moving toward her, stalking. She swallowed again, hard, but held her ground. Well, no, she backed away a bit, until she came up against the bed.

"Get your clothes off, baby." He toed his boots off, still stepping closer. He stopped a yard away and unzipped his jeans. He let himself out—his erection huge and hard, upright and seeking her. "Off, Sadie. Now."

After a moment, she moved, lifting her sweater over her head. His hands were helping then, pulling at her tee.

"I just need to be inside you. Just that. But I need it right now, Sade."

She was unfastening her bra while he opened her jeans and slid them down her hips. He pushed them down so she could step out of them and did the same with his own. Then he lifted her onto the bed and came down on top of her.

"Are you ready for me? Please, baby." He pushed between her legs and slid his fingers to her opening. She was already wet, and he groaned out his gratitude. "Thank God."

He placed the huge, pulsing head of his cock there, then grabbed onto her shoulders and pushed in, all the way. Sadie caught her breath against the tightness, the abrupt breaching of her body, her self. Then he held there, breathing hard into the crook of her neck. "There. That's all I needed. Just that." He kept breathing hard, a rough catch in his throat. He dug in with his knees to bury even deeper into her. "I'm not wearing a condom, Sadie. You can't imagine how good this feels. How good you feel."

Sadie had one hand at his head and the other circled over his shoulders. Every muscle was taut. He was pressing into her, not thrusting but still straining for the last millimeter of penetration.

She curled her fingers into his hair, gripping tight. She closed her eyes, overwhelmed by the strength of his desire, her own rising in response. He filled her, stretching her, exquisite simulation to every nerve. Sudden tingling, sparkling heat shot through her, bright, like a lightning bolt. Her body arched up against him, her breath keening out.

He clutched at her, nuzzling his face into her skin, groaning. "Stop, baby. Don't move." But he shuddered and suddenly, with one thrust, he began to come. He stroked inside her, deeply, fiercely, spurting into her. Body bucking, she plunged into orgasm too, long and intense as he filled her with the wet flood of his semen. Her cries joined his, fading gradually as aftershocks continued to jolt them.

He still grasped her, rubbing skin to skin wherever he

could. After several minutes, he lifted his head to look at her. His breath still harsh, his expression feral, he gazed at her until, with a curse, he dropped down to kiss her. His lips brushed at hers, soft at first. Then, with needy groans, he took her more aggressively, nipping and sucking, using his tongue.

Inside her, she could feel him harden again, feel that remarkable fullness as he expanded. He thrust once to take his fill of her, and then again. Each stroke was long and deliberate, and he lifted again to watch her reaction. Supporting himself on his elbows, he took her breasts in his hands. He molded them, lifting them up so his mouth could reach to suckle, his tongue rasping at her nipples. Without thought, she curved her spine, offering herself.

Then he used his thumbs and fingers to pinch, to torment, watching while he continued plunging into her.

Impossibly, he was driving her to another wracking peak. Sadie could hardly bear it. "Leet."

"Sadie. Baby."

"I can't do this."

"Yes, you can."

And he was right, she could. But it was more, more than she thought possible. Taken over, she dug her heels into the bed, arching up to accept his thrusts. Spasming everywhere, her body beyond her control, she convulsed in orgasm. And screamed.

Her hands had lifted to twine with his fingers beside her shoulders. His grasp tightened on hers, keeping her with him, bringing her back as he continued slow, deep strokes. As she gradually gathered herself, she was aware when his strokes became more determined. He ended each thrust ground into her, and held there, staking his claim. Each next lunge was stronger, held longer. Each came with a louder exhalation of his breath.

She opened her eyes to see his gaze locked on hers, hot and fierce. "Sadie." A tremor passed over his face, and his fingers clenched on hers, hard enough to cause pain. But she returned his grasp and met his gaze strongly, letting him know she was there and not afraid.

He read her right. With a primal groan, he lowered his head, teeth scraping at her shoulder. And then he let go, clenched all around her, pounding and thrusting, filling her, taking her. For long minutes, he went on, each breath an exclamation, each penetration a full and complete possession.

He growled when he came, loud and rough and long. Possessed, taken, owned, and *given*, Sadie cried out with him.

His head was buried next to hers, breath still chafing out hard into her shoulder. He held her close with one big hand clutched into her hair. He stroked with his thumb, and she knew he found the tear that trailed there.

He lifted a little and turned her head so they were face to face. His gaze took hers, penetrating, seeking, as he rubbed another tear away.

Sadie knew her heart was in her eyes.

And he saw it. Acknowledged it. Owned it.

"I love you, Sadie Benjamin."

She lifted a hand to hold his face as he held hers. There were no tears to brush away, but she knew the emotion was there, just as intense.

"I love you, Leet Hayes."

Her eyes filled again, and he stroked away another tear. He smiled gently. "Are you going to cry every time I love you, or tell you I do, or you tell me?"

"Maybe," she said, sniffing just a bit. "I will if I want to."

"It's going to happen a lot."

She gave a little one-shoulder shrug. "I might get over it."

"No need on my part."

"Okay then."

"Okay then." He rolled over and brought her along with him, her head on his shoulder, their legs entwined.

Both apparently more than content, they rested there for a long time.

"Marta snuck a pie into my truck. I saw it when I put your bag in the back seat."

"Strawberry-rhubarb?"

"I think so."

"Then what are you doing still lying here?"

"Really. Damned if I know. Ice cream?"

"Well, yeah."

He smiled and patted her bottom. "That's..."

He waited while she rolled her eyes. "Your girl."

"Hell yeah."

He chuckled through a good, smacking kiss before he pulled on a pair of old, baggy sweats and padded out of the room. Really, his butt looked very fine in anything at all.

They ate in bed, a thing Leet considered to be one of the truly fine pleasures in life. He wolfed his own piece and then finished hers—he had a couple big work-outs coming up—before they settled in snug under the blankets. He told her he'd have to leave early in the morning and would be gone again through the weekend.

He thought another upcoming separation might justify one more go-round, but he didn't want to come off as greedy. He took the gentlemanly high road. Plus, there was always the morning. He wouldn't have to leave as early as all that.

But he woke when her cell rang. He tried not to listen—*really* tried—as she talked someone through what would happen if her water was broken. There was a plan made for the morning.

She'd slipped out of bed and into his robe when she took the call, and walked over to the window. He held the blankets open for her when she came back. She came in and snuggled up against him for warmth.

"Sorry, Leet."

He grunted and tucked her in close. Maybe a little too close. *Yup.*

"Just so you know, things are gonna happen if I get woken up at night and you're here with me."

There was a smile in her voice, thank God. "Yeah? What kind of things?"

He nudged around so she'd get a clue.

"I see," she said dryly.

He hoped he wasn't fooling himself when he heard a little humor in that dryness. And sighed in grateful relief when, the next moment, she had him in her hands. She faced him on her side and brought him against her abdomen while she stroked him. In her smooth, strong hands. Along his whole length. Up and down. And again, with a little lingering extra attention at that most sensitive spot at the head. She had magic in her fingers.

"Sadie." He said it in a moan. He had in mind all kinds of things to do—things to do to her, things to get her to do to him—but he was very much interested to see where she would take this. And entirely satisfied just enjoying where it had gone already. *Really* enjoying.

So he groaned again and arched a little, giving her all the access she wanted.

She took it and ran with it.

She worked at him a little more, teasing and torturing in a very witchy fashion. Then she slithered lower and took him between her breasts.

He had to work hard to hold back when she rubbed a little spit and his own moisture around to ease the glide. She had one hand behind his back to secure him against her and used the other to hold her breasts around him. Her mouth was at his ribs, tongue stroking, teeth nipping. He was a little distracted, but he felt it when she put her lips below his heart and sucked hard. He almost came right then, aware she was returning the mark he'd left on her.

She'd started moaning, too. He was sure she toyed a bit with herself where she held him to her breasts. And his knee pressed between her legs was getting—giving—a little action.

He was amazed at how sexual—willing, adventuresome—she was. She had such little experience, but had opened up to him, for him, so strongly. He couldn't imagine what kind of idiots she'd made love to in her past that she hadn't found her pleasure.

Fucking morons. Morons he couldn't help smirking about at this particular moment. Sadie was here with him.

He couldn't take anymore. He slid his hand into her hair, wrapping it around his fingers. "Sadie, sweetheart. Come up here." He tugged a bit at her hair.

But she pushed back. "No. Roll over."

"Babe."

"No." She nudged him, and he complied, rolling to his back. What really did he have to complain about?

She came to her knees, still straddling his left leg, still rubbing herself a little there while she lifted her hands to run them through her hair, dropping it over her back, arching to give him a very gratifying view of her breasts. She really was a witch. He spoke his thought out loud, graphically, using some of those four letter words.

She gave him a wicked smile and paused as she slid her hands down her body, stopping to fondle her breasts for him. Then she took him again. He cursed and arched helplessly as she lowered her head, her mouth.

"Sadie. Don't do that."

But she had him already, deep in her hot, wet mouth.

He felt her tongue stroke, her teeth lightly graze.

A tremor shuddered through him. He was going to lose it right there. He was going to fill her mouth before he gave her any satisfaction, before—

He put his hands onto her head and lifted her, rising up at the same time so he could take her mouth with his. He held her there, swearing out her name like a curse every time he came up for air, until she did what he wanted and crawled over him, coming down on top of him, taking him in. Slick and hot, she sat down on him, taking him all the way.

He lay back, pulling her along, thrusting up into her. "Yes. God, yes."

But she wasn't done with him. She pushed against his shoulders and lifted up, arching back a little, taking control of their movements where they were joined.

He wasn't going to let her have it all her way. He reached up to touch that spot where her own faded bruise was still visible, then grasped her nipple between two fingers and played it with his thumb. He slid his other fingers between them, where she was hot and wet, and diddled her.

She arched back, undulating, whimpering as she rocked up and then took him again. Suddenly, she was wild, riding him. He heard his name chanted out over the sound of their flesh slapping together. She put her hands over his, both of them, and brought him closer, harder against her.

She tightened around him, milking him as she started to cry out. Beyond his control, he came too, arching up into her depths, shooting into her.

Then she collapsed into his arms. As they settled, he rolled her to his side and tucked the blankets up around her. He held her in his arms while they both slept.

*C*HAPTER SIX

Sadie spoke with Leet before her lunch break on Friday. He was on the road, he said, and would spend the weekend in Boston.

He'd been right in that thing he'd said about love. He said it a lot, and she said it back. And they expressed it physically, too, a lot. They'd showered together before he'd left, and one thing had led exactly to that other. They'd used the words then as well, in both the gentle moments and the urgent.

She might, as she'd said, get over getting teary about it, but she hadn't entirely yet.

He seemed very comfortable about it. He said the words easily, frequently, though not, it was clear, at all casually. He said it with his eyes on her, or on the phone, with meaning in his voice. With all of his attention.

Sadie couldn't say she felt entirely comfortable about it. What was between them had happened so fast, was so intense. She wasn't, by nature, someone who rushed into things, or who even felt comfortable just going along for the ride when they got rolling. She normally wanted to know where things were going, think about it some, and get there on her own accord.

Leet appeared to be more decisive as well as a man of action. He saw what he wanted, he grabbed it. Done. He'd ride the wave and get there ahead of it. He'd probably ride the avalanche and beat it, too.

So it wasn't entirely comfortable, but it did feel right. She knew her heart was taken, gone over. The feeling she had for Leet, the wonder of what he felt for her, filled her, made her feel not just complete but satiated, *wallowing* in contentment, in happiness.

It was enough at times to shake her. To move her to

tears. To make her a little bit afraid.

And so, over lunch, she sought out one of her favorite people. Meg Velazquez was her sister of the heart. She was a midwife, also, in the large, medical center-based midwifery practice that had been well-established in the area for many years. She'd married young and against her parents' wishes. Raul had been poor and illegal. He'd worked odd jobs, mostly yard work.

Now he had a business degree and a successful landscaping service. And a wife and five children he loved more than the world.

Their family, like Sadie's, was a blended one. Relatives from Mexico often stayed with them for long periods. It looked like Raul's aunt might stay forever. They'd come to depend on Tia Lourdes to manage the busy household.

The Velazquezes lived on the Vermont side of the river and the two families often got together. Meg and Raul's children were all high school or college age, but they loved Jace and took Tino in as a little brother.

But it was Meg that Sadie needed to see. Above all, Meg was practical, sensible, more grounded than anyone Sadie knew. She seldom gave advice, but was an astute listener. Whenever Sadie was troubled, she felt better after an hour with Meg.

She was therefore quite taken aback when Meg interrupted as she spoke of Leet.

Meg raised her hand, abruptly halting her. "Stop. You love him, don't you?"

Sadie took a breath but admitted what was obvious truth. "Yes."

"And do you trust that he loves you?"

"Yes."

"And he wants you, bad. And you appear to like that, yes?"

Even in front of Meg, Sadie had to fight a blush. She nodded.

"Then shut up. Take him." She waved her hand. "Move on."

"Meg!"

Across the table, as if they were alone rather than in the middle of a busy hospital cafeteria, Meg took her hand. "It's love, Sadie. You don't negotiate with it. You can't make it unfold to your liking. You know how that would go. You'd dither about each tiny step, forward, back, back some more. It's happened. You're in it. The full monty. Move on."

Sadie sat back and looked at her friend, not quite holding back an amazed laugh.

Meg raised an eyebrow. "Did I ever tell you about how Raul and I met?"

Sadie shook her head.

"I'd seen him around. He worked in my parents' yard—it was fall, there were a lot of leaves. I was a cheerleader."

Sadie couldn't hold back a chuckle then, for sure.

Meg blushed a little herself. "Maybe that was something you didn't know about me. I wasn't very good. It was a small school." She shrugged. "Anyway, I was practicing in the back yard. I suppose it's possible I knew Raul was out there when I went. I do remember I happened to have my best little cheerleader girl skirt on. *That* probably wasn't accidental."

Sadie grinned, entirely enjoying herself.

Meg grinned back. "Those round-offs are hard. He offered to spot me. After about the third one, he just left his arms around me. And then he kissed me." Meg's smile was sweet now. "I took him to my room. It was my mother's bridge day. We made love. Well, the truth is, he—" a wave of her hand sufficed here—"my brains out. Though very sweetly. *Extremely* sweetly. "That was it. We got married. I had Luis in the summer after my first year of nursing school, and Elena just after graduation. Raul worked hard. We were poor for a long time. But we loved. We accepted it and moved on. "You should, too."

Sadie, quiet, nodded.

"What else is there to do?" Her friend squeezed her hand and gave her a kiss. "I've got patients. Keep me informed. I'll be happy to hear every hot detail." She took her tray from the table but spoke over her shoulder as she walked away. "And I want to meet him. Raul will want to check him out, too."

Sadie sat a bit longer. It wasn't what she'd expected from her friend. But still, Meg hadn't failed her. She felt better.

This game hadn't gone so well. They'd made some mistakes—stupid ones, driven by nerves. Understandable, probably unavoidable, but still freaking frustrating.

Just three minutes left and they needed two scores. Not impossible, just extremely unlikely. They'd gotten the ball into the red zone with simple brute force—short, viciously defended runs and a couple dumps to Wes on desperate third downs.

Wesley Clinton was his clinch, go-to wide receiver. Tre'von Lewis was the glamour player, taking down long throws into the end zone with balletic leaps and magic in his fingers. When he caught a ball, it was spectacular. He got a lot of camera and headlines.

In comparison, Wes was the work-horse. When Tre couldn't get open, Wes would find a way. Even with dense coverage, Wes would get his hands on the ball and bring it in, then drive through his defenders for a few more after-contact yards. Leet's passes to him were often short, last-ditch. Because of it, Wes took a lot of hard hits. He'd be close to the scrimmage line, defenders many and ready. He'd get the yards, but it cost him. Leet had pulled him to his feet from under a pile of blue and white uniforms the last two plays. Each time, he was slower getting up. It had been a long game.

One more third down. In the huddle, a quick one, many of his players worked to catch their breath, leaning with hands on their thighs. This would be their last make or break play. A pass play. Leet met the eyes of every player in the circle. They all needed to dig deep, and they knew it. They broke huddle and with a show of energy that was a good part bravado, though gratifying to Leet, they took their places.

Leet wanted to throw to Tre. He needed to get them in the end zone and finish this drive. They needed to get the defense on the field, a rest for the offense. He needed to give Wes a break.

The play broke, and Leet scanned the field. It was always his favorite part of the game, that suspended-time moment when he opened his senses, his awareness, to the entire field. When his decision-making and actions fell in place without conscious thought.

He saw Tre, steps away from the end zone, leading left. His two defenders paced him, but Tre had better reach than anybody. He just needed two more seconds.

Wes had gone right. He had triple coverage. Leet could get him the ball, and Wes could maybe muscle his way to the first down. But it would hurt. And it wouldn't get them off the field.

Two seconds. Then one. He took his arm back for the long throw.

The first hit came from behind, from his blind side. And the next, a split second later, from the front and right. The ball was gone from his hand as he went down. He tried to roll, tried to protect himself in the fall, but it was all too fast. He hit the turf hard.

Sadie's day on the labor deck had been fairly quiet. Two women in labor were making steady progress. Both had epidurals so they were resting quietly, just waiting for it to be time to push. The husbands were happily occupied, with some of their attention on the game televised in both labor rooms. One of her own teen patients was there, being monitored after a minor car accident. Things were more rowdy in that room, but the game was a focus there as well.

She was reviewing records and signing charts when two of the residents came back. A first year and third year, both women, they didn't bring with them the happy celebration that the guys had brought back last week. Maybe the game hadn't ended so well.

She started giving them report—it wasn't a lengthy process. She was nearly done when a man walked up to the desk. He was African American, muscled under his dress coat, like Leet but smaller. He looked tired. It was the look many men wore when their wives were enduring a long labor, but she knew this wasn't one of the husbands currently on the unit.

He looked at the three women dressed in blue scrubs, reading name tags. He stopped when he got to Sadie.

"You're Sadie?"

She stood, her attention on this handsome man, vaguely aware that the women beside her had quieted and stood, too. She nodded. "Yes. Can I help you?"

"I'm Wesley Clinton." His eyes glanced to the residents for a moment, drawn no doubt by their audible intakes of breath. Sadie looked to them, too, curious about their reaction. But his next words brought her focus entirely back to Wesley Clinton.

"I'm a friend of Leet's." The man paused then, obviously in distress. "He's been hurt. He's asking for you."

Sadie's eyes never left Wesley's, even as she reached out to balance herself against Sraddha, the resident nearest her. She wavered and felt grounded only in the dark eyes that kept steady on hers. Her voice shook, barely more than a whisper. "What happened? Is he...how bad is it?"

Sraddha put her arm around Sadie, bless her, and held tight. "Sadie, do you know Leet Hayes?"

But Sadie could only keep her eyes on Wesley, waiting.

"He'll be okay. But he needs surgery, and he won't let them take him in until he sees you." While he spoke, he'd opened his phone and pressed a button. "I've got her. Here she is."

He handed the phone to Sadie. She took it and automatically said hello.

"Mom!"

"Jace, where are you?"

"I'm with Coach. Mom, Leet's been hurt. Wes is his friend. Go with him."

"Jace—what's happened?"

"Just go with him, Mom. Go now."

Sadie shook herself, trying hard to find the part of her that knew how to act in an emergency. "Okay. I will."

"Call me after you see Leet. I'll stay here with Coach."

"All right. Tell the grandmoms."

"They already know. Go."

Sadie didn't understand that but didn't argue. "All right. I love you."

"Go."

"Jace—"

"I love you, too. Now, go!"

She handed the phone to Wesley. "I have to change."

He leveled a look at her. "Do you?"

Sraddha answered for her. "No." She sent the junior resident to the locker room to fetch Sadie's coat while she bundled Sadie and Wesley along to the elevator. "We'll toss your coat down to you," she said as she waited with them for the elevator.

The labor deck was just one floor up from the lobby and an open balcony ran along the length of the waiting area. By the time Sadie and Wesley had made their way down, Sraddha was there, dropping her coat into Wes's arms. He helped her into it as they quickly moved to the doors. Sraddha spoke from above. "Call, Sadie. You have some 'splainin' to do."

Immediately outside the doors, a limo waited, still running. Wes handed her into it and then followed.

"Where is he?"

"In Boston. We have a plane waiting at the airport. We'll be there in just a little more than an hour."

"What happened?"

"Any chance you can wait for him to explain?"

Sadie looked at him, aware that she'd been a bit oblivious but not willing to let this guy off the hook. "I guess you play football."

He turned his head away for a moment but then accepted the inevitable. "Yeah."

"And Leet, too."

"Yep."

"Your team is called the Metal."

He nodded.

"Son of a bitch," she said, mostly to herself.

He stayed silent. She realized he was tired, exhausted.

"I hope you're not taken, 'cause I think Sraddha's in love."

That made him laugh. He settled into the seat, letting his head rest back. He took hold of her hand, squeezed, and didn't let go. "I am taken, and she can be mean, so Sraddha's gonna have to deal."

"What's the injury?"

"Fractured humerus. Compound."

"Right or left?"

He swallowed hard. "Right."

"Do football players recover from that?"

He paused then and slipped his arm around her shoulder until she rested against him. "Sometimes."

She put her arm around his waist so they could both take comfort. They were quiet the rest of the way to the airport.

A crowd of reporters blocked the entrance to the hospital. There were several cameras and the bright lights that accompanied them. Sadie would have looked for another way in, but Wes had his arm firmly around her. He'd slept through the short flight and seemed to have recovered some energy. In the limo that had brought them from Logan, he'd had the good sense to unclip her ID badge from her scrubs and hand it to her. "Pocket," he'd said.

Questions came from everywhere, and lights flashed. He pushed into the center of the crowd and then stopped, overriding everyone's urgent questions with a raised hand, meeting the eyes of many of them until they quieted.

"Leet's going into surgery soon. He's doing fine except for being royally pissed that we lost the game." Tre had brought in Leet's desperate pass for a touchdown, Wes had told her. But the back-up quarterback hadn't been strong enough to lead them to one more score when they got the ball back with just ninety seconds left on the clock.

"I play football. I can't answer any medical questions. I'm sure his doctors will talk to you when they're done with him." He started pushing through again until a woman reporter stood and held her ground directly in front of them. Sadie felt the sigh in Wes's chest. "Cheryl."

The woman's eyes ran down Sadie's length and back. The brunette's eyes were hard when they came back to Sadie's. "Who's the girl?"

The word was derogatory as this woman used it, and Sadie fought to not bristle visibly. Wes's squeeze at her shoulder helped.

"She's a nurse, obviously. Let us through." Then he stepped forward, causing Cheryl to move or be moved. She took the wiser course.

Finally, they were through. Wes kept his arm around her. They took an elevator, and he got them through security when they exited it. As they moved, she asked if Cheryl had some particular reason not to like her.

Wes didn't meet her eyes. He kept his face turned away as he spoke, so she barely caught his words. "Every man's entitled to a mistake."

Sadie *humphed,* but had no time for any other response as Wes pushed through a door with her.

Leet was there, on a stretcher, the back slightly propped. A liter of IV fluid ran into his left hand. A couple smaller bags had been added on—probably antibiotics in one and another, on a pump, likely a morphine drip. His right arm and shoulder were immobilized, wrapped in white bandages, and packed with ice. A black woman radiating glamour perched next to him on the edge of the stretcher, holding his hand. She stood when they came through the door, regal and gorgeous. She gave Sadie a good once-over before she moved to Wes.

Sadie recognized her immediately. She stepped away from Wes as Clarissa Brooke, top supermodel, strode toward them. The two wrapped their arms around each other and held on. With her heels, Clarissa's height exactly matched Wes's. They made a superbly handsome couple. Sadie was extremely happy the beauty belonged to Wes. She could deal with nasty Cheryl.

She'd have spent a long time enjoying watching the pair in other circumstances. But Leet's gaze had captured hers. He lifted his hand, and she moved to him. He was quiet, fighting for composure, she was sure, as she reached him. She leaned into him, taking his head in her hands. He wrapped his left arm hard around her, pulling her tight against him. A couple breaths huffed out, harsh. "Hey, blue eyes."

She murmured his name and tried to lift up, but he held her too tightly. She kept pressing until gradually his grasp loosened. Finally, she was able to lift her head enough to search his face. He was in pain, she could tell, and a little afraid.

She stroked her hand over his forehead, his jaw, using touch to relieve the tension. "I love you, Leet."

His arm clenched around her, and he closed his eyes.

She ran her fingers through his hair, soothing. "You could have told me, you know."

He opened his eyes and watched her for a long minute. "'*Student*-athlete,' you said. Football is a *game*, not life, you said. That's what you told Jace. What kind of respect for the game is that?"

She trailed her fingers along his face. "You're an idiot."
He raised his brow, looking a bit more his imposing self. "You
have a life. You went to college, yes? You worked hard to
find something besides football, work you love. Didn't you?
How could I object to that?"

His eyes searched hers, still showing uncertainty.

"You play because you love it, don't you?"

He nodded.

"Enough said."

He closed his eyes for another moment. "Sadie, I'm sorry."

She nodded solemnly. "It was a lot to keep from me. You
must have been so excited when you won last week. I'd have
liked to have seen that, to have shared that with you."

He watched her and nodded. "You're absolutely right. I
was thrilled. And dying to tell you about it. I'm sorry I
didn't." He paused. "I was afraid you'd be worried about
Jace. Me having influence over him."

Sadie squeezed his arm on his good side. "I can't think of
a better influence for him, a better role model."

He let that settle. "Thank you, Sade."

"Why aren't you in surgery already? I can see you're in
pain."

"I needed to see you."

"Humph." Sadie reached for the green button attached at
his pillow, the patient control for his pain medication. She
pressed it without hesitating.

"Hey."

She lifted an eyebrow then also pressed the call-light.

He protested. "We need to talk."

"*Yeah*. You should have told me you were friends with
Clarissa Brooke."

He didn't like that either. "What, you recognize *her*, but
you didn't know who I was?"

Sadie shrugged the obvious. "She's on magazine covers
all the time."

"*Yeah*, girl stuff. Don't you ever see a sports magazine?"

She laughed and knew they'd gotten the attention of the
other couple. "Sorry, I guess not." A nurse poked her head in
the door, and Sadie told her Leet was ready. She nodded and
left again.

Wes and Clarissa walked over, and Leet grumpily and
unnecessarily introduced the two women.

The nurse came back with an anesthesiologist who nodded to Leet as he took a syringe out of his pocket. "All set
then?"

Leet gave him a brusque, "No!" at the same time Sadie
gave him the go-ahead. He emptied the syringe into Leet's
IV.

"Wait! Sadie!" He took her hand back and pulled her,
hard, close. His eyes focused fiercely on her as he fought the
drug. "Marry me. Say you'll marry me."

Sadie touched her lips softly to Leet's as he started to
fade. "Yes, Leet. Of course I will."

His grasp on her loosened, and the nurse put the rail up
and disengaged the brake with a foot lever. They began to
roll him out of the room. But Leet wasn't done. "Wes, did you
hear that?"

"Yeah, man. You've got her in the red zone."

Sadie rolled her eyes. Football analogies. She'd been
close with the battle analogies, but not quite right.

"She said yes. She thinks I won't remember. Wes, tell me
later she said yes. You, too, Doc. You're a witness."

"You got it."

But Sadie was sure Leet was asleep even as the doctor
spoke.

Sadie and the Clintons—Wes and Clarissa had quietly
married recently, having reason to, with a child due in seven
months—were treated to a VIP waiting room. A dietary aide
came in with a fresh pot of coffee and decent food. The fur-
nishings included comfortable couches with bedding tucked
into a cabinet, everything needed for a good nap. None of
the three took advantage.

Sadie called and spoke with both Jace and Ray. Ray,
Sadie learned, had been Leet's high school football coach,
and the deputy, Will Hunter, had protected Leet's back as left
tackle. He was with Jace and Ray, as worried as the others
about Leet's injury and fussing about lack of coverage on the
blind side. She updated them all on Leet's condition and
urged Jace to go to bed. Leet was to have an open reduction
of the fracture and would probably need pins to set the bone.

He had a couple hours of surgery ahead. Sadie reassured them with a promise to call in the morning and made the same commitment in her next call, to the moms.

She also spoke with Sraddha. Her relationship with Leet was big news on the labor unit, topped only, and only in some minds, by the fact that she was currently sharing a waiting room with the famous Clarissa. Sraddha took that news with decent aplomb. She had no concerns about assuming care of Sadie's teen patient on the unit.

One more call to Meg, who agreed readily to cover if any of Sadie's home birth patients went into labor, and she had her life managed.

That done, she had nothing to do but indulge Clarissa's avid interest in all things related to pregnancy. She gave her usual honest, open, but no-pressure description of the value of midwifery care. Then they got into details that had Wes looking for some distance. Luckily for him, Metal coaches and teammates stopped by in pairs or small groups for an update and often stayed to keep Wes company for a while. Wes introduced Sadie to each of them. They all greeted her warmly, leaving her feeling a part of the group.

It was a full two hours before the surgeon came to talk with them. The procedure had gone fine, he said. There was some muscle and ligament damage, though not as much as they'd feared. The break was repaired and, with time, should mend entirely. He deferred answering any questions—these from the coaches—about Leet's future ability to play. Time and physical therapy would tell. Leet was strong and very healthy.

In another hour, the patient was moved from recovery to a surgical floor. He had a private room there, and Sadie and the Clintons were able to see him. He was expectedly groggy, but he took Sadie's hand immediately and pulled her close.

Though it was to Wes that his gaze went, full of questions.

Wes knew what he wanted. "They patched you up good. It should heal just fine. Whether you play or not in the future, probably gonna be up to you."

Leet nodded once. "Thanks." Around Sadie's back, the men clasped hands. "You should take Clarissa home."

Wes acknowledged that but looked to Sadie. She looked back. "I'll stay."

Wes gave her a good hug, and she and Clarissa exchanged kisses. Leet took Sadie's hand again and held it as
the couple walked away. But Wes paused at the door and
looked back until he got Leet's attention.

"She said yes."

Leet's gaze came back to Sadie, flashed heat. "I remember."

Wes nodded. "I thought you would."

They left her alone with Leet.

He found he couldn't let go of her hand. He should, he
knew. If he was a decent guy, he would tell her to go lie
down and get some sleep. He should tell her he wouldn't
hold her to a promise she'd made under a certain amount of
duress.

But all he could do was hold her tight and want her closer.
"Lie down here with me."

Sadie huffed out a breath. "No way."

"Come on." He tried to move over a bit, but wasn't very
successful. The anesthetics still had him feeling heavy, slow.
"There's room."

"Nuh-uh."

"Yeah, there is. We've slept together on my couch, and
there's more room here."

He believed she rolled her eyes. "First, no, there isn't.
And second, one of us didn't have a broken arm, and IVs,
and monitor wires every which-where."

"Please, baby. I need to sleep, but I can't sleep without
you here with me." That might have come out a bit pitiful.

"Yes, you will. I'm taking my hand away. Just so I can go
get a chair. I'll be right back."

She was, or at least he thought so. He couldn't be sure
how long she was gone. But he was sure when she was back,
her head resting on the bed next to their clasped hands. He
curled a strand of her hair into his fingers too, just for safe-
keeping.

He wasn't sure how much time passed between their
next words, either, or the next. Somehow, all of the night
passed, but every time he spoke, she answered, as though it

was one conversation.

"You don't have to marry me, Sadie, if you don't want to." He thought that was very big of him and likely attributable solely to the drugs in his system.

"I love you, Leet. What else would I want to do?"

"Is Jace okay?"

"He's fine. He's with Ray. We'll talk with both of them in the morning."

"And tell them you're going to marry me, right? That's what you said, remember?"

"Yes. I remember."

"Did you know that Clarissa is pregnant?"

"Yes. She told me."

"Can we have a baby too...three?" He wasn't sure if that made sense.

"Yes. Sleep, Leet."

He wanted to remember that too but wasn't sure if he would. "Are you taking birth control pills?"

"No. I have an IUD. Go to sleep."

"A what?"

"It's a kind of birth control."

"Can you stop taking it now?"

"Yeah, sure. Sleep, you idiot man."

"Will you call my parents in the morning?"

"It's already morning. They'll be here soon."

"How did they know?"

"First, they were watching the game. Second, Wes talked with them before he left. Third, I talked with them hours ago when you first asked me to."

"I forgot that. But I didn't forget about getting married. Or a baby either. Three babies. I didn't forget that."

"Apparently not."

"I don't think they do, though, Sade."

"What's that, Leet?"

"My parents. I don't think they watch my games."

"You seem to be wrong about that."

"Hmm. Thanks, Sadie."

"For what?"

"The three babies."

Sadie came back from a shower, her hair still wet. She wore green scrubs now, lent to her by Leet's nurse.

When she stepped into Leet's room, a woman standing by the bed gave her a brief glance and asked her to come back later. The tone nearly had her backing out of the room with a compliant nod before Leet stopped her.

"Sadie." He spoke with a certain amount of urgency. "Get in here."

By that time, Sadie had put together the fact that the woman who'd spoken with such authority was Leet's mother. His father was there, too, across the room, leaning against the window sill.

Sadie dug around for her backbone and entered, following Leet's clear, just short of imperious, signal to come and take his hand. Mrs. Dr. Hayes had to take a couple steps back for that to happen, and it was an awkward moment as she reluctantly gave way.

Leet squeezed Sadie's hand, offering or taking courage, she wasn't sure which. "Mom, Dad. This is Sadie Benjamin. We're getting married soon." *Very soon* seemed to be implied, but Sadie wasn't sure if anyone but she heard it.

Aletha Hayes's brow lifted, a mixture of elegance and surprise. "Leet, you failed to make us aware..."

He kept a tight hold on Sadie's hand, apparently not trusting her not to bolt, which, she had to admit, had occurred to her.

"It's happened just recently. And I've been pretty busy the last few weeks."

"Of course." Aletha found her manners. It appeared to take some effort. "Ms. Benjamin, I'm happy to...have we met?"

"Sadie. I'm a nurse-midwife. I work some at the Medical Center. You spoke at the obstetrics department business meeting last spring. I was there."

"Oh, yes. I've heard the midwifery group there is very reputable, very professional." The politically correct, faint praise would hardly have warmed the hearts of Meg and her partners.

"They are, though I'm not a part of that group. I have a small private practice, mostly home births." Sadie wouldn't have had to go there and probably shouldn't have. She gave Leet a little glance of apology. He gave a squeeze to her hand.

"I see." That was a tad sour.

Mr. Dr. Hayes stirred himself. "Well, we're happy to meet you, Sadie. We missed Leet's surgeon when he rounded this morning. Leet said you'd probably have more details about the surgery than he could remember?"

Sadie had borrowed a few minutes at a computer as well as the scrubs. She'd reviewed the medical information regarding Leet's kind of injury and the repair he'd had. So she was ready to answer the question but didn't proceed until Leet gave her a nod.

"Leet had a compound fracture of the proximal humerus." She made eye contact with the parents but then spoke to Leet with details they wouldn't need. "Compound means the bone tore through the skin. That causes more tissue trauma and increases the risk of infection. That's why you're getting antibiotics through your IV and major anti-imflammatories as well.

"They did an open reduction, using internal fixation wire and a locking plate." Again, to Leet, she said, "That means you had an incision at the site, and then wire and screws were placed to hold the bone together. They considered replacing the head of the humerus with a prosthetic one, but decided they had an adequate repair. But the prosthesis may need to be considered in the future, depending on your recovery.

"You had some rotator cuff trauma. That's typical of this kind of injury. Apparently, it wasn't as bad as they anticipated. "Recovery from the injury and surgery generally takes a full year." She was watching Leet and knew that smarted. "It requires immobilization for at least three weeks, followed by physical therapy—gently, at first.

"About ten percent of people with this injury have permanent paresthesias—that means numbness or loss of sensation. Usually, that's in the deltoid area. About the same number have some loss of motion. A lot depends on the age and health of the patient." Sadie looked at Leet again. "And his follow-through with physical therapy."

She had their clasped hands held against her abdomen. Leet kept eye contact but was silent for a long moment. "Thanks, Sade."

She nodded and looked to the parents. They'd been exchanging their own silent eye contact. The father—Nathaniel—nodded. "Yes, thank you, Sadie. That was helpful. Can you explain the delay in surgery?"

"They'd stabilized him on the field and during transport. The shoulder was immobilized and iced, and they'd already started antibiotics, in consultation with the specialists here. Surgery wasn't urgent." And Leet had refused to let them take him until Sadie got there.

"Yes, but…"

"Dad." Leet's tone resulted in a significant pause in the conversation.

Aletha broke it. "What about discharge?"

Sadie answered. "They'll get another x-ray and MRI later today. They want to check the repair once the swelling has gone down a bit. Then, if he's okay with pain control, he can go home tomorrow."

"You'll come to the house, Leet?"

Sadie honestly couldn't tell if the anxiety she heard in Aletha's question was a hope that he'd come or that he'd decline and relieve her of responsibility.

"Thanks, Mom. But no, I'll go to my place."

"You'll need some help, dear."

Leet looked at Sadie.

"I'll be there. And my family lives nearby. They'll be glad to help."

Nathaniel stepped forward. "We'll be there, too, son. As much as you need. And Sadie, we'd like to meet your parents. Maybe we can make that happen once Leet is settled and feeling better."

"My family would like that, too, I'm sure."

Aletha and Nathaniel gave somewhat awkward goodbyes. Leet didn't let loose of Sadie's hand, so they had to work around her to place a kiss on Leet's cheek.

Sadie couldn't help a bit of a heavy sigh when they were gone. Leet pulled her close to nuzzle.

He mustered a small grin—Sadie was aware it was an effort. "You used the word 'family.' You didn't mention the moms."

She gnawed on her cheek a little. "Well, your mom about had a cow over the home birth deal. I figure they're going to have to work up to the whole lesbian in-laws thing."

Leet chuckled, but it wasn't much.

She sat next to him on the bed and rubbed her thumbs at his temples. "You'll be okay, Leet."

He held her right wrist with the one good hand he had and kept her close. "I know, Sade. I will be."

"No one knows yet if you'll be able to play again."

Leet slowly nodded. "I know, babe. I can live with it either way. I have a life, remember?" He slid his hand, still trailing the IV tubing, to her face. "And now I have you. And the boys." He smiled then, with more heart in it. "And our next three, right? That's a lot more than I had a couple weeks ago."

Sadie could still see the grief behind his words. "But you love to play."

"Yes, I do. And I'll do whatever I can to get the chance to play again. But if it doesn't happen, I'll deal. All right?"

"Yes. All right." She leaned in to kiss him, softly, but he held her to it. "Yes, my love."

*C*HAPTER SEVEN

Two weeks later, Leet held a party to watch the biggest game of the year. Neither team in contention was the New Hampshire Metal, and for that, every one of the partiers was a bit sad.

They gathered in the great room off Leet's studio. It was more than the brief description he'd given Sadie. It had a huge screen and a cluster of deep, comfortable couches and recliners. There was plenty of room for tables that had been laid out with classic tail-gating fare, from wings to ribs to Wes's soon-to-be world famous chili. And a lot of beer.

One wall of the room held the photos and trophies that highlighted Leet's football career. Sadie realized it wasn't accidental that she'd never been in this space before she'd learned of Leet's pro status.

Clarissa came with Wes, and there were a handful of other Metal team members. One of them was the back-up quarterback David Zimmerman, who, Sadie was sure, struggled to balance his cocky, all-youthful-confidence against his obvious and somewhat begrudging hero-worship of the starting QB. Leet took it in stride, treating him much like a big brother would—neither too indulgent nor too hard on him. All of Sadie's family attended. Joss downed her fair share of beer and was serious about watching the game. Marta took a while to get over her awe of Clarissa but soon looked to be on her way to BFF status. Tino enjoyed most watching the game from Leet's lap but ended up sacked out there before half-time.

And Jace was in heaven. Ray had come, too, and they watched the game studiously, scrutinizing the quarterbacks' play especially. A point in his favor, David eventually joined them, as interested as Jace in Ray's very astute, professional commentary.

Meg and Raul were there with Lourdes and the three of their kids who were home. Meg sent her enthusiastic thumbs up from behind Leet's back, and even Raul gave his nod of approval. Though it made her smile, she valued their good opinion. Leet appeared to enjoy them as well. He spent a lot of time in the studio with Raul. Apparently, they made a plan to view a particular locust tree that Raul thought Leet would want to sculpt.

Sadie also met some of Leet's local buddies. Two of them she recognized from the rescue at the river—sheriff's deputy Will Hunter and the rescue squad leader, Denny. She chatted with them during half-time.

Will pulled from his pocket a couple cards made by Gracie and Jeb. He said their mom had come by the office with cookies as thanks for the sheriff's department's help in the rescue. The cards were for Leet and Sadie. She smiled as she read them, aware of Leet nudging alongside to get a look, too.

He stood beside her, marking his claim with a hand on her shoulder, thumb stroking her neck. That was all with his left arm. His right was still in a sling except for the couple hours every day he spent in PT. He clinked beer bottles with Will,, Will bringing his bottle against Leet's, held at his side in his right hand, and nodded to Denny.

Denny spoke next, looking at Sadie. "It was a hell of a rescue. That family owes you. Did someone tell you don't ever do that again?"

"Yes." That was Leet, speaking with some force.

Denny met his gaze with a tip of his bottle and a grin. Then he looked at Sadie again. "Did you do okay after? You looked about frozen solid. I'm sorry we couldn't take you in with us."

She nodded. "I know. You had to triage. I was fine. Thanks for your help."

"The morphine worked for you?"

Leet brought her closer to his side. "Yeah, it worked fine. *Really* fine. For both of us. Thanks, dude."

Those two did that one-sided bottle clinking thing then, Denny responding to the humor in Leet's eyes, even if he didn't get the full reference. Sadie did, however, and made Leet pay with a not-entirely-subtle pinch at his side. That served only to deepen Leet's smile.

A woman joined them, slipping an arm around both Will

and Denny. Denny introduced her as Prissy Parker.

She had highlighted blond hair that Sadie doubted she'd been born with. She also had a bouncy personality that made Sadie wonder if she'd been a cheerleader in her past. And that led to another thought.

"Prissy Parker?" Sadie said, smiling her welcome. "Did your parents give you that name?"

"Oh, you mean all the P's? No, I married into that. I used to be Prissy MacAvoy."

"Ah." That accompanied another pinch to Leet's side. Sadie kept grinning as he responded with a pointed squeeze at her shoulder. "Have you known these guys long?"

"Sadie." He said it in an undertone, into her ear.

The other two men were quiet, though they looked to be on high alert, if that wasn't just Sadie's imagination.

"Oh, since high school. They were all jocks together, you know. And—" this with a perfume-dispersing flip of the hair— "I was a cheerleader."

"Really?" Sadie cast a quick glance at the men, each looking a bit guarded now. "I'd love to hear more." She stepped across the circle to slip away with Prissy. "Have you met Clarissa?"

Behind them, there was total silence.

"No." This involved a little jiggle of excitement. "Is that really her? I thought so, but I couldn't believe it. Oh, wow. I can't wait to tell the girls at the shop tomorrow."

Leet watched the second half of the game with Ray, Jace, and David. The party had quieted, and everyone seemed aware that the small group was intent on watching the play.

It stung to be watching rather than playing, there was no doubt about that. Leet knew he wasn't alone—every quarterback in the league except two was wishing he was on the field that night. But it was tough—they'd had such hope, and the whole team had put heart and soul into their season. He'd let them down, and he couldn't be sure he'd ever have a chance to make it up to them.

He worked hard at accepting what would be. He was moving his arm now with only minor pain. The surgical

wound was healing well. With the help of a physical therapist, he'd adapted his workout to maintain his body's
strength and conditioning without the use of his right arm.

But the outlook for achieving normal strength and capa-
bility in his injured arm was pretty dim. Right now he was
limited to gentle range of motion exercises, and even that
showed frustratingly slow progress. He'd spoken to the specialists in sports medicine—physicians, therapists. It wasn't
impossible. But most guys with his injury never played again.

What he'd told Sadie had been true. Even without football, he had a full life. He loved his art, and his injury
wouldn't keep him from that. And he had Sadie and her sons
and their family. It was more than most had in a lifetime. He
was a lucky man.

But, lord, he loved to play. He was realistic enough to
know he only had a few years left. Still, he wanted them.
Really wanted them.

Sadie watched him, he was aware, for signs of his anxiety about this. He didn't try too hard to cover it. She knew
him well and was very present. It wouldn't be something he
could hide. It wouldn't be honest of him to try.

She was doing a pretty good job of supporting him without driving him nuts with it. It was clear she had this maternal urge to hover that she squelched fairly well—obviously
aware that it would make him crazy. He could see her bite
her tongue sometimes or watch nervously as he did some
task on his own or pushed himself hard in his workout.

She'd driven him home from the hospital and stayed with
him, just the two of them, for three days. She'd changed his
dressings and gotten him to his appointments, helped him
figure out life left-handed. He was very grateful for that time.
Each of those nights he'd lain in bed with her, needing so
much the comfort of her presence until the pain meds had
drugged him into sleep. He knew she never slept until he did,
knew she'd be there, and knew he could handle anything so
long as that was the case.

And she'd backed off as he recovered, as he weaned off
the pain meds and got more competent at handling his normal
daily tasks. He'd appreciated that, though he'd tried to argue
her into continuing to live with him. She'd been adamantly
unwilling. It was important to her to maintain home for Tino
and Jace. She wouldn't consider bringing them all to live with

him either, though Leet thought it was a perfectly fine idea.

He'd even brought up marriage then, proposing a simple, quick wedding. She couldn't object to bringing the boys to live with him if they were married, he argued. But she'd resisted, insisting he had enough to deal with already. He hadn't pushed, but it wasn't for the reason Sadie thought. He hadn't pushed because he was waiting to hear from his lawyer.

On his first day home alone, once Sadie had left, he'd called Raymond over. After a painful, though not truly difficult talk with him, Leet asked his lawyer to start the procedure to have Suhayla declared dead. They'd had a funeral. In their minds, they'd let her go. But there hadn't been a body, and in that case, a legal process was needed. Arranging that would be an inherently painful task, one neither Leet nor Ray had reason to pursue up until now.

Suhayla had been on his mind some recently. He had to own that their marriage was a failure, and that he'd had a part in it. He wasn't a man who accepted failure easily. He had loved Suhayla, but looking back, and from the perspective now of his relationship with Sadie, he considered it had been a fairly casual love. He had cared for her, about her, but he hadn't taken care of her happiness.

She'd been very young when they'd married and probably hadn't known herself what would bring happiness to her life. And his own attention had been so much on his career. He hadn't made the effort to know her, to recognize her needs.

Things with Sadie were different. She was twenty-eight and, beyond that, she was a woman who knew herself, knew what was important to her. She found the important things and held on to them. If she gave her love, she wouldn't decide a few months or years later that she wanted something different.

Leet knew himself better as well. He wanted something with Sadie, and he'd hold on hard, too. She gave him a chance to have family in a way he never had before, in a way it turned out he loved having. He understood what it meant now—having someone who would always be in his corner, always have his back, and who would rightly count on the same from him. Who would expect better of him than an indifferent shrug when things got tough. Who would hold him to a higher standard, just by having one, setting one, herself.

He would do better, be better. He wouldn't forget that

he'd failed Suhayla. That he had lessons learned from her.

Then, tonight, Will had pulled Raymond and Leet aside to share some news. Dalid, the prince with whom Suhayla had her affair, had been killed. The royal family, in exile since the revolution nearly three decades earlier, had made an attempt to seize back power in their small country. Clandestinely, loyalists had been setting the stage, inserting compatriots into the power structure.

But the extremists who controlled the country had unearthed their plot. Dalid, the last blood descendant of the old king, had been assassinated. Once again, members of the royal family fled the country.

Ray had seemed to take the news with equanimity. If anything, it perhaps closed a chapter on that troubling aspect of his daughter's life. Suhayla's affair had always caused him grief, even shame.

For Leet, too, the news gave a small sense of closure. He'd occasionally run across reports of Dalid—his presence opening night at Cannes, his participation in a yacht race. Even speculation about his young wife's barrenness. Against his better judgment, he'd read every article. It had been like picking at a scab, keeping it from ever healing.

When Will left the two of them, Ray's hand rested on Leet's shoulder, a gesture of support. Leet was very thankful that Ray appeared fond of Sadie. For sure, his old coach was tremendously attached to Jace. He hoped Ray would be a part of the family he planned to make with Sadie. And that the memories each man had of Suhayla could rest in peace.

So he took pleasure now in sitting next to Jace, watching the game with Ray. Twenty years ago, he'd been in Jace's place, learning all he could about the skill and art of quarterbacking by listening to Coach's astute observations. He still learned from it.

He knew before he felt her touch that Sadie was behind him. Without having to look, he grasped her hand. And, with Jace's help—he was down one arm, after all—he tugged her over the back of the couch to sit between them. As was only right.

It was right, later, too, when Leet had Sadie in his bed. Jace and Tino were asleep in the guest room, and the rest of the revelers had found their way home. He was pretty sure there were some extra cars in the drive, as Marta had turned out to be the designated driver for a number of the locals. He knew her van had been filled when she and Joss left.

Leet idly played with Sadie's breasts as she lay facing him. They were, after all, right there. She'd given up wearing anything to bed when she was with him. Whatever she wore was destined to shortly be tossed on the floor, so she'd finally bowed to the inevitable.

Which suited Leet just fine. It gave him something to do while she chattered on a bit about the party. It was such a girl thing for her to do that he was quite enjoying it and was even half listening. And, there were the breasts.

She'd gotten through her pleasure in worming little tidbits out of Prissy about Leet, Will, and Denny's high school days. Prissy had been a generous girl, and Leet was very thankful now that his experience with her had never proceeded beyond a little unilateral or, on one admittedly fairly memorable occasion, mutual groping in the bleachers.

Once they were safely through that, Leet tended to Sadie's monologue a little less and her breasts a little more. In fact, he was getting a lot more interested there—a lot more of him was getting interested—when he heard Coach's name mentioned. His hands paused in mid-fondle.

"What did you say about Ray?"

"That he's very attracted to Lourdes. Didn't you notice? It was cute."

Cute? And Raymond Morgan? Those two things just didn't belong in the same sentence. Even the same paragraph.

He had to replay his memory tapes. "Lourdes? Raul's aunt?"

"Um-hmm."

It seemed she'd gotten a little interested, too, judging by where she'd put her left hand. He had to work a bit to focus. "What about her?"

"Ray—he spent most of half-time with her. She fixed him a plate of her tamales. And then her flan. He walked her out to the car when Meg and Raul left."

"Wait—" Leet had to grab her hand to keep it still. "You're saying you think Ray is *romantically* interested in her?"

Sadie, bugger her, smiled in that superior, woman way. "Well, I suppose he might have been arranging her cooking services rather than a date."

"A *date*?" *Okay*, that was almost a squeal. Leet took a deep breath and considered the facts. Lourdes was a woman and, though he hadn't thought to go there—she was an *aunt*, after all—she was pretty hot, once he did think about it. Big brown eyes, long dark, just slightly silvered hair, generous curves very well-displayed in a slinky red dress, sexy little accent. Enough said, or maybe even too much.

And Ray was a guy. As far as Leet knew, he'd never been involved with a woman after Neelah. But he was a big, robust, healthy *guy*.

So it wasn't impossible. It just seemed—well, *okay*, he guessed.

And Sadie was out and out laughing at him now.

He put her hand back where it had been. "Can we stop talking about this now?"

With smarmy innocence, Sadie shrugged. "You seemed interested."

"Shut up."

Whatever she intended for a reply, his tongue got in the way of it. He settled over her, and he felt a bit superior himself as she gave a small moan and opened her legs to his marauding hand.

He still couldn't bear much weight on his right arm, so their lovemaking had been somewhat affected. Sadie had been all concerned and careful about it when they'd first gotten home after his injury. For some reason, she'd thought a little pain in his shoulder would, like, get in the way of his dick wanting to have fun.

It had taken a couple nights together for her to get over that. Then, in her totally Sadie way, she'd taken charge, and they'd had some pretty spectacular sex with her on top. The woman was fit.

But he was getting better, and he certainly could manage a little—marauding—with his right hand. She seemed to like it okay. She squirmed nicely as he rubbed at her and opened her legs more. When he took advantage of the invitation, he found her hot and wet. He slid his fingers in deep and had her groaning out his name. God, he liked the sound of that.

Using his left arm, he lifted up and centered himself over

her. Replacing her hand with his, he nudged around her opening. He pushed in just a little, getting that first feel of her tight sheath.

She put her hand on his face and opened her eyes, a question hovering.

He sank further into her. "Don't worry."

Her breath huffed a little as he breached her. "You sure?"

"Um-hmm." He slid his right hand to her breast and then took her, all the way. Her breath was heavy with anticipation. She knew what was coming and it excited her.

He loved it. He loved it all with her—having her ride him, using their mouths on each other, their hands, whatever. It was all nothing short of spectacular. But this—having her underneath him, being buried to the hilt in her, possessing, owning—this he fucking *loved*. It might lack political correctness, but he was a man. And when he had her like this, surrounding her, penetrating her, she was his woman. He felt it then like no other time.

He held back a triumphant howl. Or maybe he didn't so much. Either way, he tangled his left hand in her hair to secure her while he started moving. He went hard into her, undone by the way her body gave itself up to him, clasping him tightly but slick and welcoming. He groaned and felt his eyes roll back in his head. His back arched as he sought her very depths. And then he let go, thrusting into her, wallowing in the pleasure. Her head arched back as he tightened his fist in her hair and her breast pushed up into his hand.

He hovered there, lunging into her, nearly peaking, praying she didn't have far to catch up. He dug his knees in for more purchase and found her nipple with his fingers. He took it hard, like he knew she loved, and then, thank God, she was coming.

He didn't let her come down. She cried out; her body clenching all around him in her orgasm. But still he kept stroking, even as she initially resisted, until she was there again.

He was there, too, *more* than. He surged into her, his own rough, feral sounds joining her cries, his body seizing, his semen exploding into her.

Like a chicken with its head cut off, his body kept moving in her long past the point of climax, long past the last spurt of semen.

He couldn't stop. He couldn't stop loving her.

Finally, all that was left was the clench of their arms around each other, the entanglement of their legs, and their harsh breaths that gradually softened to sleep.

Spring had arrived, at least by the calendar. The Vermont winter hated to let go, though, and, despite the smell of maple syrup in the air and the occasional crocus poking through, snow still covered the ground.

Leet didn't mind. He was getting great work done in the studio. He could incorporate some of his range of motion exercises into his work and the strength in his right arm was steadily improving. He'd finished up a couple projects—he'd gotten the big birch done and moved outside—and was happily working on the maple while mulling over in his head and doing some sketches of the locust that Raul had shown him.

Sadie complained that she missed the birch, and Tino, too. He'd made a game of tossing balled up socks at it from the bedroom balcony, just to hear it chime and set its prisms dancing in the light. Both Sadie and her son liked to watch Leet work, and he was very pleased that his art seemed to speak to them.

He had Tino working on his own projects, starting out with some soft wire. But the boy pressed every time he was there to use the torch. He'd have to give in to the kid soon. Sadie had let him know that she trusted him to keep Tino safe, but Joss still gave him the evil eye about it. Pretty soon, he was going to stop being scared of her.

Sadie had heard, like women somehow always did, that there was some serious dating going on between Ray and Lourdes. And, also like a woman, she couldn't keep from yapping about it. He guessed she was, after all, a woman. And most of the time, he had zero complaints about that. She spent a lot of time with him and had brought the boys with her for a couple weekends. Much of the rest of the week, he was a welcome guest at the farm.

They'd had the obligatory, expertly catered dinner at his parents' place. They—the parents—had been on remarkably good behavior. To his further surprise, they'd accepted an invitation to brunch at the farm.

That had been an unusual but oddly satisfactory day. Marta and Aletha got into comparing childbirth experiences, to Sadie's avid interest. Nathaniel and Joss had distanced themselves as much as possible from that conversation and ended up tromping through the barn with the boys. Leet had to make a quick decision and chose the barn. Though there was a little goat reproduction stuff going on there. The farmhand Canaan had his eye on a nanny goat—a doe, he said, was the proper term—that appeared ready to have, well, a kid. Tino expressed a little too much enthusiasm about that, but Joss kept the group moving. Bless her.

Luckily, by the time they got back, the women had moved on to pie recipes. Now, that was a conversation worth having, though if his mother could put her hands on a pie plate in her kitchen, he'd eat his helmet. Of great note, he learned that Marta had shared her expertise with her daughter, who he was now convinced had been holding out on him. Sadie acted all innocent, like the ability to bake pies was something that might just fail to come up in conversation.

They argued about it on the way home. *Top five qualities in a woman*, he said, and counted them off on his fingers. *Looks good*—he took a hit for that one, but she was on his right as he drove, so as a responsible health care provider, she really couldn't do much more than a little swat to his bad arm. *Has some brains*. That apparently was safe. *Sense of humor*—okay there. *Likes sex*—he reminded her of his injury in an entirely manly way before she acted impulsively, so she settled for a nudge against his thigh. And five—*bakes pies!*

He teased a smile out of her when he went on at length about how he'd taken a chance on her, getting involved before he'd made certain of that final fact. He told her that, given her high marks in some of the other categories, he'd figured he could settle for just having Marta in the family.

In bed that night, he suggested she'd be smart to make sure she kept her ratings high there, at least until her pie-baking skill was proven.

He'd gotten a good swat—left side—for that one.

All in all, he was a happy man. Very happy. And he'd heard from the lawyer last week.

Tonight, he'd gotten her to dinner alone. He'd made a reservation at Two Lanterns, an inn dating back to colonial times that had a five-star restaurant. More importantly, its dining room was nicely conducive to romance. In his pocket, he had something for Sadie.

They'd finished their dinners. Well, to speak honestly, he'd finished his and hers, too, and the same applied to their desserts. Which had been nice enough but nothing approaching Marta's rhubarb pie.

The table was cleared except for their wine glasses, a small vase of flowers, and a candle.

They'd enjoyed their time alone. Sadie had told him about the birth that had kept her out most of the night before. Leet thought he was getting pretty good at feigning interest. Well, it wasn't exactly feigned. She took such obvious pleasure in her work he'd actually come to enjoy hearing her talk about it. Within limits—and she seemed to be aware of those. He wasn't hearing any more stories about water breaking, at least.

And of course, they'd talked about the boys. They'd spent the last evening at the grade school, enjoying—though that might be a bit overstating the case given its overcrowded, hot and stuffy, disorganized nature—the annual ice cream social and art show. Tino had won a blue ribbon for his tree sculpture. And a lot of attention for having Leet there, acting entirely like a dad. Tino's pride in both had meant a lot to him.

Tonight, he'd watched her across the table, aware that he was falling more in love as he sat there. Aware that was happening each day. Aware that each day it seemed impossible, but still was true.

He had her hand in his when she quieted, watching him, alert to his more serious mood. Keeping her gaze in his, he reached into his pocket for the ring box and placed it on the table next to their hands.

She glanced at it once and then looked only into his eyes. She left her hand in his, but sat back a bit against her chair.

Leet spoke softly. "After I was injured, after you said you'd marry me, I spoke with Ray and my lawyer. We'd never had Suhayla declared dead. We'd had a funeral, but of course, there was no body. The legal declaration of death was a formality that neither of us really had the heart for." He shrugged. "And no real reason to pursue.

"We had some other decisions to make, as well. Suhayla had some money, quite a bit, left in a trust from her mother.

Ray and I talked about it. We'd like to make a donation of it to an organization that funds programs to promote literacy for girls in the Middle East. That's going to be taken care of now. My lawyer let me know last week that we're ready to put the case for Suhayla's death before a judge. We've taken all the steps required to get a ruling. I'm going to be free of my past, Sade. I'm not injured or drugged, so you don't have to respond out of sympathy or feel compelled to just humor me. I'm going to ask you again. If you say yes, you're going to wear my ring. And we're going to make it happen. Soon. Not some vague time in the future, but soon." He leaned forward and brought her fingers to his lips. "Will you marry me, Sadie?"

He thought he was sure of her answer. He'd considered this all just a formality, really just a way to get them moving forward on the commitment they'd already made. But he knew a moment of panic, one he figured he shared with many a man in his position. Though knowing that didn't make him any happier when she didn't answer right away.

She looked back at him, and he was pretty sure he liked what he saw in her eyes. Then she looked at the ring box. She lifted a brow, though he thought he saw a twinkle in her eye. "I think I should get to see the ring first."

His jaw clenched and he felt his teeth grind. She could probably hear it. So could the people at the next couple tables, he was pretty sure. He didn't want to look, but he knew they were getting some attention from around the small room.

"By all means," he said. He flipped the box open with his free hand.

"Leet!" She tore her hand from his to wiggle the ring out of its box. She lifted it and turned it in her fingers. "It's beautiful! Did you make this?"

It was a teardrop diamond set into a white gold band that had been carved with tiny leaf shapes. Scattered among the leaves, and surrounding the diamond, small emeralds sparkled. It *was*, in fact, beautiful. But that wasn't the damn point.

"Sadie." He was sure there was a warning tone in that, but she didn't seem to get it. She kept admiring the ring.

"Leet, I *love* this."

"Sadie!"

That got her attention, and everyone else's, too. The waiter had gotten the kitchen staff watching them over the counters.

"What?"

"Answer the damn question!"

Both brows went up at that. "You're *swearing* your proposal at me?"

He crossed his arms over his chest. "Looks like it." That might have been overly loud.

She shook her head a little in question. "Leet, how many times have I said I would marry you?"

He grimaced, couldn't help it. "*One. Short.*" His tone was a little clipped there, maybe.

She had a little attitude herself by that time. "Well, yes then."

He muttered some fairly rude words under his breath but stood and pulled her to her feet. Then he had her in his arms and, wondering if she would drive him crazy on a daily basis or something less than that, he took her mouth. It was a damn fine kiss, and he knew she'd kept the ring in her fingers when she'd put her arms around him, so all in all, it turned out okay.

Their audience seemed to think so, too, as there were a lot of smiles and some applause. Women started asking to see the ring, but he held her back to slide it onto her finger himself before he let her go show it around the room.

The place quieted as they took their seats again, smiling at each other as they finished their wine.

"*Really*. I love it. Did you make it?"

"No. The work is too fine for me. I had a friend make it— a real jeweler. But I designed it." He held her hand and admired it. "It looks good on you."

"It's perfect. Thank you."

He nodded and held her hand some more.

"And I get it," she said then. "The next time someone proposes, I'll give my answer right away."

He grinned but nipped at her hand a little sharply. "Not gonna be a next time, woman."

She did love the ring, really loved it. On the ride home, she'd continuously run her fingers over it. In the bathroom, before she'd joined Leet in the bedroom, she inspected it closely. Closely enough that, in the better light, she'd found the one carved leaf that wasn't so much a leaf as a tiny football. It had made her laugh out loud.

Sadie was very happy. She'd been perfectly content that Leet had let their talk of marriage lapse. She hadn't known the reason that he hadn't pursued it further, but she was comfortable with their taking some time. What had happened between them had developed so fast. It suited her better to let her feelings—and his, perhaps—settle.

Plus, he'd had the issue of his injury and recovery. She knew that his ability to play more football was in serious doubt. That was a very important part of his life, and she thought it best for him to have time to take it in. To see what his future held for him. It seemed a bad time for him to make long-term decisions.

But months had passed, a couple anyway, and their relationship had remained nothing but strong. Leet had become part of her family. Tino and Jace had been easy, but Marta and even Joss had taken him in, too. He was often at the farm for dinner—even when she wasn't. She was sure that wasn't always about pie. He helped out there sometimes, too. He especially liked joining Jace and Canaan in the big, physical jobs.

Marriage wasn't particularly important to her—she'd always been a little afraid of it, in fact. But it felt perfectly right now, with Leet. Their lives had joined—his to hers, to her sons. She trusted him with their happiness.

And so the ring felt right. Just exactly right.

He'd lit candles in the bedroom. He'd taken his shirt off but still wore his dress pants. She wondered if he knew what a sight he was like that, how he made her heart tremble.

His shoulders were so broad, so muscled. When he held her, when she ran her fingers over the strength there, she felt completely protected, completely safe. His long arms were also heavily muscled, powerful, capable. The surgical scar, healing so well on his right, seemed a testament to his resolve, his determination in the face of adversity—and even added a bit of rakishness. His abs were sculpted, bronzed like a surfer, and bare except for the drift of coarse hair that arrowed down from his chest, narrowing to just a thin line at his waist.

His back was the same, strong and muscled. His lats mounded on either side of his spine. They left a little gap where his slacks rode at his hip, a little valley along his spine. She loved the feel of his muscle under her hands and was always tempted by that little space, an invitation for her fingers to explore.

She saw it now as he turned to open a bottle of wine. And when he walked toward her, one filled glass in his hand, one for them to share, his eyes glittered.

Oh, *yeah*. He knew. And he clearly took some pride in it. He wasn't *exactly* strutting as he came to her, but he was enjoying—maybe even basking in—the excitement she knew he could see in her eyes.

He handed her the wine and she sipped. He'd been trying to develop her appreciation for reds, but tonight, he'd chosen a sparkling white. He kept his eyes on her as she handed the glass back. He turned it, put his lips at the same place hers had been, and took his own sip. Then he turned it again and placed the bowl of the crystal against her breast.

She'd left her evening dress hanging on a hook in the bathroom. Underneath, she'd worn a slim-strapped silk tank over a demi-bra and her panties, and that was how she was dressed now.

Through the silk, the cool of the glass tightened her nipple. She drew a breath in and couldn't help but follow his gaze to watch along with him. She could see as her other nipple tightened in sympathy, jutting out against the silk. Moving deliberately, slowly, he tilted the glass and drew it down until the thin edge of it, that place both their mouths had touched, caught against her nipple.

He pressed the edge of the glass in, hard against the taut tip of her breast. Then he nudged it down lower, scraping over the nipple until it popped free over the narrow rim of the glass. He brought it up a bit then, so her peak protruded over the rim, lifted by its fine edge, held there.

Sadie's breath shuddered out, and she swayed a little. He held her only by that press of crystal, not touching her at all.

"Don't move."

His gaze didn't stray from her breast. Even his lips hardly moved as he gave the quiet order.

She steadied herself but moaned as he started to tilt the glass. He did it slowly, the wine edging closer until it reached her nipple. Her breath huffed out then as the cold and wet and tingle sent a shock of sharp stimulation through her.

Leet met her eyes briefly. "Stay here. Keep your hands at your sides." He turned away and set the glass back on the table. Then he walked back to her, moving his gaze again to her breast.

The silk of her tank was transparent now. It clung to her ruched nipple and showed the dark circle of her areola. It shimmered as her breath quivered out.

Leet stopped in front of her. Still not touching her otherwise, he bent, placed his mouth over the wet silk, and took her in. He drew her in deep, suckling hard, stroking her with his tongue.

Sadie swayed again, just barely keeping from grabbing at him to steady herself, to clasp him to her. He tugged harder with his mouth and shot a spasm of heat to her center. She moaned again, louder, wanting, *craving* more.

"Leet!" She needed him, needed his touch.

And suddenly, she had it. He slid his fingers between her legs and pressed up into her core. Entering her, he took the silk of her panties with him, two fingers pushing up into her. The silk pulled tight against her, stimulating, rubbing at her center. He pushed in harder so the edge of his thumb pressed against her.

She was coming, held there by the suction of his mouth and his fingers inside her. Uncontrollably, her hips rocked, flaying herself against his hand. The rough movement caused her body to jerk, pulling away from his mouth. But he refused to let her go. He just clasped harder at her with a tension that made her scream.

She would have collapsed then as the long, brutal orgasm took her over. But he was there, wrapping his arm around her, bringing her against him. With her in hand, he took a couple steps. He turned her and bent her over the bed.

He tugged her panties down just a couple inches. His breath was harsh behind her. "Show me. Give me what I want."

Sadie dug her fingers into the bedding. Her legs, still bound by her panties, were open just a little. But she knew what he wanted her to do. Groaning into the bed, she arched her back, tilting her pelvis, offering her opening to him.

"Yes."

She heard his zipper rasp open and then he was inside her, distending her, hard and deep. He pushed all the way in so the rough edge of his zipper and the fabric of his slacks abraded her bottom.

His big hands took hold of her hips. He lifted her, bringing her up against him, sinking even more deeply into her.

"Christ, baby." His voice was urgent, coarse.

She was helpless then as he began to pump into her. Her toes lifted off the floor. His grasp on her hips brought her against him with each thrust. He filled her, joining their bodies deeply, bindingly, with every plunge.

His breath was shuddering out of him now, rough and loud. Hers did the same as her body responded to this fundamental taking.

Their climaxes came together as he arched back, holding himself at the fullest penetration. His fingers gripped her with bruising strength as his semen flooded into her. He growled, his body jerking into her a couple more times has he emptied himself. He collapsed over her then, his mouth open, teeth grazing her shoulder, his hands covering her fists that still gripped the bedding.

After long minutes, his breath slowed. He slid one arm under to lift her onto the bed. He came with her, pulling up blankets and tucking her into him.

"Holy shit, Sadie," he said. It didn't seem to be any kind of complaint.

"I assume you're going to have to talk with your moms before you'll set a date."

Sadie had been resisting opening her eyes. The sun was shining brightly, the room was lit up, and she could feel the warmth of it bounce off the slate floor. Spring might finally feel like spring.

She knew Leet had been awake for a while. He'd rolled to his back and had her pulled up against him. He held her left hand up, dangling it by the ring he'd placed there last night. The sun struck the stones and he was doing his best to flash white and green sparks into her eyes. All in all, it was quite annoying. Sleep had been so nice.

"Would you stop that?"

"What? Nagging you about our wedding? I've just gotten started. Or this?" He light-speared her in the eye again.

"That one." She made a fist and tried knocking it into his forehead, but he took command and had her knocking herself. She laughed and rolled away, regretfully giving up on the idea of sleep.

He kept her hand, though, and brought it back to start nibbling her fingers. "So?"

She stretched, arching a bit. It was mostly a wake-up thing, but there was a little interest from that nibbling, too. "So what?"

"Wedding."

"Oh, yeah." The sun was on her skin now, and she had this urge to wallow in it like a cat. "Yeah, I'll talk to the moms."

"Soon, Sade."

"Yeah, okay."

"I don't mean talk to them soon—do that today. I mean choose a date that's soon."

"What about your brother? Don't you need to talk with him?"

"He'll come when I tell him."

"Doesn't he teach college? His classes probably go to the end of May anyway."

"Sadie. He'll come when I tell him, or he'll miss it. I don't care a lot."

She gave up her pleasure in the sun and rolled a bit to look at him. "Okay. Grouch."

He gave her a grin, apparently not too concerned. "And that IUD thing? I've read up on it."

"Um-hmm."

"You don't just stop taking it, do you? You have to have it taken out."

"That's right."

"Have you done that yet?"

"No."

"Well, what are you waiting for?"

She lifted up on an elbow and pulled her hand away from his. She arched her brow and rotated her hand in the sun, shooting him with a flash of green.

"You weren't waiting for a ring." He grabbed her hand again and brought it to his chest, stroking the ring with his finger.

"No. You're right. But we have to talk with the boys."

He smiled at her and slipped his other arm around her. "Yeah, we do. But they're not gonna care. We need a girl in the family. And then a couple more boys."

"That's a lot of boys."

"Yuh-huh."

"We could have three girls."

"Not from me, babe. I'm too studly."

She snorted. "I know the biology, dude. For every boy sperm, there's a girl sperm."

"Yeah, but my boys are fast little devils."

"I'll take that bet."

"Five bucks."

She put a hand to his face and smiled into his eyes. He felt it, too. They were already family.

"Are Jace and Tino yours legally, Sade?"

She sat up cross-legged on the bed and faced him. "Jace is. His parents are both gone. I fostered him, and then got the adoption approved. Not Tino, though. Seffie sees him every few months—she's come up here a couple times, but mostly we go down to the city to see her."

"That means she could want him back, and, legally, she could take him."

Sadie took a long breath. "Yes, that's what it means."

"Have you asked her to give him to you? Could you adopt him? Sadie, could we adopt him?"

She shrugged slowly. "I've never asked. When I took him, we didn't really have a formal plan. Seffie was okay with it when we moved up here. But she's still him mom—"

He took her hand and gave it a shake. "You're his mom, Sade, and I want to be his dad."

Sadie slid her hand into his hair and leaned forward to gently kiss him. "You're quite a guy, Leet Hayes."

"It's what I want, Sadie."

She nodded. "Seffie has always made the best choice for her son. She's trying hard to make a life for herself. Already she works to help support her aunt's family." She stroked her hand through his hair. "We have to trust her to keep making the best choice for him."

"You love him, Sadie. How could you let him go?"

"I try to be grateful for every day I have with him. I can't control the rest of it."

She knew he didn't like it.

He shook his head. "No matter what Seffie does, there's never going to be a better place for him than here with us, with Jace, the moms."

Sadie nodded

"Can we talk to her?"

"Can I think about it?"

He didn't answer right away. "Yes." He took hold of her wrist and kissed it, all while looking into her eyes. "You know we'll be sharing some decisions now, right? You're not alone anymore, not a single parent."

"I get that, Leet. I'm okay with it. It's what I want."

"Good, baby." His eyes still held hers. "I want to adopt Jace."

Sadie's eyes filled. "I want that, too. But..."

"Yeah, we'll have to talk to him."

"Yes, but he'll be thrilled."

"He damn well better be."

Sadie laughed, just keeping the tears from spilling over. "I'm very much looking forward to learning what kind of dad you're going to be, Leet."

He reared up and came down over her, taking her back wrong-ways on the bed. He settled his weight over her, prodding, eager for her as always. "I'm going to be the kind that tells the kids to go play outside so he can do their mother."

She laughed again, the tears gone now. "Oh, good. I was hoping..."

*C*HAPTER EIGHT

Leet shut down the torch and straightened his back, stretching a bit to relieve the knots there. He was laying down texture over the trunk of the maple. It was slow work, exacting, but he loved it. He ran his fingers over the area that had cooled. This was what gave the tree the look and feel of real bark.

He dripped sweat. It was warm now in early May. The glass doors were open in the studio, light slanting over the yard and pond as the sun set behind him. The air was fresh with just a little humidity.

He took a sports drink from the small studio fridge and downed half of it before he started to clean up. He worked around a kid named Max who was at the forge clanging away. Max was into medieval reenactment and was building a longsword. It was pretty cool. He was doing very fine work on the sword, and he'd given Leet a couple lessons in fighting. Leet was wielding the sword left-handed. That didn't matter so much, Max said. It was all about the footwork.

As Leet moved about, putting tools away and sweeping up, he rotated his arm, working in some of his PT exercises. Things were good there. Earlier in the day, he'd thrown a little bit with Jace. The shoulder was still pretty stiff, but the gentle workout had felt great. His therapist was very encouraging about his progress, but she still wouldn't give him an opinion about his chances for playing in the fall. The best indicator he'd gotten was an indirect one—the team hadn't used its draft picks to get another quarterback.

Sadie was at a birth. She'd called a bit ago on the studio phone and let him know she didn't think she'd be long—fully dilated, starting to push, and some other details he didn't really process. Jace was out with some friends, Tino was with

Marta, and so Sadie would come by Leet's place when she was done.

All in all, an excellent Saturday with the best yet to come. His favorite happy ending.

The court date for the ruling on Suhayla's death was just a week away. He'd gotten a wedding date out of Sadie that was satisfactory enough—no more than a couple weeks past the ruling. She and the moms were avidly planning, but not frenzied about it. He'd wisely made the deal with them that if they planned and organized, he'd happily finance the whole deal. He'd only asked them not to get crazy, and so far, they'd kept to that commitment. He wanted to get married, was all, he said. Simple was fine. Anything more elaborate should be fun, or sweet, whatever. But no frenzy, no finger-nail-chewing, hair-pulling madness, and *no tears*.

He had to allow the possibility of a few happy, poignant tears on the day itself. He figured the moms would never hold it all in. And he'd be entirely fine with just a little damp-ness in Sadie's blues as she gazed at him and said her vows. That, he could live with.

In fact, he was looking forward to it.

If there were flower or cake issues or whatever, at least they weren't coming to him. It was good to be a man.

He was aware that his ploy to have Tino extol the virtue of wedding pie over wedding cake had failed, but that had been a low percentage play from the beginning.

His brother Matt would be there, though that had cost him a week, and would stand up with him along with Will and Wes. Sadie would have Meg with her and a couple college friends. Will had ferreted out that there was a tall, red-headed volleyball player in the mix.

Leet's parents would be present. His mother had even given up a conference she'd planned to attend. He'd put his foot down at waiting another week for that.

Life was good.

Done in the studio, he showered off then took a glass of wine and a book out on his bedroom deck to wait for Sadie.

It was full dark when Sadie got there. The birth had taken a little longer than she'd thought it might. It was a first baby, and the new mom was a college professor. It had taken her a while to get over thinking she had control over her body in second stage. Pushing a first baby out was gritty, untamed work. Not something where the intellect, even a prodigious one, played a big role.

But she'd done it and was very proud of herself in the end, as she should be. The baby had taken to the breast like a natural. Sadie had left them safe and tucked in for the night. She would visit them again in the morning.

She came up the stairs to Leet's room quietly, thinking he might be asleep. And he was, sort of. Dozed off, at least, in the recliner out on the deck, an open book resting on his belly. She smiled, enjoying the view of him for a minute. He was such a physically active man—she didn't see him being still very often.

She left him there while she went to shower. Perhaps he wasn't as asleep as she'd thought. When she stepped out of the shower, he was waiting for her with a towel.

He wrapped her in it and pulled her close. "Hello, midwife." His lips took hers in a very sweet kiss before she could answer. "Everything go okay?"

"Yes. It was lovely." He was doing a pretty good job of getting over his squeamishness, though she still enjoyed torturing him once in a while with gratuitous details about childbirth. She'd spare him tonight, though, given the sweetness of his kisses.

"That's good."

Or maybe the kisses weren't about sweetness but a purely defensive tactic. Either way, she decided it was in her best interest to let it go. Particularly given the fact that he'd swept her up in his arms and was on his way to the bed. There were candles again and a glass of wine.

He set her on the bed and handed her the wine. "Did you get dinner?"

She took a sip and tried not to grimace. A Merlot. He liked it, but it was just too bitter for her. She handed it back and saw by the indulgent roll of his eyes that he'd read her assessment. "Yeah, I'm good."

"I stopped by the farm after Jace's practice. So there happens to be some apple pie in the fridge."

"'Some' apple pie? You mean Marta only gave you a couple slices?"

"No, it was a whole pie, okay? But there are a couple pieces left." He objected when she mimicked his eye-roll. "Hey, I had help. Max was here."

"That's right. Blame Max." She giggled and stroked a hand through his hair. "Thanks, but I'm okay. Anyway, I'm guessing you're planning an apple pie breakfast."

He'd been waiting for the word, obviously. As she declined, he took her lips and laid her back on the bed, coming alongside her. "Well, yeah. But I'd have shared if you were really hungry. Play your cards right, and I still might."

With that, he tugged at the towel she'd tucked around herself. "Play my cards right?"

"Yeah, you know." He had the towel loose and started rubbing her breast with it, the cloth chafing lightly at her nipple. "If I get to have my way with you."

She arched a little as a tremor slid through her. His lips trailed kisses along her neck. "There's a reward for that?"

"Hey, I reward you every time." His knee came between her legs, pressing high. "Don't I, baby?" He pressed a little more when all she did was give a small murmur. "Come on. Admit it."

"Hmm."

He pulled the towel down, tight against her, until her nipple sprang free. Then he slid his tongue over it. "Sometimes more than once, right?"

He lifted his head to look at her. She knew he was gauging her response to his lovemaking, saw by the flare in his eyes that he was satisfied with it. The flare sparked stronger when he slipped his fingers inside her, where she was hot and wet. "Sadie?"

"Yes." The word rasped out as he had her arching, opening her legs for him. He worked his fingers deeper, stretching her, stroking.

"Sometimes more than twice, right, Sade?"

She tossed her head, arching up as he slicked his fingers over her center. "Yes." That was huffed out as he moved his fingers faster. He took his mouth back to her breast, finding her nipple and pulling hard at it.

"Come, Sadie." He pressed his knee against her leg, holding her open as his fingers plundered. "Now. Right now."

She was held captive by his strength, her thighs spread

wide, her core exposed, vulnerable. Compelled to his bid-
ding, helpless against his determined assault. She cried out,
unable to move except for the little jerks that quaked
through her as she peaked. He kept at it, stimulating her,
prolonging her climax until she'd had too much. "Leet!" She
grabbed his hand, stilling his movement.

Soothing now, he stroked his lips over her face, her
mouth. "That's it, baby." He slid his arm around her and held
her close as she settled.

Sadie closed her eyes and enjoyed the comfort. She
knew this was just an eye of the hurricane kind of moment.
He wasn't done with her.

So she smiled when she felt him move, lifting up off the
bed. She opened her eyes and watched with appreciation
while he took his t-shirt off over his head. He left his jeans
on—she could see the bulge that marked his own arousal. He
looked back at her, his gaze slowly traveling the whole length
of her.

"That was once."

The man loved a challenge. Just those words, and the
heat in his eyes as he took her in, were enough to have her
blood stirring again.

And he knew it. A blaze of primal satisfaction crossed his
face.

He lifted the wine glass from the bedside table and took a
good swallow. Then he came up onto the bed. He put one
knee between her legs, straddling her thigh, and sat back on
his heels.

He dipped two fingers into the wine. He reached forward
and rubbed her lips with the wine. "First wine. Then my
mouth."

Good as his word, he leaned over her and brought his
mouth to her lips. He took his time at it, but soon took it further, invading her mouth, bringing with him the sharp taste
of the wine.

He took his time there, too.

Finally, he lifted back up. He took another swallow of wine
and dipped his fingers again. He looked her over at his leisure,
considering. He chose a nipple next, sliding his dripping fingers
over her, painting her. Then followed with his mouth.

He used his tongue, gathering up the drops of wine. He
rasped over the peak, erect now under his avid attention. His

lips followed, caressing, taking. Gently, at first, just a whisper.

She wanted more before he gave it to her. Her breath was catching, a quiet complaint at his restraint. Her body tensed, rocking a little against the denim-covered thigh that prodded just a bit between her legs. He gave a little grunt of approval but teased for another minute before obeying her implied command.

Abruptly, he sucked hard at her, drawing her in deep, pulling, abrading. Sadie moaned, passion shivering through her. She arched, lifting herself into his mouth, a willing participant in his taking of her. Without pause, he pinched her other nipple with wet, wine-soaked fingers. Then he followed with his mouth, aggressively tending to that side, too.

In a few moments, he lifted up again. Her breath hummed out of her as he dipped his fingers again. He rubbed them over the sensitized nub at her core. Then he dipped them again, taking them this time to her opening. He slipped his fingers inside, mixing the wine with her own moisture. When he brought his fingers out, he swirled them in the wine. Then he drank, watching her, letting her know he was savoring her taste as well as the wine.

He set the empty glass aside. With a hand at each of her knees, he brought them up and out. He held her there, her legs open, waiting, watching her, until she arched. Offered herself.

He took her then, capturing her in his mouth, stroking and sucking at her taut little bud. And pushing inside her, thrusting with his tongue. He replaced his tongue with his fingers, stimulating, stretching, stroking, while he went back to torture her nub with his mouth.

Sadie's breath was rasping now, in rhythm with the forceful thrusts of his fingers. He groaned his own satisfaction, using his mouth harder against her now.

He kept at it, deeper, harder, until she shuddered into orgasm. Her body shook, spasming as he drew the last bit of pleasure out for her.

He didn't give her even a moment to settle. She opened her eyes as he sat back, his knees still propping her legs wide. His eyes were hot, his expression full of want. Need. He came up on his knees, looming over her. "Twice," he said.

She watched as he took his hands to his jeans. He opened his fly and let himself out. His erection was huge and hard, throbbing with the steady beat of his pulse. He stroked himself as he looked her over, his gaze a hot caress at every intimate body part.

"Lift yourself up."

Sadie arched, offering herself once more. Without otherwise touching her, he positioned himself at her entrance. Watching her eyes, he sank into her deeply. Then he bowed back and she was suspended there, impaled by the strength of him.

A low, satisfied growl explicitly communicated his intense pleasure. He took her hips in his hands and held her, securing her body's acceptance of his deepest penetration, his body's complete invasion of hers. And then he started moving. Slowly at first, so she felt every bit of his withdrawal, every inch of his return. When he reached her depths, he held there, grinding in, rocking, pulsing against her. Achieving the ultimate extent of physical union, making them one. Gradually, still watching her, he increased the speed of his thrusts, not sacrificing depth as he plunged into her, but moving faster, faster.

He came over her, propping himself on his left elbow and holding her head in his hand. Just inches apart, his eyes focused on hers, kept them spellbound. Their breaths were harsh, synchronized, increasingly urgent.

Sadie slid one hand over his shoulder, locking fingers into the curls at his neck. She slipped the other along the sleek, slick muscles of his right arm to where his fingers still clutched her hip. She entwined her fingers with his.

He pumped faster yet, nearing the end of his control. He urged her over, rasping out her name, giving her his instruction with harsh exhalations. "Now," he said. "Hurry. Sadie. Now."

They went over at the same moment, bodies crashing together, muscles clenching, hands grasping. Through it their gazes held, their breaths took the same air. Before it was even over, he was kissing her, a long, binding kiss that ended only with their last shudders. When he lifted his head, he slid his thumb along the path of a tear that had trailed down her cheek, every bit as though he knew it would be there.

He rubbed his thumb over her lower lip, spreading the moisture of the tear, then taking it with his mouth. "I love you, Sade."

She smiled, heart incredibly full. "I love you, too."

He pulled her along as he rolled over so they were facing each other. She waited for it.

"That was three."

"You just had to say so."

"Well, yeah."

"Like I might not notice."

"Just making sure."

They both laughed quietly, immersed in pleasure, in happiness.

Sadie's eyes closed a few minutes later, though she was pretty sure Leet had started to think about pie.

The thought of pie did cross Leet's mind, but he was really just too damn content to move. Sadie started to doze, and he pressed his lips to her forehead, savoring his great satisfaction in the moment.

He'd almost joined her in sleep when Max knocked at the door and called his name.

He lifted up, covering Sadie. "Yeah?"

Max spoke through the door. "Will Hunter called on the studio phone. He's trying to reach you. He said it's urgent."

He'd felt his cell buzz in the pocket of his jeans a few minutes ago—his jeans that were still on, more or less. But it had been at a critical moment—not a time to be answering the phone. "Thanks, Max. I'll call him."

Sadie was awake and held his gaze as he worked his phone out of his pocket and dialed. He tucked his arm around her as Will answered.

"Will. What's up?"

He closed his eyes and took short, controlled breaths when he heard Will's news.

Will was on patrol in the village. A car had passed him, heading south, a luxury sedan. A woman was at the wheel, and he thought it was Suhayla.

Leet swallowed hard. "Are you sure?"

"No, I'm not sure," Will said, frustration obvious. "How can I be? She's supposed to be dead. How could it be her? But I effin' think it was. And if it was, it looks like she's on her way to your place."

Leet held Sadie, held the phone to his ear, and couldn't find words.

"You'll know in a couple minutes. If it's her, she should about be there."

"Yeah. Thanks, Will."

"Let me know."

"I will."

He closed the phone and spent a few seconds trying to hold on to his life. But he knew Sadie was watching him, questions in her eyes. Reluctantly, he turned his head to look at her. Then he made himself move.

"Get dressed, sweetheart. Quick."

"What is it?"

"Maybe nothing." He was out of bed already, fastening his jeans, looking for his shirt. "I'm not certain. But—"

He looked at her again, knowing she would see the anguish that had started to overtake him. She spent a couple moments reading his face, then she moved.

He suspected it was her midwife mode—reading a situation, evaluating, then taking action. She dressed quickly, without fuss, without further questions. She slid her feet into her clogs and was ready when he took her hand. And followed, trusting him, supporting him, he thought, as he led them to the stairs.

He stopped before he took a step down and turned her to face him. "Remember I love you. Remember how much I love you."

Sadie's face was pale, but she nodded.

Then he took her down.

Leet knew the truth before they reached the last steps. He stopped there, Sadie's hand still in his, when he heard the front door open. He closed his eyes, almost swaying, and listened to the sharp clatter of high heels on slate. The sharp clatter of his life changing, falling to bits. Just a few steps, enough to bring her to a view of the stairs, and the sound stopped.

He held on to Sadie's hand like it was his lifeline—and it was. He opened his eyes and saw Suhayla.

She looked—older, more mature. Very much a woman with none of the girl that he remembered left in her. Her clothes were sleek, elegant, and, at a wild guess, just off the runway in Milan. She wore slim white slacks that shimmered into silver. There was a little slit at the ankle, the better to show off the strappy silver, very high heels that adorned her prettily pedicured feet. Her top was sleeveless, slinky, in that same shimmer of silver-white. It caressed her small breasts, giving teasing glimpses. Tasteful jewelry in silver tones sparked with diamonds.

Her hair just reached her shoulders in carefully styled disarray. Makeup was artfully applied, adding drama to her dark eyes. She was slender as a wisp, her bearing regal.

She was stunning.

But he held Sadie's hand in his—Sadie, in her jeans and clogs, with her sexy curves and warm, true heart. In his hand, he held his life.

Suhayla's gaze met Leet's. He'd seen her quick evaluation of Sadie, her quick dismissal.

Little did she know.

She lifted her chin another majestic notch. "Leet." Her voice matched her bearing, cultured, confident to the point of arrogance. "It's so good to see you."

Leet took a sharp breath in, clutching so strongly at Sadie's hand that he knew he caused pain. Anger coursed through him, and outrage at this betrayal. And most of all, fear.

Suhayla's gaze swept over Sadie again. She let condescension show in her face. "I'm Leet's wife."

It was a dismissal, Sadie knew, intended to cause her to shamefacedly slink out the door, revealed as the no account slut she was.

The woman was so good Sadie could almost imagine it working. Almost, it did.

Leet had a wife. That was a piece of news that settled like an icy stone in her chest, chilling her heart, making it hurt to breathe.

But Leet kept her hand held fast in his, grounding her.

He'd believed his wife was dead.

Sadie was sure there was only honesty and not deception in his feelings for her. In his love for her. *Remember*, he'd told her. She would.

Suhayla was the deceiver, the betrayer.

Leet was as much a victim of it as Sadie was. What kind of woman would leave a man, even one she didn't love, thinking his wife was dead for three years?

She struggled to take it in. Leet had a wife.

And suddenly, even though she remembered, this wasn't her place.

Sadie turned to face Leet there on the step where they'd come to a halt. She put her free hand on his forearm, stroking it, trying to gentle his clasp on her hand.

"I'll go home, Leet."

Looking half dazed, he tore his gaze from Suhayla. He made a slight movement with his head, shaking it. *No.*

But she nodded. "Come on. Walk me to my car."

He glanced again at Suhayla and relented. "Yeah. Okay."

He let go of her hand only to circle his arm around her shoulder and pull her tight into his chest. Moving somewhat stiffly, he took her down the last four steps. He kept them distant from Suhayla, sidling around her to the door. Sadie glanced at the woman briefly as they passed, getting a glimpse of her expression, one that flaunted her sense of superiority.

Leet glanced back too, before he closed the door behind them. Sadie was sure Suhayla wore a different expression for his benefit.

He pulled her away from the house to her car. When they had some distance, he stopped and took her hard into his arms. "Sadie."

"I know, Leet." She spoke, muffled, into his chest.

"I didn't know."

"I know, Leet. I believe you."

He pressed his face against her hair, sinking into her. "It doesn't mean anything."

Sadie took a deep breath and lifted away, pressing her palms against his chest until he gave her just a little distance. Enough for her to be able to look up at him. "It does mean something, Leet. It means you're still married."

He shook his head. "No."

Sadie had to dig for strength. She'd have liked to deny it, too. "It won't help to pretend it's not true."

Leet let go of her and turned, pacing away. He turned back and looked at her, then kicked the tire of her car.

In any other situation, she'd have objected. Sadie almost laughed at the thought. Who'd have ever foreseen this situation?

He faced her, hands at his hips. The length of the car separated them, symbolic of the gulf that now divided them.

"I love you, Sadie. And you love me. I know you do. That hasn't changed. And it won't."

"No," she agreed. "It won't."

He stepped closer, near enough to slide his hands through her hair, to hold her face up to his. "We'll get through this."

"Yes," she said. "But we're not through it yet."

His eyes blazed. "What does that mean?"

Sadie tried to step away, but he held her. She slipped her engagement ring from her finger and held it up to him. "It means I can't wear this."

He stepped away then, backing away from her offering. "You put that back on."

She shook her head gently, sad to her toes. "I can't wear it."

"I won't take it back." He had his hands behind his back, signaling his refusal.

Sadie didn't know what to do. He looked wretched, and she felt the same. She swiped tears away from her face before she slid the ring into the pocket of her jeans.

Whatever held him back broke then, and he rushed to her, lifting her up against him, arms tight around her. Sadie clung to him, holding on every bit as tightly as he held her. She kept her sobs inside, but couldn't prevent the tears.

He held her, rocking, a long time until their breathing eased.

He set her down then and took a half-step back, his hands steadying her at her waist.

"On Monday I'll see my lawyer. I'll start the divorce process." He took a breath and shook his head. "I don't know how long that takes."

Sadie didn't either. It was information she never expected to need.

"You have to talk with her, Leet. You don't know what's happened to her, where she's been."

"There's nothing I need to know."

"You married her, Leet. You loved her."

His jaw flexed, just visible in the light from the house. "There's none of that left." His hands squeezed her. "I know who I love. You know it, too."

She looked over her shoulder at the house. "She's very—"

Abruptly, he put a hand over her mouth and brought her back to face him. "Don't fucking say it. There's nothing beautiful about a woman who would let me think she was dead for three years. Who would let her *father* think it. There is nothing about her that is going to attract me now. You can fucking take that to the bank, Sadie."

That settled her some, though it might have been small of her to admit it. Suhayla *was* beautiful, with a style and glamour that was way beyond Sadie's reach. That kind of chic, feminine allure wasn't a thing she valued, was never a goal she'd set. But in a circumstance like this, it was enough to shake her. His reassurance helped.

She nodded, thankful for his words, trying her hardest to accept them as truth. Nonetheless, her point had value. He had loved Suhayla once. "Still. Go talk to her."

"I'm not going to stop seeing you, Sade."

She shook her head. "We can't be—together, Leet."

He cursed viciously. "If you mean by that we can't make love..." He shrugged, anger visible now. "Whatever. I can live with that. But I don't want to stop seeing you, and I *won't* stop seeing Jace and Tino. I made a commitment to them, too. That was part of the deal, remember?"

She remembered. She remembered cautioning herself to go slowly, reminding herself to protect her sons, to guard their young hearts. It was now clear she hadn't been cautious enough. She scrubbed her hands over her face in regret.

"Stop that." He took her forearms and gave her a little shake. "Stop thinking what you're thinking. You weren't wrong to fall in love with me. You weren't wrong to let the boys get close to me."

He pulled her in again, but she held her arms against his chest. This time, she couldn't find it in her to hug him back.

"We'll get through this, baby. Don't even think about giving up on us." He put a finger under her chin to lift her face to his. His eyes searched hers. "You hear me?"

Finally, she nodded. It was true. She trusted him, she trusted them.

He watched her until he was satisfied with her response.

Then he kissed her, hard and long.

He opened her door and ushered her into the car. "You go to bed. I'll talk with her. And I'll come see you in the morning." He closed her door, but spoke to her through the window. "I am always going to love you, Sadie."

Leet didn't turn back to the house until Sadie's car had reached the road at the end of his drive. Even then, he didn't move any closer. Looking at the house, he felt that loss, too. He'd built it. He loved it. It was his home.

Now Suhayla was in it. Her name had been on the deed—still was, no doubt—and her very presence in it took it from him.

He pulled out his phone and dialed Will. "You were right," he said as soon as Will picked up.

A short pause, then, "Holy shit."

"Ay-yah."

"Where the hell has she been?"

"I don't know. I haven't spoken to her. Sadie just left."

"Shit."

"Yeah. If you hadn't called, we'd have still been in bed when she walked in."

"Ouch. How'd Sadie take it?"

"She took off my ring."

"Fuck, man. I'm sorry, buddy."

"I have to go back in and talk with Suhayla. Then I suspect I'll need a place to sleep."

"You know where the key is. Grab a blanket and pillow from the closet and push Beowulf off the couch." It wouldn't be the first time Leet had to wrestle the dog for rights to the couch. "I won't get in until the morning, six or later."

"Yeah. Thanks, man."

"Are you going to talk to Coach?"

Leet glanced at his watch. It was after midnight. "I'll do it in the morning. Maybe I can give him some sort of explanation then."

"Yeah, maybe." Will didn't seem to have any more confidence about that than he did. "Good luck, Leet."

He closed his phone and slipped it into his pocket. He only had one thing left to do.

Inside the house, Leet searched the living area, then followed the sound of quiet voices to the studio. He looked over the railing and saw Suhayla below, talking to Max. She was leaning in casual elegance against the stair banister, sipping a glass of red wine. Max seemed to be resisting her charms. *Yay, Max.*

Suhayla caught Leet's movement and looked up at him.

Max followed her gaze. "Hey, Leet." He took a couple steps closer, aligning himself with Leet. "Everything okay?"

Leet nodded. "Yeah." *Maybe, someday.*

"I shut the forge down. I was going to bunk here overnight. I should be able to finish up tomorrow. Is that okay?"

Leet nodded again. "That's fine, Max. Goodnight."

"Yeah. See ya in the morning."

He nodded to something Suhayla murmured then took himself off to the living quarters. Lucky him.

Suhayla languorously came up the stairs, holding her pilfered wine in one hand, the other caressing the smooth wood of the railing. He'd built that rail, painstakingly sanded and varnished it, and he found himself irrationally resenting the way she seemed to casually possess it.

She stopped a few steps away and lifted her brow. "Did your friend leave, then?"

He couldn't go there, not without images of violence springing into his head. "I saw Dalid was killed. I'm sorry for that. If you loved him."

Her cool poise wavered for just a moment. "Thank you, Leet, for your concern."

"Is that why you came back?"

"You're trying to have me declared dead, Leet."

And that made him the bad guy? "Yes." If she wanted to know more, she'd have to live with the disappointment.

She lifted an elegant shoulder. "That made things difficult for me." She went on when he let his indifference show. "Dalid provided for me, but I wanted access to my own money. I've found I can no longer draw from my accounts."

"For three years, you let Ray and me think you were dead. I should care that your lover didn't leave you enough money to satisfy you?"

She stepped closer, lifting a hand to brush at his chest. He took her wrist to lift it away and then stepped back

"I am still your wife, Leet."

"I'll see my lawyer about that on Monday."

She made a little moue with her lips. "Don't be too hasty, darling."

"I am entirely about haste in this matter."

She frowned in a pretty way that was surely supposed to make her look innocent and helpless.

Pettily, he thought she must practice in the mirror.

"I will hope that you reconsider."

"Hope away, Suhayla. There is nothing between us."

She lifted her left hand, twirled the ring she wore there. The ring she'd taken off sometime before she'd left him. "We have a marriage between us. We loved each other once, didn't we?"

"Water under the bridge, Halie. It's over. It was over even before you left me for another man."

"Perhaps that was a mistake."

"If it was, it can't be unmade. Would you like me to drive you down to the Junction? I'm sure we can get you a room at the Arlington. In the morning, I'll take you to see Ray. Then you can move on."

"I don't intend to move on, or to sleep at the Inn. I plan to stay here, Leet, in my home."

He nodded, regretfully unsurprised. "I'd appreciate it if you'd use the guest suite then."

She gave that little frown again. It didn't really work this time either.

"Goodbye, Suhayla."

"Leet. Would you mind? My luggage is in the car."

"Can't help you." And he couldn't. It may be ungentlemanly of him, but he would not, could not help her move into his home, his life. "Ask Max if you want to."

He walked around her to the studio stairs. He'd grab his travel bag from his locker and be gone.

"Where are you going, Leet?"

He didn't answer. There were worse ways to spend the night than fighting for turf with Beowulf.

As much as anything, Sadie was relieved when the alarm

went off. She hadn't been asleep anyway, and she hadn't had a new or welcome thought in hours. She was scheduled for a shift at the hospital, and that seemed as good a way to pass the next twelve hours as any.

Leet had said he'd come see her this morning. He'd known she was committed to work but had obviously forgotten about it in the drama of last night.

Sadie wasn't sure she was ready to face him.

She was too...bereft. She'd spent some of the hours of the night thinking of how to describe her feelings. She wasn't heartbroken, exactly. She could trust that Leet loved her and that he hadn't done anything deliberately or even just carelessly to cause her grief.

She felt like a small child who'd just had her favorite treat in hand, then had it taken away and been given, like, Brussels sprouts instead. A long diet of nothing but Brussels sprouts.

She'd had something she wanted very much. Leet, their relationship, had become incredibly large, critical parts of her life. To be without them now left her empty.

Bereft.

She'd done her best to keep perspective. Leet was stalwart, true. He would do his best to keep his commitment to her and to Jace and Tino.

But he couldn't control everything in life.

Obviously.

He'd had an important attachment to Suhayla. He still had one to Ray. Could he really promise now that his feelings for her were all in the past? Could he truly be certain that, as he heard the story of her last three years, there would be nothing to draw his sympathy? Nothing that would evoke feelings of concern, of caring?

Shower, dress, get through the day. Sadie worked to clear her head of fruitless thoughts and regrets. She couldn't change what happened next. She could only trust Leet to watch out for her and the boys, to do his best by them.

Shower, dress, get through the day.

She left the A-frame and drove out of the yard. Joss would be up, probably in the barn already. Marta was likely in the kitchen, already working on breakfast for Jace and Tino.

It was cowardly of her to leave without talking to them, but it was the best she could do. *Drive to the hospital. Change into scrubs. Get through the day.*

Lourdes was in the kitchen when Ray showed Leet in and had him sit at the table. Leet was very glad he'd called ahead, or things might have been more awkward still. Lourdes had coffee to pour but obviously was only just getting started at making breakfast. Leet's call had perhaps been every bit as well timed as Will's had been the night before.

Ray had clearly picked up from the phone call that something was amiss. He sat steadily through a long pause from Leet and grasped Lourdes's hand at his shoulder when she came to stand behind him.

Leet lifted a shoulder. "There's no good way to say this, Ray. Suhayla's alive. She's at my house."

Ray dropped his head back until it rested against Lourdes. He was seeking comfort there, and she gave it, sliding her free hand along his head then across his chest, hugging him close against her. Ray clasped that hand, too.

Leet watched them together, thankful for what he saw was between them. He shook his head. "I haven't really spoken to her yet. I told her I'd bring her here today to see you."

Ray's head moved back and forth just a little. "I don't know what to say. I don't even know what to feel."

Lourdes patted his shoulder. "A father always loves his daughter, no matter what she's done." She was watching Leet as she spoke. "It's different for Leet, though. He has to take care of Sadie." Enough said, apparently. With one more pat, she went to the refrigerator. "We'll have breakfast. Then, Ray, you will see your daughter."

By the time Leet drove to the farm, he'd remembered that Sadie had planned to work that day. Still, he had to bite back some disappointment that her car was gone from the yard. He didn't have a clue what to say to her, but he surely would have liked have her in his arms. For a good hour or two.

He climbed out of his truck and headed to the barn. He figured Joss might be there and he'd bring her to the house with him. The big doors were open, and sunshine was lighting a good part of the interior. Goats waiting for their milking were putting up a small fuss. As his eyes adjusted to the dim light in the back of the barn, Leet spotted Canaan working silently as always. He paused and looked up when he caught Leet's movement but didn't speak.

"I was looking for Joss."

"Tino called her and Jace in for breakfast."

The man's little used voice was soft with a bit of a drawl that hadn't come from anywhere in the Northeast.

Leet nodded his thanks and turned away.

The walk to the house felt like a long one. Even before he reached it, he could hear the small family. They were in the dining room, loudly enjoying each other and what was no doubt a big farm breakfast.

He paused at the doorway, aware that Marta and Joss watched him carefully even as Tino called out his name and jumped off his chair. He ran to him and leapt, clearly expecting to be lifted up into Leet's arms. Leet complied and gave the boy a good, long squeeze. Jace came, too, to greet him, but he was tuned to his grandmothers' reserve and was more cautious. Leet met his eyes, nodded, and put a hand on his shoulder.

Marta spoke first. "Have a seat, Leet. Do you want a plate?"

"No, thanks." He took a chair, though, and kept Tino in his lap.

"We saw Sadie came home last night." That was Joss. "We didn't expect her. Then she snuck out of here this morning without checking in with us. Problem?"

He looked back at her, then at Marta and Jace. "Yeah."

Joss sat back with her arms crossed over her chest. He had a small flash of her Viking foremothers. Marta leaned toward Jace and took his hand.

Tino leaned back against Leet's chest; even he finally cued into the serious atmosphere.

"You know I was married to Ray's daughter, Suhayla." He made eye contact with the women but spoke mostly to Jace.

"She died. That's what Coach said."

Leet nodded. "That's what we thought. But we were wrong."

Marta gripped Jace's hand more tightly. "Suhayla's alive?"

"Yeah." He looked around the table again. "She came to

my place last night."

"You're still married." Joss spoke bluntly, though not without sympathy. He thought.

Jace stood. Marta got up with him and put her arms around him. Otherwise, Leet was pretty sure he'd have taken off.

He stood, too, still holding Tino.

"I love your mom, Jace, and you and Tino, too. That's not going to change. We're going to work this out."

There was anger in Jace's eyes. Leet knew that was easier than the tears he could see there, too. "How?"

"I'll get a divorce."

"Mom doesn't like divorced guys."

"Jace." Marta pulled him closer, but Jace pushed away.

"She likes me, Jace. She loves me."

Jace faced him. "She says guys who get divorced don't keep their promises." He turned then and strode toward the door.

"Jace, stop!" Leet spoke in a command, as a father would have the authority to do. He was conscious of it, and maybe Jace was, too. Either way, he stopped and turned around again. But nothing in his attitude was friendly.

Leet stepped toward him, passing Tino to Marta on his way.

He stood in front of Jace and put his hands on the boy's shoulders. "You're hurt. So is your mom. I'm as sorry as I can be for it. But I'm not giving either of you up."

"Me either!"

Leet turned his head to look at Tino who was watching avidly from Marta's arms. He took a good breath in and let it out. "Fuck, no!"

That satisfied Tino, enough so that he turned to Marta and Joss to tell them that Leet had used a bad word. Like maybe they hadn't heard.

He turned back to Jace who looked like he was trying to chew back a smile. He lifted a brow and spoke intently to him. "You can trust me, Jace. Your mom can, too. I'll do whatever it takes to work this out."

Jace grinned just a little. "You're going to have to grovel."

Leet nodded. "I'm fully aware of that."

This time, it was Suhayla who sat with Leet and Ray in Ray's kitchen. Leet watched her and was aware, finally, that Suhayla had never fit in here.

The kitchen was homey. It was comfortable and informal. It was a place to relax, to enjoy food and friends, family. Leet loved it. Ray loved it. Suhayla had never been happy there.

Many years ago, to please her, Ray had remodeled and refurnished the living and dining rooms. Those were now elegant but unused spaces. Ray had his kitchen and his den, and those were the rooms where he lived.

He'd greeted Suhayla with moisture in his eyes. He held her close for a long moment. It was not quite a full hug.

Leet knew Ray had wanted Lourdes to be there. Ray said over the phone that he'd asked her to stay—begged her, nearly, he'd said. But she'd insisted that he and Leet needed to see his daughter alone, at least this first time. She'd come, she said, as soon as Suhayla was gone.

Leet had forced himself to leave the farm. He'd have very willingly spent the day there, the week. Forever, in fact. But Joss had started to give him the eye, and he knew he couldn't avoid what was ahead of him.

So he left, grounded by a good hug from Marta and a reminder from Tino that Leet had committed to spending some time with him in the studio that afternoon.

He'd gone home, entering the house through the open studio doors. Max had been there, working at the forge. Max was a young man of firmly held opinions and few words. With one long, direct look, he managed to communicate that he wasn't happy with Suhayla's presence and that Leet was tasked with keeping her out of Max's hair until he was done and gone.

Leet sent him a direct look back. *Deal with it*, he conveyed. If anyone had a right to feel unhappy here, it was Leet.

Suhayla, clearly having been rebuffed by Max, lounged gracefully on a sofa in his living room. She probably wouldn't look so pleased with herself if she knew what he'd done to Sadie on that very spot where she reclined.

He drove her to Ray's in his sedan. He'd been tempted to

use his truck just to annoy her, but he'd been sure she'd re-
quire him to help her into it, and he wasn't going to go there.

They maintained an uneasy truce during the drive over.
When it had become clear to her he wouldn't respond to her
attempts at conversation, she'd shut up.

Leet searched his conscience once. Was he justified in
being rude? Could there be some explanation for her behavior that could excuse it, that could rouse sympathy for her?

He couldn't imagine it. He didn't want to chat pleasantly
with her. He could barely keep from hating her.

Maybe not even that.

In the kitchen of the old farmhouse, Leet went to the
counter to start another pot of coffee rather than sit longer
with father and daughter. Ray faced Suhayla over a corner of
the table and held her hand.

"Did some woman really die in that plane crash, Suhayla?"

"Honestly, I don't know." Suhayla spoke quietly, more
humbly than she had with Leet. "It was complicated. Dalid's
family didn't want me to be with him."

She touched her free hand to her lips, moved by grief to
all appearances, though Leet didn't trust that they'd get a
single honest emotion out of her.

"I truly did love Dalid, Papa." She glanced over at Leet
then moved closer to her father.

Leet really couldn't say whether he wished to hear her
story or not. Whether he hoped she had some reasonable
explanation for her behavior. But he loved Ray and owed
him, and so he walked over and took a chair at the table.

Suhayla met his eyes for a minute and then turned back
to Ray. "We wanted to be together. He wanted to marry me.
But years ago, as a boy, he had been promised to the girl,
Ladiah. It was an arranged marriage.

"Dalid thought that it no longer mattered, with the royal
family scattered. He thought that no one would care if he
married as he desired. He wasn't aware that there was a plot
to reclaim the throne, to re-establish the royal family as rul-
ers of his country. He wasn't political. He didn't care, even
when the old king's majordomo came to him and told him of
the plot.

"But the king's retainer had the backing of the old aris-
tocracy, those who waited many years to return to their
lands. And of the upper echelons of the military. He needed

Dalid, the only living descendent of the king, to take the throne. And he required Dalid to marry Ladiah."

She paused, looking briefly at Leet again before she continued her story. "The majordomo, Jibran Hafir, planned to do away with me. To kill me. He and Dalid fought over it. Dalid gave his agreement—to marry Ladiah, to accept the crown—in exchange for my life.

"The jet I was to take to Milan had been rigged with a bomb. Just before I was to board it, I was taken away. Armed men in a limousine took me back to Rio. Weeks later, after the wedding of Dalid and Ladiah, I was flown to a compound in Italy.

"Dalid was there, with his wife, waiting for the right time for the coup that would place him as king.

"He did his duty by Ladiah, his duty to his country, to secure an heir for his family's lineage. But he lived with me." Suhayla's bitterness was obvious, but so was her pride. "Before his marriage, Dalid had made no secret of his relationship with me. We were seen in public many times, in many places. Jibran insisted on the appearance of my death, if not the actual fact. Even without me on board, he blew that jet out of the sky."

"He murdered the pilot?"

Suhayla looked at her father and shrugged. "I do not know. Perhaps there was a plan for him to be rescued, to parachute to safety. I know only that Jibran wanted me dead, wanted Dalid to appear totally committed to his marriage. How many people had to die to achieve that appearance was of no concern to Jibran. Dalid saved my life. But it was required that my death be believed. I was not able to contact you."

Ray spoke at last. "But you're here now. They just let you go?"

Suhayla's eyes flashed, her voice was cutting. "When Dalid died, they had no further concern about me. They had what they wanted—a few months ago, Ladiah finally conceived. They have confirmed that she carries a boy. They still hope that Dalid's son, the king's grandson, will one day be king."

There was a question, maybe even a reprimand, in Ray's next words. "Dalid died more than three months ago. Why did it take you so long to come home?"

Leet knew. And he knew that Suhayla wasn't home. She

would never consider this place of Ray's her home. He didn't even believe her claim on his house. He was sure he hadn't heard the full story of what Suhayla wanted from him.

She paused, making no eye contact with Leet. "I wasn't sure of my welcome. I had let you think I was dead. For many years now, I have not been a good daughter." Now she looked at Leet. "Or a good wife."

Leet pushed back from the table and went to stand at the sink. He looked out the window at Ray's backyard. The sun was high now, casting few shadows. Trees were in bloom—an apple, he saw, and a weeping cherry. He'd remembered that particular cherry tree when he'd worked in his studio. There was more comfort to him out there—the trees, the many birdhouses and feeders that Ray enjoyed, the fresh green of the grass—than in this room with the woman who was supposed to be his wife.

Neither of the two at the table spoke. Finally, Leet turned to face them. "Ray, she's your daughter. You make your own call on this. Whatever it is, I'll support you. Suhayla, you abandoned our marriage. You abandoned it long before these circumstances you describe, that you say required you to leave us thinking you were dead. You loved Dalid. You wanted him, not me. Obviously, you'd still be with him if he hadn't been killed. So I don't know what you want with me or why you're here. I don't see why you would claim a marriage that you rejected, by your own will, many years ago. I told you that I would see my lawyer tomorrow and I will. I consider our marriage to be nothing but a legal contract that is now empty of meaning. I am going to put an end to it as soon as I can."

He dumped his coffee down the sink and rinsed his cup. "I have some things I've promised to do today. I'll get Max and we'll drive your car up here. If you insist on staying in my house—" He lifted his hand to stop her objection. He didn't want to hear her claim it as hers, too. "Have at it. I'll learn tomorrow if I can keep you from it. In any case, I won't live there until you're gone." As he walked past the table, Ray raised his hand. Leet clasped it, and the two of them held the grip for a good long time. "See ya, Ray."

At seven, Sadie was in the locker room changing out of her scrubs. It had been a busy shift, and for that, she was grateful. She'd done one thing, then another. She'd gotten through the day.

She'd talked with Marta briefly before noon and learned of Leet's visit to the farm. She heard Marta's sympathy and understanding, and her support of Leet. And from Tino, she heard the story of Leet's bad word.

Leet had called twice and left brief messages. The first was a reminder of his love and commitment. The second was blunt, frustrated, and contained yet another bad word.

He called again now as she walked to her car. Taking a deep breath, she answered. "Hi, Leet."

"Baby."

Neither of them spoke for a long minute. Sadie just settled in to this connection. Limited though it was, it felt good.

Leet broke their shared silence. "I've got Jace and Tino." He paused and then huffed out a little laugh. "Well, that sounds like I've kidnapped them. What I mean is, we're in the village and just ordered pizza. Why don't you come join us? You can have a slice with us then take the boys home."

How strange that felt. Sort of like a divorced couple, passing off the children, one parent's time with them, then the other's.

Though it was more, in this case. Leet was making clear his intentions. He wasn't letting go of her sons. He wasn't letting go of her.

Sadie felt she ought to find it in her to object. This was battle strategy Leet, master manipulator, making sure things happened the way he wanted.

But it was what she wanted, too. It felt good, knowing that he was there, a part of her life, of her boys' lives. It wasn't all that she wanted, surely not all that he wanted. But it was what they could have for now.

She waded into it, accepting. "Yeah, okay. I'm on my way."

He understood her thought processes. "Good girl."

The pizza shop was full of activity this Sunday evening—

some families out for an easy meal after a busy weekend, a junior soccer team still in their game gear, and a couple groups of teens. Leet sat at a booth table with Jace and Tino across from him.

Sadie had a flash of what this meant to him—the ability to be at home here, simply another town resident. The group of kids who had walked in the door ahead of her had greeted him, the guys giving him high fives, and nodding to Jace. Leet knew their names. They'd stayed and bantered a minute, especially asking Leet about his arm—which he was moving very well now—but then they'd found a table and settled in.

No big deal that Leet Hayes was among them. She knew that sense of belonging, that acceptance, was important to him. It was something he valued. Just like he valued the sense of family he'd found with her.

Sadie got a more enthusiastic greeting. Tino jumped up onto the seat and crawled over Jace for a hug. Jace reached up for a hug and a kiss, too. Leet was on his feet, waiting for her.

She turned to him after she'd emptied her arms of Tino.

He was watching, his eyes hungry for her.

It was clear news had traveled, because the whole shop was quietly watching, too.

"Hi, Leet."

"Hi, baby."

She stepped closer, and he brought her against him. She rested her head against his chest, and he dropped his down close so they were together, breathing the same air. He had one arm around her and with the other, held her hand against his heart. They stayed there for a long moment, his thumb rubbing a circle on her back, his hand keeping hers close against him.

Finally, he lifted and pressed a light kiss over her lips. Then he ushered her into the seat ahead of him. He lifted a slice of pizza onto a plate and set it before her. When he was done, he put his hand under the table, settled it above her knee, and left it there.

She looked across the table at Tino.

"Leet made me sit over here."

He objected to that, of course. His usual spot would be next to her. Leet's hand on her thigh squeezed.

"He would, wouldn't he? How was your day?"

Tino was nothing if not distractible.

"I got to use the torch. I made a...a sapling." He looked to Leet for confirmation of the word.

"Cool. What kind of tree?"

He looked at Leet again. "So far, it's—"

Leet filled in for him. "It's generic. We'll decide what it's going to be when we choose some leaves for it."

"Yeah. Leet says we have to go for a hike and find my favorite leaf. We're going to go to Fallbrook."

Sadie started in on her pizza, enjoying the first happy moments of her day. "That'll be fun. We haven't gone down there in a while."

"Yeah, that's 'cause last time we went, you squealed whenever I got within three feet of the edge," Jace said.

Leet nudged her and spoke into her ear. "Told you, you're a squealer."

She smiled up at him. "I'm pretty sure that was you."

He smiled back as their eyes met, and she entwined her fingers with his under the table.

She arched a look back at Jace. "It's a long fall, dude."

"Yeah, but why would I fall over?" He looked at Leet. "She got all nervous when I crossed over the brook on a tree that fell across it, too."

Leet shrugged. "Moms."

Jace grinned back. "Yeah."

Sadie ignored them and spoke to Tino. She held up her hands—well, one hand, since Leet wouldn't let go of the other—and turned it. "Let me see your hands. No burns?"

Tino showed her his hands, both sides. "Nope. We had to do a safety lesson first. And I got leather gloves to wear."

Leet added, "And a helmet."

Tino nodded. "And an apron."

"But not a girly one."

"No, a manly one." Tino smirked, and he and Leet fist-pounded over the table.

Sadie obligingly rolled her eyes.

"We brought the s-sapling so you could see it. It's in the truck. But then it goes back to the studio 'til we finish it."

"I can't wait to see it."

They lingered over the meal, past the time when all the families left. After a while, a couple of the teens who were on the football team brought chairs over and joined them. Sadie was happy just being there with Leet, knowing that he was happy too just holding her hand.

She called an end to it only when Tino began to flag.

"Let's go, guys. We've got to get home. School tomorrow." She looked around at Jace's schoolmates. "You guys, too. Your parents will be looking for you. Do you all have a ride?"

Reassuring her of their way home, and amidst minimal grumbling, they all got to their feet. Jace lingered a bit with his teammates. Leet lifted Tino out of the booth. "Come on, buddy."

Once outside, he showed Tino the electronic lock control on his key and sent him on to the truck. Thinking ahead, he called out. "Tino!"

"What?"

"Don't put the key in the ignition!"

"What does that mean?"

"It means, don't try to steal my truck!"

"Okay!"

Then he put his arm around Sadie as they lagged along behind.

"I miss you."

She looked up at him and received a light kiss. "I know. I miss you, too."

"I'll talk to you tomorrow after I see my lawyer."

"What did you learn from Suhayla?"

He shrugged. "I really don't know what she's after. I'll tell you more when we can be alone." He stopped their forward movement and held her with him. "When will that be, Sadie?"

"Leet—" She didn't know what to say. It had felt right, superbly right, being with him this evening. It had felt how it should be. But she couldn't forget that there was a woman who claimed him as her husband. What was the right thing here?

Tino saved her. "Look, Mom!"

She turned away from Leet, aware of his frustration, his dissatisfaction. She hadn't answered his question. She was sorry, but she didn't know how to answer it.

"Tino! That's very good."

And it was. He held a little tree—indeed, a sapling. It

consisted of a trunk the diameter of a fat pencil with three small branches stemming out, and a few twigs—awaiting leaves—splitting off of each. It had a small, flat base with the root system visible on its surface.

She loved it and loved the man who helped her son build it. She looked at Tino as he held it out to her from the back seat of Leet's truck. When Leet came up close behind her, she turned her face into his chest.

"Hey." He lifted her face up and wiped her tears. "What's this?"

"You got a car seat for him."

She ducked her head back to his chest and felt his chuckle as he wrapped his arms around her. He gave her a squeeze. "All this and you cry over a car seat. You are such a girl."

Tino had more to say, so she turned her head to see him. But she stayed in Leet's arms.

"It's cool, isn't it?" Tino was showing her the safety seat. "It's camo. And Beowulf got to ride back here with me."

"It *is* cool. Who's Beowulf?"

"He's Deputy Will's dog. He's h-u-g-e. We took him for a ride 'cause Leet is sleeping on his couch."

She scrunched her face, trying to follow. "Leet is sleeping on whose couch?"

"Beowulf's."

She looked up at Leet, who shrugged. "Well, it's Will's couch, though there's some controversy about that, at least in Beowulf's mind." He looked at her more seriously. "Either way, it's where I'm sleeping now."

Sadie smiled a little but had to fight back another wave of tears.

Leet kissed her forehead, leaving his lips against her. "Life's complicated, huh?"

She took a heavy breath, sighing it out as Jace joined them. "I guess it is."

Leet lifted Tino out of his truck and carried him to Sadie's car. He held Sadie at the door once the boys were both in their seats. He wrapped her tight in his arms and kissed her, hard and long. "I love you, Sadie."

"I love you, Leet."

Then she drove home without him.

CHAPTER NINE

Three weeks passed, and Leet was still sleeping on the couch. Well, it was just a bit better than that.

Leet had learned that, according to Vermont law, desertion, or abandonment of a marriage, required seven years to establish. Living separately for six months or more constituted grounds for a no-fault divorce, but only if both partners agreed that there was no desire to reconcile. In the case of a contested divorce, the petitioning spouse had to prove grounds, such as adultery. In that case, a legal hearing was to be held thirty to sixty days after the complaint was made. Suhayla was contesting. And the hearing still wasn't scheduled.

Even then the outcome wasn't certain. Years ago, Leet's lawyer had advised him to hire a detective and document Suhayla's affair with Dalid. He hadn't done it. He hadn't foreseen this circumstance he was in now, he hadn't wanted to make things worse for Ray, and, most of all, he just hadn't wanted to. The thought of it had seemed sordid, and he really didn't want proof of something he hadn't even wanted to think about.

That had been a mistake. With Dalid dead, Leet's petition for divorce was much weaker. He couldn't prove now that Suhayla's affair with Dalid was a sexual one. She'd admitted as much to Leet and Ray, but that was only useful if he asked Ray to testify in court against his own daughter.

Better late than never, though not much, Leet had now hired a detective. He had him working to find acquaintances of Dalid and Suhayla's who might testify to the affair. Little progress had been made, since most of those players lived in Europe or the Middle East and were likely to still have loyalty to Dalid.

Once he'd learned it would take more than a month at best to obtain a divorce, and that Suhayla had a legal right to live in the home they'd owned together, Leet helped Will clean out the extra room that was supposed to be Will's office someday. He'd bought a bed and a dresser, and let Beowulf have his couch back.

The weeks had proved unsatisfactory in more ways than his living situation.

He'd spoken with Suhayla on a regular basis. Though he'd moved out of the house, he couldn't move his studio and gym. He still spent most of his days there, and she was often present.

For a couple hours or more each day, he worked out. He often ran, but he still needed the equipment in his gym. And he needed a place to meet with his physical therapist. He was making a lot of progress there, and even the therapist was beginning to grudgingly admit that there was a chance he could play again.

Also, he needed to work. Often, he was in the studio late into the night. He was producing great work, he thought. Conception and design required his full attention, and that helped center him, distracting him from his longing for Sadie and his anger with Suhayla. And the physicality of it, the gritty, sweaty work of it, helped relieve his frustration.

He needed his woman.

He saw more of Suhayla than he did of Sadie. He'd been with her just a handful of times.

They'd had a couple outings with the boys, family events similar to their pizza night. Sadie had joined the guys for the Fallbrook hike, and he maneuvered her into dinner after. And Jace, his stalwart ally, had invited Leet to the end-of-year athletics program at the high school. He'd had a sweet moment helping Jace with his tie. The women of the family had all laughed that he'd had to put it around his own neck to get the knot right, but he pointed out that it was more than any one of them could do. He figured he who smirked last smirked best. Then he sat with them in the auditorium, next to Tino, next to Sadie, with the moms on the other side. Afterwards, he talked them into a stop for ice cream.

Marta asked him once to Sunday brunch at the farm. That had been awkward and annoying. Marta had displayed a veneer of cheerfulness that overlaid her obvious anxiety.

Joss had been nearly curmudgeonly. Sadie was clearly uncomfortable—seeming more at ease interacting with Canaan,
who'd also joined the family at the table, than with him. Every time she spoke to the farmhand or smiled at him, Leet
wanted to do murder.

He'd seen Canaan practicing tai chi and some other mar-
tial art that Leet didn't recognize, one that involved a stick.
Quiet Canaan had hidden depths, and Leet was pretty sure
he himself would come out on the short end of any skirmish.
Still, it was tempting. A little man-to-man combat would feel
damn good.

But he'd behaved himself, short of a few pointed glares
that appeared to merely amuse Canaan. And he'd walked out
to the truck with his arm around Sadie.

He'd thought that was pretty decent of him, given that
what had been on his mind was something more like tossing
her over his shoulder and carting her off to her bed in the A-
frame.

He'd wanted to linger there when he'd wrapped his arms
around her and leaned up against the truck. She'd rested
against him nicely, but there was so much sadness in their
silence that he'd known it was hard for both of them.

After a few quiet minutes, he'd kissed her and left.

And today had totally sucked. It was a Saturday filled
with bright sunshine and blue skies with a few pretty, puffy
clouds. The trees were decked out with their new leaves, the
fresh, spring green of sugar maples, the bronze tones of
copper beeches, and the maroon of Japanese maples. A few
late-flowering trees were still in bloom, lilacs and lilies of the
valley were scenting the air, and roses and peonies were
showing their buds.

It was a perfect day for a wedding.

He should have been out back at his pond, under an ar-
bor, exchanging his vows. This was the day he should have
been making Sadie his forever.

He'd started it early, with a painful call to Sadie before either of them had gotten out of bed. Like with their last en-
counters, they'd found little to say. They'd kept the connection for several minutes, the tenuous link proving an equal
mix of comfort and torture. He was pretty sure that if he'd
been with her, he'd have been wiping away her tears.

Will had been aware of the day's significance and had

tossed him out of bed shortly after he'd hung up from Sadie. The two of them had taken Beowulf on a short run and then met Denny and some others at the gym for a little b-ball. They had a late lunch and shared a couple pitchers of beer down at the Tap and Mallet after. But the efforts of his good buddies to cheer him couldn't dispel his gloom. Eventually, he acknowledged their intent and his appreciation and took his miserable self home.

There, he took advantage of something he'd learned from Max, that whaling away on hot steel with a six-point-six-pound straight pein sledge hammer was a good way to vent an excess of anger and frustration. He put Bruce Springsteen on loud and was enjoying even more the god-awful racket of hammer on steel. He kept at it past dark, past the time his body was tired, drenched in sweat and beginning to ache. He didn't consider it too small of him to hope that he was keeping Suhayla from sleep.

In fact, she was lucky to not get hurt when she surprised him with a touch at his back, mid-stroke with his hammer. He glanced back at her and saw that she held out a cold sports drink.

Her implication was correct. He'd been overdoing it, pushing himself past exhaustion, soaking his clothing with sweat, not even being careful to re-hydrate. He got a grip on himself and went through the motions of shutting down the forge. Then he walked over to grab a towel and turn off the music before he went to her, took the drink, and downed it.

He looked her over in the sudden silence.

She hadn't exactly approached him in a sexy negligee, but it was near enough. She wore a slender, slinky pearl-white dress that was just short of translucent. Even so, it left little to the imagination. The fabric clung—outlining her breasts beneath the draped bodice, her erect nipples visible behind it. It followed the slim curves of her waist and hips. She'd cocked herself onto a stool just right, so there was a little evocative, vee-shaped fold of the silky cloth where her thighs met, framing her mound.

He rubbed the towel over his head, drying his face and hair, then slung it over his shoulders. He went to the fridge for another drink, wishing for a good shot of whiskey instead. Then he faced her.

"What do you want, Suhayla?"

She gave that practiced little pout. "You know what I want, Leet."

He cast his gaze over her suggestive pose. "You want me to fuck you?"

That made her flinch, but she covered it quickly. "I want to be your wife."

"You were my wife. You didn't like it. Remember?"

She shrugged, aware, he was certain, of the way that action made her breasts move under satin cloth. "We were different then."

He shook his head and took another stool, across the workbench from her. He leaned his elbows down on it, grounding himself in this place of his work, his art. "I don't think so, Halie. I think you still want glamour and parties. That's not what I want now, just like it wasn't back then. You weren't satisfied with me then. You won't be now either."

"You're famous now, Leet. You can have so much more."

"Fame really isn't what I'm after. And you know I was injured. You know I might never play again."

"But you mean to. I see you with your therapist. I see you working out. You'll play again, Leet. You could play for one of the top teams. You don't need to stay here."

He knew wicked satisfaction gleamed in his eyes. He didn't care. The Metal were contenders, and he'd helped make them so. "I *do* play for one of the top teams, Suhayla."

"Phht. You know what I mean. You could move. You don't even have to change teams if you don't want to. You can live in New York or Washington, or on the West Coast. You don't have to stay here."

He stood. "I like it here. I *love* it here, Suhayla." All he wanted, *everyone* he wanted, was here. "You want to live elsewhere, that's fine. I'll give you money." He pressed his hands on the table and leaned toward her. "I'll give you all the money I have, right now. I mean it. Every penny." Leet had made the offer before. He spoke slowly, letting her hear his sincerity in every word. "Take it all and go live where you want. You don't need me. You don't even want me."

She stood then and slid her gaze over him. "I do. I do want you."

Leet wasn't falling for her pretended seduction. She'd had sex with him, but she'd never felt desire for him. He'd suspected it before. Now, since he'd been with Sadie and learned a woman's passion, he knew it. He moved quickly around the bench, stepping aggressively close, leaning his body over hers.

Automatically, she stepped back, her cheeks paling.

He crossed his arms over his chest and lifted his brow.

She looked suddenly lost, childlike. "I need you, Leet."

Finally, he thought he understood. She wanted—needed—a man. She needed an arm to cling to, a male to complete her. To showcase her, actually. She was the adornment, the sparkling jewel that drew the attention. She was beautiful, ethereal—untouchable. And that only worked if a man held ownership over her.

A prince would be perfect for the role. A fledgling quarterback, not so much. A star quarterback might do in a pinch, if he played his role properly.

It helped to understand. But he still couldn't give her what she wanted.

He shook his head. "I'm not what you need, Halie. You shouldn't need anyone in that way. You'd do better to find your own happiness. I've found mine. I want you to let me have it. *Please*."

Suhayla's voice shook, and he knew tears threatened—real tears, not the false ones she'd tried on him a couple times in the last three weeks. "Have *her*, you mean. She is no different than I. You have fame, you have money. Of course she wants you. Why would you choose her over me?"

He lifted his head once. "She loves me."

Tears spilled then. "I can love you."

Maybe she could love someone. She said she'd loved Dalid. He wondered if it was true. He suspected she was a long way from having love for anyone. Even, perhaps most especially, for herself.

"I'm sorry, Suhayla, for any part I played in your unhappiness. I was young and careless, and I regret not trying harder to know you, to understand you. Our marriage was a mistake. You knew it was when you left. That's *why* you left. It's too late to make it right now. My offer of money stands. Anytime you're ready to take it and let the divorce go through, just say so. Otherwise, we'll fight it out in court, and I'll keep at it until I win. I promise I will." He turned away, heading toward the shower. "In the meantime, don't ever come swishing your ass at me again."

He spent a long time in the shower. It wasn't enough.

—⸻

Sadie had gotten the boys to bed and finally gave in to the misery she'd been trying to hide all day. No one had bought her act in any case, and she just didn't have the energy for it any more.

She didn't even have the energy to open up the mindless paperback she'd picked up before she'd plopped down on the couch. The room was dark but for the reading light she'd left on, and even that was too much. She lay on her back, threw her arm up to cover her eyes, and wallowed.

The day had sucked. She was pretty sure she hadn't hidden her tears from Leet when he'd called first thing in the morning. She'd opened her eyes once to the bright, beautiful day and then burrowed head and all under the covers. Somehow, it would have been better if the weather had been cold and rainy, if a natural disaster or terrorist strike had marked it as an inauspicious day for a wedding. Well, she couldn't quite hope for that. But the lovely day did somehow rub salt in her much wounded heart.

She'd stayed under the blankets through that painful call from Leet. She might have stayed there all day except for the guilt she felt when it became clear that the moms had corralled Tino and Jace, sneaking them out of the house to leave her in peace.

Finally, she marshaled herself to rise and shower. She caught up with the boys and worked with them and Marta, tidying up the vegetable garden behind the house and the flower beds in front. Digging in the dirt was pretty good therapy, and the company of her family was soothing. Meg, bless her soul, called to invite the whole gang to join hers for a late afternoon picnic. It would be sinful, she claimed, to waste such a lovely day.

The impromptu get-together had featured good food and company and some boisterous backyard volleyball. Meg's hugs had been supportive and understanding. It was the best possible way to spend those hours.

Given that she wasn't spending them getting married to Leet.

More than anything, it had been a relief when dark fell and her little family trooped home.

And when she could finally collapse on the couch for the purpose of wallowing.

She counted her breaths, one, then another, trying to find acceptance, to let go of her jumbled emotions and replace them with peacefulness.

There was, after all, no real villain in this story. Certainly, it wasn't Leet, who, she trusted without doubt, had acted with honesty and integrity. He'd had no intent to deceive her. He had pursued her while truly believing that Suhayla was dead.

Even Suhayla deserved a certain amount of compassion. She'd been born essentially an orphan but for the benevolence of a man who had briefly loved her mother. She'd been raised with love, but entirely isolated from her natural family. Leet had been nearly a brother to her, one of just two dependable, present human beings in her life. It wasn't surprising that, as a young woman, she would seek safety in marriage to him.

And then to find that it didn't suit her when she spread her wings a bit, when she was exposed to other people and lifestyles. She wasn't the first woman, and wouldn't be the last, to fail to recognize her own needs, her own *self* at such a young age.

It was nearly impossible, though, to find sympathy for Suhayla's experiences of the last three years. She'd discussed it with Meg and Lourdes, who'd heard more of the story from Ray than Sadie had from Leet. She found she couldn't talk about it with Leet, that their own sense of loss was too strong to allow reasoned discussion of Suhayla's behavior.

Through their work, Meg and Sadie frequently saw the sad outcomes when women lacked power in their lives. Lourdes had lived it. With them, Sadie could begin to have some empathy for a woman whose love—perhaps a true, honest love—put her in an untenable position.

Yes, she could relate to that.

Sadie sought to act with compassion in her life. Yet here, so many hearts were involved—some of them entirely innocent, like her sons, some of them perhaps less so. How did one find the right answer?

She couldn't, at least not on this day that had been so achingly painful. She missed Leet. She wanted him.

She didn't move, arm still covering her eyes, for many moments after she heard the quiet tapping on the glass of the sliding door to the deck. Compassion, right—she'd been juggling these concepts for too long.

After another breath, she reached up, turned out the light, and went with her heart.

She opened the door to him in the dark, not questioning his presence. He'd come on foot, a gentle lope that had covered the five miles to the farm in less than an hour, not even enough to cause him to break a sweat. He hadn't wanted to deal with the awkward question of where he should park his car. It didn't feel right to drive up to the house, announcing his presence. It also didn't feel right to park somewhere off the road, deliberately hiding his intention.

He'd stopped thinking about whether this was right or wrong somewhere around mile three.

He went with his heart.

That meant, as soon as the door slid open, he stepped in and took Sadie in his arms. She was there and willing, wrapping herself around him, accepting his kiss. Hungrily, their mouths met, seeking, finding this connection they'd been missing, that they needed.

He kept her against him with one arm while he turned to close and lock the door. Then he gripped her, holding her hard against his erection, and took her to her bedroom.

He laid her on the bed and separated only enough to unzip her shorts and slide them off with her undies, then take off his shoes and socks and lower his running shorts enough to free himself. Then he was on top of her, pushing into her, whether she was ready or not.

She was just moist enough for him to shove his way in, all the way, to her depths. Her breath caught just a little, making him aware he might have hurt her. He couldn't help it. She'd have to deal. He'd needed to be right there, sunk into her, filling her, connected.

He took several deep breaths, taking in her scent, settling himself. Then he lifted up enough to find her face.

There was a half-moon casting dappled light over her bed, over her. Her eyes were dark, glittering, watching his. He lifted over her and used his lips to take her tears. He kissed her eyes closed and waited until her breathing eased. Then he started to make love to her mouth.

He kissed her gently, letting her feel his longing, his love. He spent a long time at it, coaxing, loving. He didn't move where he'd thrust inside her, hoping she understood that he needed the connection, the union that made them one. That he couldn't fucking live another moment without it.

Her lips moved under his. Softly they played, rubbing, lightly nipping. Their breaths were gentle, sighing.

Then he used his tongue, deepening the kiss, making more of it. She opened for him, and, at the same time, he could feel her relax around him, her increased moisture easing his way. He groaned involuntarily and flexed his hips once, sinking deeper, taking advantage of her welcome.

His mouth took her more aggressively, his lips tugging, tongue thrusting, teeth abrading. She was there with him, rising up to seek, opening to let him take.

Finally, he lifted again to look at her. Their breathing was rough now, wanting. He held himself on one elbow and put his hand on her breast. He cupped it, massaging, and stroked his thumb hard over the nipple. The cotton of her sleeveless summer blouse was soft, little hindrance to his possession. None at all, even, when he sucked her into his mouth.

He drew on her hard, causing her breath to seize, causing her to arch up. He resisted the urge to respond when her pelvis tilted, rocking against him.

He suckled, teasing with varying intensity. He used his free hand to stroke her other breast, pinching and tugging at the nipple.

Then he lifted again, and watched for what was revealed as he slowly undid her buttons. He kissed the skin that he bared, sliding his tongue over her sternum and then the rise of each breast. He grasped the edge of her pretty summer bra with his teeth and tugged it down so he could reach her nipple with his tongue. Finally, he undid the front clasp and opened the bra to expose all of her.

Her breasts jutted up, rising further with each urgent

breath. His gaze went to hers, heat searing, before going back to watch as he circled each breast with a hand and lifted them higher, brought them closer together. He took her nipples with his mouth, moving the short distance from one to the other, nearly able to grasp both at the same time.

He sucked at them, stroked with his tongue, grazed with his teeth. In the end, he held them, pinched by thumb and forefinger, as he looked up again to watch her.

Sadie writhed beneath him, her breath panting, her hips rocking, urging him to motion. Her eyes flashed, and her hands, one clutching his t-shirt, one clasped at his hip, signaled her need.

Done holding back, Leet acquiesced to her demands. He pulled out slowly and then sank into her again in one long, exquisite stroke. The stimulation of that one motion, the tight, wet heat, clasping and yielding at the same time, was his undoing. He arched back, growling out his passion, eyes rolling back in his head.

And then he moved, thrusting deeply, charging into her. He kept his grip on her nipples, pinching in time with his lunges, driving her on. Faster, each motion took him deeper, stronger, until he was lost in it.

He heard Sadie's muted cries with her first powerful orgasm. But he didn't stop, didn't even pause. He needed more, was determined to take more.

He pushed into her harder until she was with him again. Until her hands clutched at his back and her body rocked with his. Until she took all of him, accepting him, meeting him, needing each stroke.

They came together, Leet clenching his body over hers, filling her, fiercely spurting into her. He pressed a hand over her mouth and buried his own face in the mattress at her shoulder, hushing the rough sounds of their pleasure. His orgasm went on, his thrusts driving her higher in the bed, driving her higher in her own peak.

When it was finally over, he collapsed against her, barely able to hold some of his weight off her. It was minutes before their breathing slowed, quieted. Her hands dropped from his back, and she slid them up to entwine her fingers with his.

Another long time passed. He was still inside her, had even hardened again, but all they could do was lie in silence, together.

Finally, he lifted up and kissed her softly. He gently pulled out of her and stood up. He covered himself with his shorts, then sat on the side of the bed to put his shoes on. When he was done with that, he clutched the hand she'd held out next to him. Then he stood and walked out of her room. Out of her house.

Leet was loath to leave his bed the next morning. He could hear the bustle of churchgoers—cars filling parking lots in the village, friends calling out to one another, bells ringing.

He knew Will had already left for his early shift. Beowulf was welcome at the station and in the squad car, so he didn't even have canine company.

He'd gone to sleep wondering if those brief, passion-filled but wordless moments he'd spent with Sadie would have him waking feeling better or worse.

The answer was, it still sucked. A little bit better for having made that connection, for the comfort of knowing she missed him, still wanted him, as he missed and still wanted her. A little bit worse for the reminder of how much he, they, had been forced to give up.

He wondered for the first time if Sadie and he would have been off on a honeymoon this day. He hadn't gotten around to thinking of it, to making a plan for it. The truth was, he was so looking forward to having her with him every day—in his home, in his life—just that had seemed like it would be honeymoon enough. He'd have been entirely happy just being with her.

Thinking about it now—where he might have taken her, what they might have done—apparently didn't make matters any better.

Eventually, he got himself up, cleaned up, and went to his studio. Suhayla's car was gone from the drive and the house felt so empty he went upstairs to investigate. He knew she'd complied with his request to use the guest suite, so he went there. Her clothes still filled the closets—the woman did love fashion—but he guessed a couple pieces of luggage were missing. Two large suitcases were still tucked into one closet, but there were no overnight or carry-on bags.

She wasn't gone for good, but he guessed she was gone for a while. He gave Ray a call, thinking she might have confided her plans with him, but all he got was a voicemail message. He wandered back to the studio, though he didn't accomplish much more than a mildly rousing game of garbage can basketball with one of Tino's old, balled-up socks.

It was a week before he saw Suhayla again, and the circumstances were not what he'd have predicted.

CHAPTER TEN

Sadie was in her office, reviewing charts for her teen prenatal clinic that afternoon. Her cell phone buzzed, displaying Leet's number.

She hadn't spoken with him for more than a week, since the night of their almost-wedding when he'd come to her in the dark. Not that they'd spoken then, either. Somehow, that urgent taking had seemed less real for its silence, less remiss.

But no, it had been real. And she'd wanted it, needed it, too.

She couldn't have turned Leet away to save her life.

It had brought pain, though. Tears after he left that wouldn't stop. Days—nine of them now—she'd had to force herself through. Days of having to work hard to find her balance, her joy.

She'd nearly broken. She got up that Sunday morning and hung her head in the shower. For twenty minutes, she cleared her head of all thought. Banished every commitment to respect vows that had been made, to set an example for her sons, to live by some sort of code that she could defend, could honor.

Carefully disciplining her mind, she dressed and left the house. She was going to find Leet. She was going to *be* with Leet.

But Canaan was on her front porch, reclined in one of the two brightly-painted wooden rockers that Leet had brought her when spring had finally settled in. He pointed to the other. "Sit, Sadie," he said.

She hadn't wanted to. It was obvious he knew that Leet had come to her last night. Canaan seemed always to be aware, to see things one wouldn't expect. Like the way she knew he was tuned in when Tino was out in the barn. Canaan was always there before Tino could find trouble. She'd come to count on him for it. She knew that she could trust him to watch out for Tino. And for Jace, and the moms.

And now, maybe for her, too.

Not sure she appreciated it, she begrudgingly plopped down in the rocker. When he held out his hand, she put hers in it. He didn't speak. Apparently, a hand to hold was all he was inclined to offer.

It was a comfort to sit there with him—he radiated a kind of peace in his stillness. It wasn't enough, quite. Finally, Sadie's anger and frustration bubbled over. "I can't live this way."

Still, Canaan didn't speak. What he did do was to lift up one foot and prop it on the porch rail. Then he tugged up his pant leg, nearly to his knee.

His action revealed a prosthetic leg—a high-tech one, like Sadie had seen on news stories about wounded vets returning from Afghanistan.

He still didn't speak, but when Sadie turned her head to look at him, he turned his and looked back.

"Dammit," she said, and looked away over the farmyard. "Sometimes you have to learn to live with shit."

He chuckled a little. "Yeah." He stood then and shook down his jeans. She knew he was ready to walk away.

"I'm sorry, Canaan. I know my shit will get better eventually. Yours won't." She let out a sigh. "I kind of suck."

He laughed a little more at that, then bent over her, hands leaning on her chair arms, and kissed her forehead. "You don't suck, Sadie. You're okay."

Then he did walk away, not a bit of his handicap showing in his gait. And Sadie spent the day with her family, learning how to live with her shit.

Now she took a good long look at her phone. And let her pulse settle a little before she answered. "Hello."

She wasn't sure what inflection was in that word when she uttered it. Hope? Embarrassment? Longing?

Whatever it was, the mood changed suddenly when a woman's voice responded. "This is Suhayla. Leet was hurt in his studio. You should come right away."

She stood, though she was hardly aware of it. "Where is he?"

"At home. Come now."

"Does he need an ambulance?"

"No. Come alone."

The call ended then. Sadie hung up and slipped her phone into her pocket. She grabbed her bag with her car keys. On her way out of the office, she explained quickly that there was an emergency and asked her nurse to look for another midwife or possibly a resident to help her with the afternoon group.

The drive to Leet's seemed endless, though she had no recall of it as she pulled up outside his garage. Suhayla's car was parked in the drive. She entered through the front door, calling out Leet's name. At the balcony over the studio, she leaned over the rail and peered down.

He was there, lying on the floor. She could just see his feet and legs. They were still.

"Leet!" Sadie ran down the stairs. He was unconscious, or nearly so, curled on his side by one of the benches in the locker area. She crouched beside him, talking to him, calling his name as she searched for injury.

She paused, becoming silent, when she saw the nylon bands that secured his hands around the metal base of the bench. She touched his shoulder and shook him a little. "Leet!"

Slowly, he turned his head. His eyes rolled as they opened, taking a moment to focus on her face. "Leave, Sadie." His words were quiet, slurred, but nonetheless urgent. "Hurry. Run."

He had to know that wasn't going to happen. She slid her hand underneath his head, cushioning it where it lolled against the floor. She found no signs of trauma. Suspicion that he'd been drugged flitted through her mind. "Leet! Did Suhayla do this?"

He opened his eyes again, trying, she knew, to look stern. "Please. Sadie, go. Now."

She wouldn't leave him and knew it was too late anyway. For she'd seen Suhayla now, coming from the great room. She had a gun in her hand and was pointing it with authority.

"Stand up, Sadie."

Sadie shook her head no. She wouldn't leave Leet.

Suhayla arched one brow, managing to convey a certain imperial disdain. "If you don't stand up, when I shoot you, I might hit Leet as well."

Well, that made the woman's intentions clear enough.

Leet apparently understood, too. Groaning, he tried to

lurch up onto his elbow, looking over the bench at Suhayla. "Sadie, don't move. Suhayla, stop this."

The effects of the drug—if, indeed, that was the cause of Leet's lethargy—seemed to be lifting some. Leet's words were clearer, his eyes more focused.

Suhayla stepped closer, keeping the bench between them, and directly faced Sadie. "Stand," she said, "or take your chances."

Leet was yelling at her, yelling at Suhayla, though the sound seemed somehow muted as she slowly rose. She kept her eyes on Suhayla and saw no remorse, not even a flinch, as the woman fired the gun.

It felt like a punch into her side. Sadie took a step back with the force of it, on legs that seemed suddenly not entirely under her control. She pressed her left hand against her side, ironically aware that she'd been hit in that spot below her rib where Leet had once marked her. She lifted her hand and saw that it was streaked red. Automatically, she put it back over the wound and brought her other hand against it, applying pressure.

Leet cried out her name. His voice became more distant as she kept taking slow steps backwards, though she knew from the rush of sound in her ears that it wasn't just distance causing that effect. She could feel blood seeping between her fingers despite the pressure she exerted.

Her back came against the stairs and she was grateful for that bit of solid support. She leaned against the rail, then went with the wobbliness of her legs and slid down to the floor.

Suhayla hadn't moved but was watching dispassionately. Leet had his head on the floor again, but had twisted around so he could see her. "Lie down, Sadie. Keep the pressure on, but lie down." His gaze was on her, his words directed simply to her, as though they were alone.

Sadie knew he was right. Propping herself up against the stair like she had would only increase the flow of blood. But once she'd gotten to that position, she seemed unable to move further. She focused on Leet's eyes, feeling now like his gaze was the sum total of her world, her one connection to it.

His mouth moved, but she no longer heard the words.

Leet struggled hard against the fog that gripped his brain. He still called Sadie's name, still gave her urgent instructions, but he wasn't sure she was still with him. Her gaze was vague now, and she didn't respond to his words. Most of all, she hadn't lain down, and he could see the effect that blood loss was having on her color. He could also see the steady trickle of it over her fingers. The pool of it that was forming on the floor beside her. She was slipping away.

He wasn't sure why Sadie was here when she should have been at work. He'd woken to her calling his name, pushing at his shoulder when all he'd wanted was to sleep. Then he'd registered the fact that he was lying on the floor of his studio, his hands bound around the leg of a bench.

When his muzzled brain began to function just a little, he recalled having been at work in the studio. He'd been doing some heavy welding. Sweat ran in rivulets from under his helmet, his shirt was drenched.

As she'd done before, Suhayla had come up behind him. He hadn't seen her for a week. And so, instead of ignoring her as he was tempted to do, he'd shut down the torch, took off his helmet, and turned to face her. With a nod, he took the drink she held out to him and downed it.

That had been a possibly fatal mistake. If not for him, perhaps for Sadie. That horrid possibility faced him now as he watched Sadie's awareness fade. Reluctantly, he let go of her glazed gaze and turned back to Suhayla.

His motion was extremely limited. His body was sluggish and tended to forget what it was doing. His hands were useless to him, cuffed under the bench—a bench that was securely bolted to the floor. He had to focus all his will to keep Suhayla in his view.

"Halie, what are you doing? Stop it now. Call an ambulance."

Suhayla circled around him. She pulled a stool over, placing it so that when she settled onto it, he could see Sadie as well as her. In relief, he dropped his head down again, able to keep them both in view without having to struggle against his logy brain.

"Suhayla, please." He groaned, knowing Sadie was slipping further away, her eyes closed now, her body still. Just that trickle of blood that signified the life still in her. "What do you want?"

She kept the gun in her hand, resting it incongruously on the shimmering silk of her skirt. Her posture on the stool was almost prim, her expression benign, unconcerned.

"You know what I want, Leet." Her voice, too, was correct, unemotional. "You brought this on yourself."

"I'll do it. Whatever you want, I'll do. Just get help before it's too late."

"It's already too late, Leet. It was too late when you chose her over me."

"Goddammit, Suhayla. You left me. Don't you fucking remember that?"

"You should have wanted me back."

Leet closed his eyes, by just a hair resisting the urge to pound his head against the floor.

"When I came back, you should have wanted me. Remember, when we were married? Remember saying how much you wanted me?"

Eyes open again in disbelief, Leet glared at her. "That was a long time ago, Halie. Before you left me. Before you fell in love with another man. Before you let me think for three years that you were dead."

"I needed you to want me again, Leet."

"I'll do it, Suhayla. I'll give you what you want."

She stroked the gun. "No. I've figured out a better way. I'm going to be your widow, Leet. You and Sadie will die today. Once I came back, you spurned her and chose me. She found us making love, and in a jealous rage, she tried to kill us. But she died instead—you had to kill her in order to save me. Though not before being fatally wounded yourself, of course. You'll die in my arms while I weep."

He guessed that might suit her—the role of the tragically grieving widow, with plenty of drama. There would be lots of attention—bright lights and cameras. He shook his head. "No one will believe that. Too many people know I'm in love with Sadie. They know I wouldn't cheat on her."

"They'll believe you changed your mind when I came back." She smirked, obviously perfectly able to visualize it. "And I'll have proof."

"You can't prove that, Suhayla."

She nodded her head with a smile. "I'll have your semen inside my body."

He shook his head again. "No. You will not."

"I assure you, I will."

Leet rolled, getting his elbows underneath his chest as well as he could and lifting up onto his knees. With all the strength he could muster, he pounded his back against the bench. Again, and again. He had little hope that he could loosen it, but he would try for all he was worth. He kept at it until Suhayla fired the gun.

He rolled back over and frantically searched for signs that Sadie had been hit a second time. Her eyes had opened again, and she still pressed her hands to the only wound he could see. After another moment, he saw where some wood on the stair had splintered under the force of the second bullet. It was very near Sadie's head.

"I've been practicing," Suhayla explained as she moved back into his line of vision. She held his gaze, slowly drumming the pistol against her thigh as she stood over him. "Do what I say, or the next one will kill her."

"Suhayla. You don't have to hurt Sadie any further. Just me. Your plan works if you kill me." He heard Sadie moan, a pitifully weak objection that he felt entirely free to ignore. "Sadie doesn't have to die."

Leet could no longer see Sadie. He could only watch Suhayla, could only regret the harm that had been done to Sadie. Could only hope that he would find some way to see that she survived this.

"She's innocent in this. I'm the one who hurt you. Please, *please*, leave her alone."

"She is *not* innocent." Suhayla practically spit. "I see how you want her. I know what she lets you do to her."

Leet groaned, frustrated beyond limits, scared to his soul. And finding no way to reason with the craziness he saw in Suhayla's eyes. He tried once more. "Suhayla. This isn't you. I admit I never made the effort I should have to know you. But I know this isn't you. Stop what you're doing. It isn't too late."

There was nothing but a disdainful smirk in her eyes. She stepped over him, standing one foot on either side of his hips. She lifted the skirt of her dress and he saw that she was naked underneath. He turned his head, able to see

Sadie now. He met her gaze and held it.

Suhayla went to her knees, straddling his thighs. A soft clatter signaled that she'd put the pistol on the bench. Her hands started working at the fly of his heavy work jeans. He watched Sadie, silently swearing to her and to himself that this would not happen.

Before she got his jeans loose, Leet heard Suhayla's breath catch. The motion of her hands halted. He looked up at her, then followed her gaze toward the glass doors. Three men stood there, outlined by the bright sunlight behind them. They were dressed in suits and wore dark glasses. All three appeared to be Middle Eastern, muscled, and resolute. They had guns—much, much larger guns than the one Suhayla had brought.

Suhayla stood and faced them angrily, gesturing back to the doors. "Amir! Get out!"

One of them faced Suhayla and inclined his head. "Cousin." He spoke to the other two, directing them. Nodding, the two left, one going past Sadie and up the stairs, the other setting off into the great room adjacent to the studio. Then the first, Amir, spoke into a communications device clipped to his suit jacket.

Leet realized that he recognized the man. He was Suhayla's cousin, met many years ago in a New York night club. He was the one who'd introduced her to Dalid.

Suhayla strode to him and pushed at his chest even as he spoke. The man took no notice.

"Get out, I said! This is none of your business."

She flailed at him until he grasped her arms and gave her a rough shake. "Be quiet." Suhayla appeared defeated, dropping her head and turning away.

One more man came through the door. He carried a black bag, and Amir motioned him to Sadie.

The man moved to her, looking her over.

Leet called out to him, hoping in this bizarre situation that the man was the doctor he appeared to be. "Help her! She's been shot. She's lost a lot of blood."

The man took a stethoscope from his bag, knelt beside Sadie, and began listening to her heart.

That wasn't enough. "She needs an ambulance!" He looked from the doctor to Amir and urged him to call for help. Both men ignored him entirely.

The doctor stood up. "I need her moved so I can work on her. To a bed or a table."

Amir acknowledged him with a short nod. "It'll have to wait until the others get back. I need the house secured first."

"I'll move her," Leet tried, but again, the men paid no attention to him.

The man who'd been sent into the great room reappeared and nodded an all-clear. Amir motioned him over to assist the doctor.

"There are beds back through there," Leet told them, no doubt unnecessarily.

The doctor and his new assistant lifted Sadie and carried her out of the studio.

Leet turned back to Amir. "Let me go with her. Please."

The man had removed his sunglasses. He looked at Leet then at Suhayla, whom he still held by one arm. Leet thought he wanted to roll his eyes, but had too much control.

He tried again. "Let me go with her. I'll do whatever you say."

Amir made no response until the third man came back down the stairs. "Clear," that one said. "Her clothes and suitcases are in a room upstairs."

Finally, Amir motioned him to Leet. "Cut him loose. Let him go with the woman." He looked at Leet with the next words. "Keep your gun at his back and shoot him if he does anything you don't like." Then he spoke to Suhayla. "Go with them. Sit down in there and behave."

He spoke into his radio again, though not in English. Leet didn't care, didn't try to stay to listen. Once his hands were cut free, his only goal was to get to Sadie. He swayed once when he pushed himself to his feet and felt the muzzle of a gun prod his back. He moved carefully then, making sure of his balance.

He brushed one hand past the pocket of his jeans and learned his cell phone was gone. He saw it on a table as he passed through the great room.

They'd laid Sadie down on the island counter that edged the kitchen area. Her eyes were open and found his when he got to her.

He took her right hand and held it against his chest with both hands. The doctor worked on her left, setting out supplies for an IV. He opened a thick gauze pad and placed it over Sadie's wound. "Put pressure on that," he said.

Leet used one hand to do as he was told but kept hold of Sadie with the other. The doctor got the IV started and taped it in place. He pumped up a cover over the bag of fluid, making more pressure so it would run fast, even when he laid it down on the counter. Then he motioned Leet's hand away and began looking at the wound.

Leet was aware there was more activity in the room. Two more men had arrived. Amir sent one out of the room with instructions to pack up Suhayla's belongings.

The second was much older than the others, his dark hair graying at the temples. He stood before Suhayla, who had quietly followed orders and taken a seat.

She spoke first, bitterly. "Jibran. You have no business here."

Leet listened in, even as he spoke soft, reassuring words to Sadie and ran his hand over her forehead again and again. Jibran Hafir. The old king's man.

"Things have changed, Suhayla. You have once again become my business."

Suhayla made a dismissive noise. "I am not your business. I came to you for help after Dalid died, and you had no concern for me. Leave now. I will have no more to do with you."

"You have made quite a mess here."

"I have it in hand. Take your men and leave."

"It is in my hands now. As I said, things have changed."

The doctor had bared Sadie's abdomen. He'd taken a device from his bag that Leet deduced to be an ultrasound—he'd squirted out some gel, moved a probe over Sadie's skin around the wound, and looked at a hand-held screen. He spoke to Jibran, paying no heed whatsoever to Leet.

"The bullet appears to be lodged in a rib at her back. It looks like it nicked her spleen, which is where the blood is from. I don't see any free air, so I don't think the bowel was struck. That's good in regards to the chance of infection. I would treat her with an antibiotic in any case. The bleeding is slowing, so the IV fluids will maintain her volume for now. If she's going to a hospital, they'll want to transfuse her."

Leet understood what that meant. Sadie's bullet wound wasn't fatal. Her life, *their* lives were in the hands of this man who was in charge of the men with the big guns. He had the power to decide what happened next.

That man, Jibran, nodded to the doctor. Apparently, the medical man took that as a positive sign for Sadie's future. He reached into his bag again, speaking this time to Leet. "Does she have any allergies?"

Leet's eyes burned as he grasped at this small sign of hope. He shook his head, "I don't know." The much-too-late thought came to him that he probably should have asked that question before he'd shot her up with morphine. His breath huffed out as Sadie squeezed his hand. He looked at her, seeing more awareness in her eyes.

"No," she said.

Leet gripped her hand hard and pressed his forehead against hers, unashamed that a couple tears fell against her cheeks. He kissed her lips once and watched as the doctor drew medication from a small bottle and administered it into the IV. He taped the little bottle to Sadie's shirt. Leet figured that was to let the hospital staff known what she'd been given. The original IV bag was nearly empty, so the guy got out another to replace it.

"You can make her comfortable. Put a small pillow under her head. Use some larger ones to elevate her legs. Don't jostle her—you don't want to disrupt the clot that is slowing her bleeding. Cover her with a blanket. The blood loss and the fluids will make her cold." As he spoke, he placed another thick pad over Sadie's wound and secured it with wide bands of elastic tape pulled tight to form a pressure bandage. Leet didn't know what else the doctor had in his bag, but he was clearly prepared for gunshot wounds.

Squeezing her hand one more time, Leet lifted away from Sadie. He didn't move any further until the gun that had been pressed into his back was removed. And that didn't happen until Jibran gave a nod to the man who held it. "Stay with him."

So, with a gunman on his ass, Leet went off to a bedroom for pillows and blankets. His heart was perhaps unreasonably hopeful, given the situation they were still in, but he couldn't hold back. Sadie had looked at him, had spoken, had moved her lips just a little when he'd kissed her. That made things all right in his world.

Even if his world had taken a significantly bizarre turn.

When he got back and gently tucked Sadie in, the gunman joined his partner, watching outside at either end of the windows. The partner pointed through the glass and spoke quietly, including Amir who stood now at his shoulder. "One man with a rifle—there, on that rise beyond the pond. He let himself be seen, so there could be more who didn't. I'd guess over there on the right, in the trees."

Leet listened as he held on to Sadie. He could only think that Will was out there, having his back yet again. He figured Sadie must have somehow gotten in touch with him. He felt tremendously better for the company and could only hope that no one was interested in a shoot-out.

Amir made a noncommittal noise. "Watch him. Look for others." The men nodded, and one scanned the woods with a pair of compact, high-tech binoculars.

Suhayla and Jibran were both seated now, Jibran in a chair he'd brought closer to face Suhayla. Leet started listening in on their conversation. It seemed that Dalid's young wife had suffered an unexpected, late miscarriage of the baby boy she'd carried.

Suhayla turned her head in disdain. "So. You have lost your last hope of claiming the throne for your king's heir. I am not sorry. You demanded too much."

Jibran leaned back in his chair, but watched her closely. "You are wrong. There still lives a descendant of the king."

"Not true. Dalid had no siblings, and now, no children. Let it go, Jibran. Your foolish quest is over."

"The king had one other child, Suhayla. By the queen's personal assistant. By your mother, Neelah." Jibran looked at her, hard.

Suhayla stood, a look of revulsion on her face. "Me? You lie! My father was an officer of the king's guard."

Jibran stood, also, and spoke gruffly. "Neelah's husband was a king's guard. He served his king."

"You mean he allowed this, this—"

Jibran stepped closer and his words were sharp. "He served his king."

"And my mother? She agreed?"

Jibran shrugged. "Neelah was unaware."

"What? Do you mean they inseminated her?"

The man shook his head once. "The king would not agree. He took your mother every night until she conceived." He continued through Suhayla's objection. "She was—

medicated."

Suhayla's voice was a whisper. "They raped her."

Jibran dismissed her concern. "In the end, it seemed to be unnecessary. The queen had also conceived and, for once, after many losses, her pregnancy survived. Furthermore, she carried a son. When it was learned that Neelah bore a girl-child, her pregnancy was no longer...significant. The revolution took place, her husband died, and she was allowed to immigrate." Suhayla strode to the windows, though she did not look out. Her way was blocked by the two sentries who moved to stand before her, shielding her, confining and protecting at the same time. Her head was bowed, her arms wrapped around herself as she shuddered through a shiver. When she turned, Leet could see tears coursing down her cheeks. She pressed her fingers to her face, looking up at Jibran over them. "Dalid was my brother."

"Half-brother."

She shook her head. "How could you let him, how could you let us—"

He looked at Amir. "Your cousin was Dalid's bodyguard. He was unaware of your lineage when they met you in New York. Otherwise, we'd have stopped the affair before it started. It was too late when we learned of it. And it seemed of little consequence then."

Suhayla scoffed. "Of little consequence!" She swiped at her tears and strode forward to square off with Jibran. "Because I was a woman! And not 'significant!'"

Jibran faced her. "Yes. It was of no concern. He would not be allowed to marry you. We cared little that he used you as his whore."

She slapped him. The two sentries stepped forward, but Jibran lifted his hand to stay them.

"What if I had conceived?" This was spoken in horror.

"You did not. We made sure that you did not. Even with him—" he nodded his head toward Leet "—we made sure that you did not."

"How did you? How could you?"

Jibran lifted one shoulder. "The shot that your doctor gives you. That he says is for your thyroid."

She turned away from Jibran and faced Leet. "Why would you care if I conceived or not in my marriage?"

"You carry the king's blood."

A small breath left her, almost a moan. "So that is why I did not die. That is why I was taken from the jet. It wasn't because..." The words were quiet, almost a whisper, while she looked at Leet.

Leet still held Sadie, one hand grasping hers, the other stroking her hair. He could do nothing but return Suhayla's gaze levelly. And wonder about how his marriage, his life, would have been different but for the interference of these fanatics.

Suhayla looked back over her shoulder at Jibran. "Did Dalid truly fight to save me?"

Jibran gave no answer.

"Did he ever know I was his sister?"

"He knew before he married. He would not have Ladiah otherwise. He'd been determined to marry you."

"But, once he knew—"

"He would not give you up."

Suhayla sank into a chair and rested her head in her hands. She was quiet for a long time. "And now, you want—"

"You are a princess, Suhayla. Now, you are our queen."

"You will not stop this foolishness, will you?"

"It is a vow I made to your father, my king. A sacred vow. I will see the monarchy restored."

"And I am to be your puppet."

Jibran straightened. "You are to be queen. My queen."

Suhayla shook her head. "I have no desire to sacrifice my life to your hopeless cause."

"It is not hopeless. The mechanism for our return is still in place. The people—your people—are rebelling against the repression of the current regime. They await a leader. They await you."

"You speak eloquently, but you are talking about my death sentence."

Jibran moved to stand in front of her. "I am not." He knelt before her. "I will protect you with my life."

"Dalid just died in service to your obsession. Tell me, did you offer to protect him with your life, as well?"

Jibran bowed his head low. "That was a grievous error. Dalid failed to follow my direction. Yet it was my responsibility. I will pay for it with my life if you but wish it."

He motioned to one of the gunmen, who came to stand next to him and place his gun against Jibran's temple.

Suhayla sat taller, assuming the regal bearing that had always suited her so well. She was royalty. That would appeal to her very much, Leet knew. Jibran was aware of it, too—he'd bet his life on it.

She made a small motion with her finger, and the gunman stepped away. Jibran lifted his head but stayed on his knees.

"Rise," she said, and Jibran stood.

Suhayla sat back a little, moving into her role. "I am still married," she said, directing a nod toward Leet.

"Your marriage to Leet Hayes has been erased. It is as though it never existed."

"I suppose you will find me a husband."

"A queen's consort, from a royal family."

"But I will rule."

"You will. In the future, your son will rule. Then you may live your life as you will."

"And your role will be to..."

"Advise, my lady."

"And if I do not take your advice?"

Jibran looked back at her, his own bearing just as proud as hers. "My duty is first to my country. Your life is sacred to me, but only until you give birth to a son. That is an event that will be made to happen as soon as it is possible."

"And beyond that, I am once again of no consequence."

Jibran was silent.

"Yet another royal jet could be sacrificed. With me on board, this time."

The answer was obvious in the cold eyes of the king's man. "As you say."

Suhayla walked away, closer to Leet now, and looked at him for a few moments. Still looking at Leet, she spoke quietly. "Have I a choice?"

She turned to Jibran for his answer. The man looked to the doctor and then back at Suhayla. He didn't speak, and didn't have to. The implication was clear that the doctor had more tricks in his medical bag. The "medication" used on Neelah was no doubt one of them.

Suhayla straightened her shoulders. "I will do as you say."

Things happened quickly then. Suhayla's luggage was brought down and taken through the glass doors. The sentries moved outside, standing at the door and under the deck, still watching the back—the pond and the woods.

Amir stopped to nod to Leet before he left. "I'm glad we didn't have to shoot you. We're Washington fans, but the Metal are okay."

Leet nodded back. *How to respond to that*? He also was glad he hadn't been shot. He thought the Metal were okay, too. But Amir was so not his buddy, and Leet just wanted all of them gone.

The doctor nodded to Leet as well and followed the luggage. Finally, it was just Jibran and Suhayla left in the room.

She looked again at Leet. "Good-bye, then." She glanced at Sadie. "I'm sorry for hurting her."

Leet nodded once. "Go see your father, Suhayla." She glanced in question over at Jibran, but Leet kept going. "You're the queen, Halie. Act like it. See your father before you leave here."

She inclined her head once and looked at Jibran without the question in her eyes. "I will."

With that, she strode to the door, but Leet called to her. "Suhayla."

She turned, arching a brow.

"Be a good queen."

She held his gaze for a moment and then was gone.

Jibran spoke once more. "I assume the man with the rifle is your friend the deputy. He apparently called an ambulance, which is waiting at the bottom of your drive. He may have called others as well, others with official status. It would be a mistake to involve them. Talk carefully with your friend. My party is leaving this state, and in two hours, we will be out of the country. You care about the woman. You care about her children. You probably even care about her mothers' goat farm."

Leet got the message. Jibran knew how to make Leet suffer.

"If we leave this country unmolested, I will forget all that I know about you and the woman."

Leet nodded. Jibran turned to leave, but Leet had a final question for him. "What you said about my marriage to Suhayla. Is it true?"

"Yes. All records of the marriage ever having occurred are gone. Officially, it never happened."

"I have a copy of the certificate in a safe in my room. My

lawyer has one, as well."

Jibran held his gaze. "You'll find you are mistaken."

"But—"

"You may have had a ceremony. You may even have witnesses to it. However, a legal contract of marriage was never made." He walked to the door. "You are unwed and free to marry as you will."

That night, Leet slept in a chair with his head on a hospital bed. He was holding Sadie's hand in his. He hadn't let go of it, in fact, since Jibran and his men had left his home. Not when Will had strode into the room, rifle in his hand. Canaan was with him, face painted and outfitted in woodland camo. That one carried a sniper rifle, also camouflaged. He looked comfortable with it and competent in the extreme. And a little scary.

It turned out Sadie had called Will as she drove frantically to Leet's place, after Suhayla had phoned her. She'd thought Suhayla had sounded wrong. She'd made the right call on that. Will had stopped by the farm for Canaan—clearly, he knew some stuff about Canaan that Leet hadn't known.

He hadn't let go of her as he'd told the two of them about Jibran's threats. As he'd argued Will out of his natural urge to call in all the troops. As he'd been forced to settle for Will's reluctant agreement to hold off on a decision. And as he'd watched the two men leave, determined to confirm for themselves that Jibran and his men left the state.

He'd kept her hand when Denny came with the rescue squad to cart Sadie off to the hospital. Denny had made one attempt to back Leet off then shrugged when he got a good look at Leet's face. After that, the squad worked around him.

The nurse in the emergency room had tried, too. She was tough, but he was tougher. She said if he didn't let go, she'd have to cut Sadie's clothes to get them off. He said, okay. She said she wouldn't be able to get Sadie's hand through a hospital gown. He said, too bad. She'd threatened to call security. He'd looked at her and told her to do it if she thought it would work. She took her own good look at him then and gave up as well.

Sadie had taken her own stab at it. She'd been awake through transport and the whole hospital evaluation, sometimes clinging to his hand as much as he did to hers. Some of the procedures she'd gone through had hurt. Anyway, she told him he'd have to eat or go to the bathroom or something eventually. So far, he'd proved her wrong. He still had her hand.

She hadn't needed surgery. The doctor with the scary black bag had been correct in all his diagnoses. The injury to the spleen had clotted off. She was to be on bedrest for another forty-eight hours, then limited activity for an additional week. She'd had four units to replace the blood loss—Leet, Will, and Canaan had all volunteered to donate, but apparently, that process took longer and Sadie's need was urgent. So Leet had had to watch while some strangers' blood dripped into her. He was alternately grateful to the anonymous donors and crept out by the sight of it.

The bullet apparently was safe enough where it was. They would watch it as the rib healed and make sure it stayed put. The rib had been broken, but the only treatment for that was a tight wrap to stabilize it and pain meds. They'd been told there were no dangerous bone fragments to worry about. Sadie didn't like the narcotics and so mostly just avoided taking deep breaths.

She was still getting antibiotics, and they were watching her for fever and other signs of infection. She'd refused anything for sleep, even when her doctor told her he wasn't just offering it, but recommending it.

The woman had a stubborn side.

The moms had come with Jace and Tino for just a brief visit. It was enough to reassure them all that Sadie was okay, but not so much as to allow for a lot of tears. Though it was a close call for Marta and Tino.

Leet's parents had come by and stayed with them for a while. It felt good to know they were keeping an eye on Sadie's treatment and lending their weight to her care. Even better, Sadie's friend Meg had come and settled into the room for a good long time. She kissed Sadie, and Leet, too, then sat in the corner quietly knitting. But he knew nothing happened to Sadie that Meg didn't know about, didn't watch. She'd stayed through the evening, not going home until after midnight. She'd brought him food before she left, but Leet hadn't eaten it yet. He still wasn't ready to let go. He just put his head down to doze.

When he jerked awake, he knew he'd woken Sadie, too. He rubbed his face, one-handed. "Sorry, babe."

"You should go home and sleep, Leet."

He put his head back down. "Not gonna happen."

She didn't argue what she had to know was a lost cause. "All right, then. Why don't you eat the dinner Meg brought, then go wash your face? When you get back, I'll scoot over and you can lie down here with me."

"No way. That didn't happen when I was lying in a hospital bed. Not gonna happen tonight either."

"This bed is bigger."

"Nuh-uh."

"Well, I take up less space."

He raised his head to look at her, indicating a fault in her logic.

"Come on. You're keeping me awake. And I need to sleep. The doctor said so."

"You fight dirty."

But he got up, went to use the little bathroom in her room, and washed up. When he got back, he poked around at his dinner tray and ate a little. Sadie arched a brow when he pushed it aside, so he bowed to her authority and finished it—it just seemed simpler that way.

Then she did, indeed, scoot across the bed. He laid down next to her, on his side, and wrapped one arm around her down below her bandages.

"I love you, Sadie."

"I know, Leet." She was quiet for a moment. "Don't think I didn't hear what you said to Suhayla. Bargaining with your life."

"I never could have dealt, if this had been worse—"

She soothed her hand over his arm. "You'd have done what you had to. You're strong. We both are."

He lifted up to touch her lips. "This was my fault."

"You know it wasn't."

"It was."

"Ray will think the same thing. You going to let him go on thinking it?"

Leet put his head back down, rubbing just a little against her shoulder with his jaw. "But I brought you into it."

She pressed her forehead against his, nudging him up so their eyes met. "Yes. And I'm very, very thankful for that. Aren't you?"

His voice was rough. "You know I am, Sade."

"Okay then."

He managed a small smile. "Okay then."

"Go to sleep, my love."

Leet dropped his head again and snuggled a bit closer. "One thing, though."

"Hmm?"

He'd heard her quiet sigh but ignored it. "The wedding's back on. Pronto. As soon as you're on your feet."

"No argument."

That pleased him plenty. So he pushed his luck. "And that IUD thing has to come out. 'Cause I'm ready."

"Already done."

"Good." In a minute, he opened his eyes wide and lifted his head. "Wait. What's already done?"

"Well, the IUD is out."

He kept watching her. "And?"

She turned to look at him and gave a little shrug. "Maybe."

A shrug? He searched her eyes while his heart settled into what seemed like a new rhythm. "That night I came to you? The day we were supposed to get married?"

She nodded. "Maybe," she said again.

"When will you know?"

"A test should be positive in a few days."

"Sadie." He closed his eyes and let it sink in. But on another thought, he opened them again. "What about this?" He gestured around the room, all things medical. "It can't be good, getting shot in early pregnancy."

She smiled. "Yeah. I tell all my patients it's one of those things to be avoided, like unpasteurized cheese."

He was serious, though. "I mean it. Could something go wrong?"

She lifted a hand to his face, trailing IV tubing. "Of course something could go wrong. Something can always go wrong. But women's bodies protect their pregnancies very well. We'll be hopeful. And trust. Like all couples have to do."

"Oh, Sadie, Sadie." He touched her lips with his, fighting tears for a second time that day. "What a lucky man I am."

ℰPILOGUE

Sadie was already near sleep when Leet crawled into bed with her. He'd rocked the baby down—little Rachel had just turned a year and still ruled the roost during her waking hours—while Sadie had gotten Jace and Tino squared away in the other room of the hotel suite.

He spent a few moments watching his wife at rest in the king-sized bed. He was pretty sure she was pregnant again, though she hadn't told him yet. That amused him—like she didn't think he'd notice that there'd had to be no accommodations made in their lovemaking for the past couple months? Plus, she was showing signs of fatigue. Like now.

It was almost, but not quite, enough to cause him to let her sleep. He lay down, spooned against her, letting her feel his hard-on. He'd make sure she was satisfied. More than once. He knew how to please his woman.

But she elbowed him away, or tried to. "Hey. Forget it, bub. You have to save your energy for tomorrow."

It was a good point, a valid one. He had a game to play the next day. A big one. The game that closed the season. The one that was played in February. There was a ring to be won.

He kissed her shoulder, sliding his tongue along her soft, sweet skin. He was gratified by the little shudder that slipped through her. "Come on, blue eyes. Making love to my wife before a game hasn't stopped me all season." And it hadn't. The Metal had had a spectacular season and he'd played great. Fucking great.

He'd missed the first half of the previous season as he completed rehab and then worked his way back from second position to starting quarterback. The team had been set back, though they'd ended with more games in the win column than loss.

It had been a hell of a year anyway.

The moms had scrambled, and he and Sadie got married

just two weeks after she'd been shot by Suhayla, not even a full month after their original plan. He hadn't cared much one way or the other about the ceremony itself, but he'd been satisfied to the bone by the sense of completeness it had given him. The sense of possession. Though that wasn't a thought he shared openly with Sadie, he was pretty sure she got the idea.

Then he'd watched her grow round with his child, his daughter. She'd been beautiful—his slim, fit Sadie with this gorgeous, ripening belly. Her breasts had swollen, too, and he found he couldn't keep his hands off her. He was hot for her *all* the time. Luckily, the pregnancy had not dampened her response to him either, and he made love to her to the very end.

She'd given birth to Rachel at home, in his—their—bed. Meg had been there, and Marta, too. He'd suffered through the labor with Sadie, though of course she scoffed at that. But she'd been a champ—coping with it in her competent, athletic way. And then he'd lain with her in that bed, many, many nights, watching her nurse their girl to sleep.

Who'd have ever thought that would make the desire in him burn? Like it did always. Like it did now.

He slid one hand around to cup her breast, tweaking at the nipple that had stayed so sensitive even after Rachel had weaned. "It could even be bad luck to change the pattern now. I don't think we should take any chances."

She snorted a bit at that. "So, I'm taking one for the team?"

"Some things just have to be borne." But he was serious now. He pressed his teeth into her shoulder and squeezed her nipple a little harder. Predictably, and to his ever-fucking-lasting gratitude, she was responding to him. Her breathing was faster now, and she arched a little, bringing her bottom tight against him. God, he loved this woman.

He tilted her forward and drew her top knee up. From behind, lying partly on top of her, he pushed inside her with one long, deep stroke. She was wet and hot and gave a very encouraging moan. For a minute, he went with it, letting it take him, humping into her, almost lost to control.

She was there with him, every bit as urgent as he was, accepting as always. But he got a grip on himself, needing more, not wanting it to end. He pushed deep into her once more and held, grinding in for that last bit of penetration.

Still holding there, he moved over her, between her legs. He slid his hand under her hips and lifted. "Come on. Up on your knees."

She rose up, arching to him so she didn't lose the depth of his taking. Her breasts jutted out proudly in front of her and he covered them with his hands, kneading them, working the nipples. Her hands covered his, pressing him closer.

He sat back on his knees, holding her against him, his thighs spreading hers wide. He moved one hand to touch between her legs. She was tight, so exposed and sensitive, with her legs wide and his body filling her, stretching her. She flinched at the first touch and then moaned as he fingered her, just light, rubbing strokes that sent her over almost immediately. She rocked back onto him, taking him deep, crying out. He took his hand from her breast to cover her mouth as she fell forward in paroxysms of orgasm.

Still keeping her legs spread, he thrust into her a couple times as she came down. He smoothed one hand down her back and gave a hard squeeze to her bottom as he stroked into her again. He bent down and licked a line up her spine. With a smile, he chided her. "Did you forget we have three children asleep in this suite?"

She spoke into the mattress. "That wasn't my fault."

"I think it was."

"It was you. You made me scream."

"Uh-huh." He lifted her up against him again and, still buried deep inside her, nudged his way up the bed.

"What are you doing?"

"Making you scream some more."

She shook her head. "No—way." He was pretty sure she'd almost used his favorite "f" word.

"You say that now." He pressed her fully against the tall, solid wood headboard. He took her hands up and curled her fingers over the top. Then he sat back, withdrawing so he was almost out of her, the widest part of him just at her opening, keeping his place.

She was beautiful. Her tawny hair fell in gentle curls over her shoulders and partway down her back. Her sleek, supple back muscles narrowed from her shoulders to her waist and then flared out again with the curve of her hips. Below her arms, he could see the rounds of her breasts where they flattened, compressed as they were against the headboard.

He stroked her with his hands, his eyes, and told her just how beautiful she was. He did use the "f" word.

Just looking at her, touching her, stoked his desire. He gripped her hips hard for purchase and watched as he slid back into her, slowly, filling her once more.

He grinned when she moaned again. She never, ever won the argument about whether she could have one more orgasm. "You like that?" He did it again, still watching. "You ought to see it from here. It's a fucking incredible turn on. How you open for me, stretch to take all of me. How I come out of you wet with your desire." He moved faster now, harder. His words were harsher. He lifted up further, pounding into her. He slipped a hand around her and used both now to stimulate her, one from the front and one behind. Her body jolted a little with his thrusts, and he knew her breasts were tugged along the bed board each time.

Her every breath was hard now, a whimper that wanted to be a wail. He saw her bite her lip, trying to keep reasonably quiet. He almost laughed as her efforts failed, but he was too far gone himself. She cried out in the last moments, lifted off the bed with the force of his final thrusts. His piercing need to have her, take her, hard and deep, tore howls from his own throat as he came. They shuddered through it together, brutal spasms coursing through them.

Their panting breaths slowly gentled. He'd been every bit as loud as she.

Well, hell. The kids had slept through worse.

Maybe.

He eased out of her, caught her as she collapsed, boneless, against him. Smiling, more satisfied than a man had a right to be, he laid her down on the bed. He covered her with himself and the blankets.

Sadie might have dozed for just a minute, but she was very aware that Leet surrounded her with his warmth, his strength. And that his hand lay over the lower part of her belly. She put her hand over his.

"You're growing my son in there, aren't you?"

She smiled and turned her head toward him. "Your third son?"

"Yeah." She heard the deep contentment in the word. Jace had been his, legally, since just after their marriage. And Tino now, too. His bio mother had agreed to an open adoption. He'd been theirs since just before Thanksgiving.

"Or maybe your second daughter."

"You think that if you want."

She rolled the rest of the way over and put up a hand to stroke his face. She knew his love for Rachel brought him to his knees. "How'd you know?"

He left his hand where it was, but his gaze, filled with male satisfaction, was on hers. "You haven't waved me off in a couple months."

She lifted an eyebrow. "Waved you off?"

"Yeah, you know. Like a plane coming in to land but the runway is, uh—"

"Uh...?"

"Out of service?"

"Out of service." She kept that brow up.

"Closed for repairs?"

"Um-hmm."

"Down for routine maintenance."

She gave up and laughed out loud, entirely content.

"Temporarily off line," he whispered in her ear. But then he was serious, kissing her softly. "And you've been tired." He nipped at her ear. "And even more beautiful than usual, like you were with Rachel."

Now she had to fight back tears. Lord, the man was good.

"Plus," he said, touching her lips with his again, "I know when it happened."

She smiled through tears. "Do you?"

He nodded, watching her intently. "Christmas Eve. I remember. We stayed up late, wrapping gifts, stuffing the stockings. I cussed my way through putting that damn bike together for Tino. Finally, you took pity on me and led me up to bed." He took her hand and kissed her fingers. "And Santa got to enjoy one Christmas gift a little early."

She smiled. She remembered, too. And he was right, it had happened then.

"When we made love, it was incredible. You had your eyes open. You let me see you when you came and when I came inside you." He leaned over her now, and she could feel that he was hard. He put his thumb along her cheek. "And when we were done, I wiped your tears away. Like now." He kissed her softly, but deeply, longingly. "You told me how happy I make you." His lips slid over her face. "Like you make me, Sade. So happy I can hardly contain it." He moved further over her, centering himself between her legs. "You know what I need, Sadie, don't you?"

She nodded gravely, matching his serious tone. "You need to be inside me."

"Yeah." He pushed into her, slowly and gently, but all the way. "Connected."

As one. It was what he wanted sometimes—that very physical, primal sensation of union. The entirely concrete demonstration of the fact of the bond between them. She knew it was heartfelt.

And it didn't detract from the meaning of it that usually— perhaps *always*—it ended in more lovemaking.

Tonight, he held above her for a long time, stroking her, tenderly kissing, taking her in with his eyes. After many minutes, his intense arousal became clear. He entwined his fingers with hers and grasped hard. His chest rubbed against her sensitive breasts, and his mouth took her more aggressively. He began to rock just a little into her, the barest movement giving her incredible stimulation.

Soon, she arched up against him, opening herself, presenting her most sensitive element for his taking. He used her compliance against her, for her, applying exquisite torture with each hard, deliberate thrust.

"Leet." Her eyes rolled back, her grasp where their fingers held every bit as strong as his. She dug her heels into the bed, her whole body tensing, straining, determined to receive the full measure of every possession.

"Sadie!" Passion tore at his control and, with a hopeless groan, he gave over. He rocked fast and hard into her, clenching around her, spasming into her.

She was with him, clutching him in her arms, lifting her head to burrow into the crook of his muscled shoulder. She felt the spurts of heat as he filled her, emptying into her. Her body wracked in bliss; her throat rasped out the long, harsh exhalation of her orgasm.

They held each other as their breathing slowed. Gradually, her muscles lost their tension, and she sank down onto the mattress. Murmuring loving words, Leet tucked blankets around her, holding her close against him. She was asleep before her next breath.

The next day, Sadie was bundled against the snow and cold, surrounded by family, enjoying the final minutes of the game. It wouldn't be touted as the most exciting game ever—the Metal had taken a commanding lead early and held onto it decisively. But she'd already heard it discussed as flawlessly, brilliantly played, and memorable for that.

Leet had just walked off the field to a standing ovation. He was taking the bench, letting David Zimmerman finish out the game. As he walked off, straight across the fifty-yard line, he took off his helmet. He looked up to where his family was clustered, threw out a victorious arm, finger pointing at them all, and blasted out a grin that would be on a hundred different front pages in the morning.

Beside her, Jace was cheering ecstatically. Coach Ray was next to him, equally joyous. He turned to smooch his wife beside him, Lourdes, who had claimed a turn at holding Rachel. Rachel was entirely entertained by the happy noise of the fans that surrounded them.

Sadie knew that Ray got an occasional letter from Suhayla. The money that Leet and Ray had planned to donate to the girls' reading program, she'd forwarded to that account. And added more out of royal funds. Apparently, she was being a good queen.

He'd also been fending off inquiries from college coaches who were all hot about recruiting Jace, even though he wasn't even a senior yet. Ray enjoyed dashing their hopes— Jace was quite determined to attend his father's alma mater, UVM. He was going to be a Catamount.

Tino had spent most of the game sitting on her other side but was in her arms now, frantically waving back to his father. Marta and Joss were also there, as well as Leet's parents.

Leet's parents were, indeed, good grandparents. They doted on Rachel and spent a lot of time with the boys as well. Aletha had a hand in helping Seffie, Tino's biological mom, transfer to the local college. She was pre-med now and, though Sadie held out some hope that she'd develop an interest in obstetrics, she seemed to be leaning toward cardiology. Aletha and Nathaniel had invited her to live with them while she finished school. She'd taken Leet's old room. Leet and his brother Matt just shook their heads about it— maybe their mother had needed a daughter to rouse her maternal instincts. Anyway, it was working out well for everybody, so there were no complaints.

Marta and Joss missed having Sadie and the boys with them on the farm full time, but they still got plenty of time with their grandchildren. Leet was away for much of the season with practice and games, so the kids still had plenty of sleepovers while Sadie was working. Their hand Canaan had become more at ease with the family after he emerged all camouflaged out of the woods on the day he and Will had come ready to rescue Leet and Sadie from Suhayla and Jibran Hafir's men. At Marta and Joss's urging, he moved out of his room off the barn into the A-frame. And he joined the women for almost every meal now. He was teaching them tai chi.

Sadie had more happiness than she had a right to expect, and then some. And now, as the game ended, she was thrilled for Leet. He'd worked so hard, had wanted so much to bring his team to this place. He was aware that he had, at best, only a few more seasons to play. Between seasons, he'd had a hugely successful showing of his art. He would be more than satisfied with his second career. But he loved football and was determined to enjoy every moment of play he had left.

The game ended now, with a roar of delight from the many Metal fans. She exchanged victory hugs for twenty minutes with family and strangers alike. Finally, as the awards were done and the cameras began to clear, she and her group were let onto the field. Leet ran to them, took Rachel and Tino into his arms, and still managed to hug every one of them. Through it all, he had his gaze on Sadie's, and a part of his smile was just for her. Finally, his arms were empty, even of Rachel and Tino. He stepped to her, kissed her madly, then lifted her and twirled, again and again, as though he would never stop.

ABOUT THE AUTHOR

Rebecca Skovgaard is a midwife in Rochester, New York. She and her husband are raising (yes, *still*) their three children, who give them great pride. She believes that if you live in Rochester, you can never have too many spring bulbs in the garden or Christmas lights in the trees.

Under the pen name Rachel Billings, she has published several erotic novels.

CPSIA information can be obtained
at www.ICGtesting.com
Printed in the USA
FFOW03n1617120215
11036FF